Submission

The Middleton Series
Book 2

Lisa Lang Blakeney

Writergirl Press

LISA LANG BLAKENEY

Love reading novels featuring hot alpha men who fall for smart women? Then join <u>MY VIP MAILING LIST</u> at https://LisaLangBlakeney. com/VIP and get a FREE book just for joining!

FOLLOW ME

Follow me on Facebook
Join my Fan Group
Follow me on Amazon
Follow me on Bookbub
Follow me on Instagram

License Note

This book is a work of fiction. Any similarity to real events, people, or places is entirely coincidental. All rights reserved. This book may not be reproduced or distributed in any format without the permission of the author, except in the case of brief quotations used for review.

The author acknowledges the trademarked status of products referred to in this book and acknowledges that trademarks have been used without permission.

This book contains mature content, including graphic sex. Please do not continue reading if you are under the age of 18 or if this type of content is disturbing to you.

Books By Lisa

Bronx - Bronx & Karma
Seven - coming soon

The King Brothers Series

Dive into this series of interconnected standalones featuring 3 alpha hot brothers and the women they lay claim to without apology.
Claimed - Camden & Jade
Indebted - Cutter & Sloan
Broken - Stone & Tiny
Promised - All King Brothers

The Nighthawk Series

Sexy, smart sports romances set in the professional world of football. All standalones.
Saint - Saint & Sabrina
Wolf - Cooper & Ursula
Diesel - Mason & Olivia
Jett - Jett & Adrienne
Rush - Rush & Mia
Freak - Freak & Willow
Brick - Brick & Kaya
Dak - Dak & Katrina

Valencia Ice Mafia Series

Hot hockey romances set on the college campus of Valencia City University.
Neo - Neo & Violet
Shane - Shane & Kennedy
Bass - Coming Soon

The Middleton Series
(Club Blue Whiskey)

Dark, age-gap, romantic suspense trilogy, set in the underbelly of Los Angeles featuring dangerous billionaire Hunter Middleton and the object of his obsession, Megan.

Obsession

Submission

Possession

MASTERSON

Meet Alpha Roman Masterson
Free For A Limited Time!

"Our passion is incredibly intense. The connection between us borders on the possessive. Our feelings are absolutely forbidden. The question now is...what the fuck are we going to do about it?"

DOWNLOAD NOW
Available exclusively through this link.

Chapter 1

I've Said Too Much

Megan

I pride myself on getting out of bed every single day and doing the work of moving forward with my life. I go to school, I go to work, and I do my best to leave the past where it is... behind me. But the call from my sister has disrupted all of that positive momentum and put me in the worst of moods.

I'm tapping my fingers impatiently against the desk in my last class of the day, waiting for my professor to finish talking about the upcoming exhibition.

"This year's exhibition should be incredible and I'll expect to see many of you there, supporting your fellow students who were selected to exhibit their pieces."

Ashley is sitting a few seats away from me, and I notice she's wearing a foreboding expression on her face. The hint of glee I feel is immense and seems to calm my nerves.

Based on the rumors floating around, Ashley was close to suspension when the Dean found out that she bribed her way onto the winners' list. Of course, her parents conveniently made a sizable donation to the college a day or so later as their version of an apology. Throwing money around to influence an outcome seems to be a family trait.

I see her stiffen and then immediately whirl her head around to catch me grinning. The malice in her eyes makes me wince. She's an evil-hearted bitch.

I start shoving things in my bag so that I'm ready to make a break for it as soon as class is over. My head hasn't been into it all day and frankly, I'm in no mood to deal with Ashley's wrath if I can avoid it. But when I look up, I see another pair of eyes staring in my direction.

Ever since Hunter put Ricky in his place, I haven't had any problems with him. He actively goes out of his way to avoid me, but lately, I've noticed him watching me with a pensive expression. I don't know what he's thinking, but he hasn't reported what happened with Hunter to the college. I have a feeling that he's terrified.

Now that I think about it, nobody's been bothering me. And while Ashley may give me a side eye now and then, she hasn't been getting in my face, which is odd because she makes it a point to track me down and make my life miserable. It had gotten so bad; I was beginning to wonder if I wasn't back in high school. I always thought college was for adults and that these sorts of antics wouldn't take place. God, was I wrong.

My bag is already in my hands as I watch the clock. As soon as the professor dismisses us, I'm on my feet until the instructor calls my name.

"Miss Taylor, please stay back."

My stomach knots.

Double fuck.

I trudge down the steps toward her, "Yes?"

From the corner of my eyes, I can see Ashley taking her

sweet time, putting her things in her bag, and watching me as Ricky stands next to her.

"It's about the exhibition," the professor says, studying me. "Make sure that you've arranged for the proper formal attire. The guest of honor is Dante DiAngelo. He's from a very prominent family in Southern California and is a well-known art collector. Aside from him, I'll email you the guest list. You have to remember that you're supposed to mingle and network with the people attending. A lot of these people have the ability to advance your career, so make sure you know their names, and you find some topics of conversation. This is an opportunity you need to make the most of."

Excitement thrums in my blood, and I nod eagerly. "I understand. I'll be ready."

She smiles at me. "Good, I'll email you the list this evening. If you don't have a dress, I can share some stores that allow rentals."

This college caters to art students from wealthy families, kids who are just passing the time until their trust funds kick in, not students with my sort of background. So, while the professor's tone is kind, and I know she means well, I also understand why she's offering.

"I already have a dress." I beam at her. "But thank you."

"Good, then." She starts rearranging her papers. "That's all I had to say."

I scurry off, and just as I exit the room, Ashley steps in front of me, her eyes enraged but her tone sugary sweet.

"What was that all about?"

I adjust my hold on my bag.

"Nothing you need to worry about. Now, if you'll excuse me-"

I can see Ricky standing a few feet away, watching us intently but remaining a purposeful distance from us.

"It seems your boyfriend really pulled some strings for you," Ashley comments maliciously. "Not surprised. I heard you got yourself a sugar daddy."

I go still at her mention of Hunter and she takes the opportunity to lean forward, her voice low.

"What's it like spreading your legs for a little bit of money instead of for free, like you usually do? I was wondering how you managed to buy your way onto the winner's list. Now I know how."

"I didn't buy my way onto anything," I hiss, suddenly furious. "I didn't have to. I wouldn't stoop to your level. And the only reason you're coming at me right now is that even with all your money, you couldn't take something which was never rightfully yours. Your insecurities are not my problem!"

Her face tightens at my words. "It seems you need another lesson in respect."

"What?" I don't bother lowering my voice. "Are you going to try to beat me up again? You know, you act like some stuck-up socialite half of the time, but then you reduce yourself to acting like a bully in some public high school bathroom. Grow the fuck up, Ashley."

Her face twists in anger and I'm not surprised. It's not like I never stood up to her before, but I've never been so confrontational and so confident. I dare her to fuck with me.

Something shifts in her eyes, and she sneers, "You should really be careful how you talk to me, Megan. Do you think you're safe right now because you're letting some old man fuck you? Where will you be when he throws you aside like some used-up whore? Because he will, and I'll still be here waiting for you to fall apart like the talentless tramp you are."

Her words conjure a painful throb in my chest because many of them are triggering for me, like whore and talentless. Many of those words remind me of another person I avoid like the plague: my sister. I recall our brief but disturbing conversation.

"You're a hard one to catch up with," Rachel said after I answered the phone.

Immediately, I recognized the voice, and all those sour feelings of childhood rushed back.

"How did you get this number?"

"Did you move?"

"What do you want, Rachel?"

She always wants something, and it's never a good thing for me.

"You're still a rude bitch, I see."

"I'm hanging up."

"I want to come to see you," she blurts out.

"For what?"

"Do I need a reason to visit my sister?"

She's never once acted like a sister to me and allowing her back into my life would be a huge step backward.

"I've got to go," I told her, knowing that if Hunter heard our cold exchange, it would raise more questions about my past that I'm not ready to answer.

"This conversation isn't over!"

"Yes, it is."

And I hung up.

Evacuating a bad situation for my own mental wellness is not something I would have normally done in the past, but this is a new day, and I'm a new Megan. It's time that both of these toxic women understand that.

"You know, from the way you're so invested in my love life, I have to wonder if you're not just a little bit in love with me. I mean, nobody has ever cared so much about who I sleep with as you do."

When her face blanches, I smile ruthlessly and know that I've got her right where I want her.

"And before you go around calling me a whore to whoever will listen, you should get your facts straight about who I'm involved with. He's not as forgiving as I am."

After saying that, I brush past her and begin walking away.

"You cunt!" She screams at me. "I should–"

"Megan!" a familiar voice full of warning calls out, and Ashley falls silent as Miss Maverick approaches us.

Her smile is sharp like she knows what she's interrupting. "Just the girl I was looking for. Can I have a minute of your time, or are you two busy with something important?"

I glance back at the red-faced bitch standing a few feet away from me, and then I nod my head. "Sure, we were just finished."

Miss Maverick walks with me to the entrance of the college, not saying a word. I glance at her curiously, and when we come to stand at the front doors, I finally ask, "What did you want to talk about?"

"Nothing," she responds. "I saw the way that girl was harassing you, and since I was asked to keep an eye on you, I removed you from the situation."

"An eye on me?" I blink, taken aback. "By whom?"

"He didn't tell you?"

"Clearly not."

"Then I've said too much."

She's about to leave, but I stop her as a deep realization sinks into me.

"Wait, was it Hunter?"

She just smiles, and this queasy feeling intensifies within me.

"Is he having me watched here?"

It's already enough that I know he can be a cold-blooded killer, but I draw the line at stalking. As if one is truly worse than another, I think to myself.

"No," Miss Maverick denies. "I was just asked to look after you, and if I saw anybody making you uncomfortable, he wanted me to deal with it."

I let out a breath, "Oh."

Okay, the gesture borders on oddly sweet and a tad bit stalkerish, but I'm willing to look past it. It's better than having Lars and Parker scare half of the students to death by glaring at them all day.

"I see."

I'm about to say thank you when I stare at her, and something else occurs to me. Something I'm almost afraid to ask.

"He didn't have anything to do with the outcome of me showing at the exhibition, did he?"

"Of course not," Miss Maverick chuckles. "The panel was very confident in the quality of your work. Mr. Middleton simply advised us to make a fair judgment."

I feel like my entire world has been shaken. First, my sister calls me out of the blue with her bullshit, and now this.

"So all this was his doing? He got the previous winners overthrown?"

"You make it sound manipulative when it wasn't that. He simply wanted everything to be fair as it should be."

"How could he even have a say in what goes on here?"

"Mr. Middleton is a very popular patron of the arts.

He's well-known in the arts community. When he approached me, he told me that all he wanted was a just evaluation of your work and that if you didn't make the cut, he'd figure out something else for you. But he was right. He knew you should have been on the shortlist to exhibit your work, as you were at first. He showed me a sketch you drew, and I was confused about how you'd been replaced myself. Your work is truly remarkable for someone who didn't study at a professional art school."

I should be furious that he interfered, but my heart is feeling so full right now. He didn't say a word to me, even when I was so nasty towards him. I made it clear that I didn't trust him, didn't trust us, but he still championed me in the background.

"I feel like an idiot," I breathe, pressing the heels of my hands to my eyes.

"It's fine." Miss Maverick pats my shoulder. "And I do hope you believe that the results weren't rigged. I was only brought into the mix as an impartial judge to give you and all the students here a fair chance. I have too much integrity to do otherwise."

"Thank you for telling me."

I mull over everything Miss Maverick revealed as I head home. Everything she said rings true to me, but I still feel really overwhelmed by this new information by the time I reach home.

Do I have any idea of who the man I'm sleeping with really is or what he's capable of? Does he really have my back or does he want something more from me?

And more importantly, am I strong enough to give it to him?

Chapter 2

What Happened With The Plumber?

Megan

When I enter my apartment, I'm not surprised to find that Naomi isn't home. She's been a little wary of me lately, especially after the break-in at Hunter's place and seeing my injuries. Of course, I can't tell her everything, but she's smart enough to know that Hunter's world is much more dangerous than she initially thought. That's why her initial encouragement of me to enjoy myself with Hunter has faded. Not that I can do much about it since I already find myself falling for him.

I examine my reflection in the mirror, and while the same Megan is staring back at me, for some reason, I feel like a different person. There are noticeable changes. All my bruises are gone, and I've been sleeping better, so the bags under my eyes have faded, too, but that's not it. I can't put my finger on what exactly is different, but I'm definitely changing.

"Of course, you're changing, you wacko. You're dating a

billionaire who has professors watching you at school," I tell my reflection. "And you like it."

I literally wash away today's interaction with Ashley as I wipe down my face with a clean washcloth, then return to the living room, picking up the résumé that I left on the coffee table last night. The girl in the photo who's staring back at me looks young. Too young to work at the Blue Whiskey.

She's quite pretty. Her hair is a beautiful chestnut color and her eyes are a dark brown, almost black. Her resume states that she's eighteen years old and has finished high school, but I doubt it. She definitely looks younger than her listed age, but then so did I a few years ago. Days of nothing but dollar-store ramen tend to have that effect.

Hunter agreed to give her a trial run in the kitchen tonight, so I'm going to work earlier than normal. Since my promotion to manager, my workload has decreased, but my duties have changed. One of my major responsibilities now is to manage employee turnover at the club. Hunter doesn't particularly like new hires because of the clientele he caters to. I guess gangsters don't like a lot of change.

I realize that most college students aren't given the responsibility of managing a bar, which is precisely why people keep talking about me behind my back, but I can't really control the staff's opinion of me—besides, it turns out that they're right.

I am fucking the boss.

I wander over to the large windows of the apartment and look outside. I'll never get used to it. The shimmering lights of the cars whizzing by. The stunning orange sunset every night. The view is spectacular.

There are definite benefits to working for Hunter and sleeping with him, too. It sounds materialistic, but I'm glad I finally let my guard down with him. Otherwise, I would have never traveled to Paris, and I'd still be living in that tiny apartment, avoiding my creepy landlord and stressing about how I would pay for next semester.

I walk across the room and click the power button of the television remote. My eyes dart up to what I hear, and I press my lips together.

They found Mickey's body floating in the Los Angeles River. The police have concluded it was an accidental death, and according to them, he's been in there for at least three weeks.

"Damn."

I wonder what it says about me that I don't feel bad about my old landlord's watery death.

It's not like I don't have a conscience, but I have suffered so much from other people that the part of me that has been silent in its suffering is enjoying this retribution.

"Am I a psychopath?" I ask the reporter on the screen. "I should feel something aside from satisfaction that a man is dead, right?"

Of course, there's no answer. The news anchor has moved on to reporting about an attempted smash-and-grab in a downtown jewelry store.

A moment later, I squint my eyes as a light almost blinds me.

"What the fuck?" I step back. I look toward the building where the flash came from, but it's gone. I probably watch too many crime shows, but feeling uneasy, I draw the drapes. Let's remember, it wasn't that long ago a man almost killed both Hunter and me in this very same building.

I have some time before I need to be at the club, so I take a shower and change before making myself a cup of coffee. I'm searching for creamer in the fridge when I hear a knock on the door.

Surprised, I head to the door and peer through the peephole.

"Yes?"

"I'm here to check the leak," comes a man's voice.

"What leak?" I ask suspiciously. "Everything's fine in here."

"There's a leak in the apartment below yours. You're responsible for the damage if you don't address it, but it's up to you, miss. I have other apartments to check as well."

"It's after six," I say through the door.

"Plumbers work twenty-four hours, miss."

"Fine," I mutter to myself as I unlock the door.

On the other side is a tall man, wearing a steel grey maintenance uniform. He strides inside with a serious look and a toolbox. He's wearing a baseball cap, which hides most of his facial features, but he walks straight towards the kitchen sink and gets to work.

"How long will this take?" I ask, dialing the number for the front desk, however nobody answers.

"Not that long," he mutters as he looks underneath the sink.

I feel a little foolish for suspecting him when he's clearly just doing his job. I'm just a little spooked by everything that's happened, I guess.

"Okay."

"Can you tell me how many people live in this place?" he asks abruptly. His question takes me by surprise and without thinking it through, I respond immediately.

"Two."

"I see."

Now that the man's question has sunk in, it strikes me as

odd. Why does a plumber need to know how many people live here?

"Why do you need to know that?"

"Just want to know how much water is being consumed."

"What does that have to do with a leak?"

"It gives me an idea of the extent of the damage."

I continue to call the front desk with my cell to verify his story as he wanders into the bathroom that Naomi and I share.

I trail quietly after him to watch him work; his methods seem a bit strange. He's not really doing anything. He's just tapping things and looking under the counter.

"I'm going to have to check whether there's some water leakage on the floors. What room is on the other side of this bathroom? Is it a bedroom?"

"I think I would know if there was water under the floors or in the walls," I say, frowning, a sense of unease creeping up on me.

"Miss, please let me do my job," he replies tersely, yet he never looks me in the eye.

Not once.

"There's nothing wrong with the bedrooms," I insist, suddenly not wanting him to continue. "Which apartment downstairs is having the problem again?"

Before he can answer, there's a knock on the door, and a familiar voice calls out my name. "Megan? Are you home?"

I frown at the plumber, who seems a little tense now.

"Were you expecting somebody?" he asks as if it's an inconvenience for him.

"I think it's time for you to leave," I say sharply, moving towards the door in quick steps and opening it to reveal Vaughn and Christian standing there.

"Hey, Hunter changed the locks, and we need a place to crash for a few hours. You don't mind, do you?"

Normally, I would have been a little put off since I barely know them, but seeing their faces brings me only a feeling of relief right now.

"Come in," I say quickly.

"Is everything okay?" Christian asks, studying my face.

"Yeah," Vaughn stares at me, his eyes narrowed. "You look a little too happy to see us. We didn't even think you'd open the door."

"Uh, yeah." I look over my shoulder. "There's just a plumber here and, well, would you like to sit down?"

Christian gives me a steady look before walking past me. "No, I think I would like to talk to the plumber."

Vaughn follows him. "Where is he?"

"He was there." I look over my shoulder to see that he's no longer in the hallway. "He wanted to check my bedroom for any leaks. I told him not to go in there."

I feel nervous yet also angry when I see him exiting my bedroom, now face-to-face with Hunter's friends.

"Hey, man?" Vaughn steps in front of him. "Which company are you from?"

The plumber digs out a card and hands it over, not saying a word. I wonder why he's suddenly gone so quiet.

Vaughn hands the card over to Christian, who studies it before saying, "You're not the usual repair man. There are three assigned to this building, and I know all of them by face."

This time, the man speaks, but his voice is more gravelly than it was a few minutes ago.

"Henry had today's shift, but he came down with a cold, and nobody else was available, so I was asked to come in. I still have three other floors to check. Excuse me."

The man swiftly walks past them and out the front door. Vaughn stares after him before looking at me, his voice sharp.

"Has that man ever come here before?"

I shake my head. "No, everything works fine in here. I tried checking with the front desk about why he was sent up here, but nobody answered."

Vaughn and Christian exchange a look, and then Vaughn takes out his phone. "It's probably nothing, but let me check it out."

Christian walks over and puts his hands on my shoulder, guiding me to the couch.

"I'll stay here with Megan," he tells Vaughn. Then he turns back to me. "Do you have anything to eat?"

"Um, some leftover pasta."

He takes out the whole container from the fridge and grabs a fork. "I missed lunch."

"I can heat it up for you," I offer.

"I like cold pasta," he tells me. "Relax."

"I was actually getting ready for work. I need to go in early today."

"At least fix yourself another coffee before you head out. Your first one must be cold by now."

Compared to Hunter, both Vaughn and Christian are way more relaxed and personable. I'm not even sure how the two of them are friends with someone as intense as Hunter.

"So, I heard you're an artist."

"I'm a student," I reply, feeling a little shaken by the sudden presence of Hunter's friends. "What is Vaughn doing? Where did he go?"

"Don't worry about it." Christian gives me an easy smile. "Just checking out the plumbing situation."

I want to ask why when they clearly don't live here, but then I decide it's better if I just let them handle it.

"So why did Hunter lock you out?" I ask curiously.

Christian shrugs. "Because he's a cold, unfeeling bastard? Who knows why he does some of the shit he does."

"I see." My lips twitch. "How long have you known him?"

"Quite a few years." Christian grins.

"So, do you work for him?" I ask, trying to figure out the exact nature of their relationship.

"Nah." He takes a large forkful of the pasta, chews, and then swallows. "I have my own law firm, Christian Lee Esquire. Hunter is one of my biggest clients."

"What about Vaughn?"

"He's a data broker and runs his own company as well, Exalt Logic. We both work alongside Hunter."

The name of the company sounds familiar for some reason. Both names do.

"Oh," I murmur.

"I think I'm insulted that Hunter doesn't talk about us." He finishes his last bite. "We're his only friends."

I just shrug my shoulders. "He doesn't talk much."

Ugh, that sounded dirtier sounding than I intended it to.

"Are there any other questions you have for me?" he asks, clearly trying to hold back a laugh.

"Can I get you some coffee?" I ask, wanting to keep my hands busy.

"Make that two cups," Vaughn says, strolling back in the front door.

"I thought I locked that."

"Nope."

"What happened with the plumber?" I ask, feeling tense.

"Don't worry about him," Vaughn says casually. "But next time someone asks to come in, and you don't know them, don't open the door. Someone from the main office will let you know in advance if they're sending a repairman, and you will not be alone when they come."

I'm starting to realize that Vaughn and Christian didn't just happen to get locked out of Hunter's place. Hunter probably *sent them.*

I start another pot of coffee and put on the sports channel on the television while Vaughn takes a peek inside my fridge. I've never really had semi-strangers just invite themselves over and make themselves at home, but it's not a bad feeling. Since Naomi is keeping herself busy with cosmetology school and whatever else she does afterward to avoid me, it's nice to have the company.

"That's a foul!" Christian snarls at the screen.

"Only because you're blind!" Vaughn shoots back. "He barely touched him!"

They've made themselves completely at home, and I wonder how to feel about it. It's a little strange for me, but not the worst feeling. It's while I'm steaming the milk for my coffee, my thoughts a little distracted, that I hear my phone ping. Thinking that it could be Naomi, I set aside the cup, wiping my hands, and pick up my phone. The number on the phone is an unsaved one, but the message has me going still, my mouth dry.

God, not again.

I slowly set down my cell phone on the counter and make sure to keep my voice steady.

"Guys, I must step out for a second before heading to

work. You can stay here if you want and watch the game. Just lock the door behind you."

"You don't mind us hanging out here when you're not home?" Christian asks.

My head is reeling so much that I don't even consider the fact that I'm leaving two strange men in my apartment.

"No, I'm sure Hunter has his reasons for sending you two to keep an eye on me."

Vaughn gives me a knowing grin. "Who said he did that?"

I'm rushing as I grab my tote bag and check my hair in the mirror on my way out.

"I may be younger than you three," I tell them. "But I'm nobody's dummy."

Christian kicks his feet up on the end of the couch, grinning the entire time.

"Ain't that the truth."

Chapter 3

Maybe I Should Tell Daddy

Megan

My new neighborhood is in somewhat of a residential area but it's got quite a few nice cafés to choose from. I select one that's far enough from my building but close enough to walk, not paying much attention to the flowery decor inside.

My hands are wrapped around a hot cup of coffee as I anxiously tap my foot against the floor. It's not a very crowded place, and I'm grateful for that because I'm feeling a little claustrophobic right now.

I shouldn't be here.

I should have deleted the message.

Better yet, I should have just changed my number again.

I hear the bell on the front door of the café jingle as somebody walks in and when I look up, it's an attractive girl, a few years younger than me. Her fake blonde hair is done up in curls, and her makeup is dramatic, making her brown eyes appear larger and almost doe-like. She looks like the sweet hottie next door.

She isn't.

From the corner of my eyes, I can see a few men check her out but she doesn't pay them any attention, walking straight over to me.

"Sissy." She beams, still using her ludicrous nickname for me. "How've you been?"

"Rachel," I murmur her name, my voice cautious. "Why are you here in LA?"

She sits down across from me, pushing her blonde weave back from her shoulder and smiling. "Aren't you going to order me something, Sissy?"

I point towards the counter. "This place is self-service."

"So, then go get it for me." Her smile still lingers but her tone is hard now.

"I have to leave in ten minutes." I shift in my seat, ignoring her words that I know were meant as a challenge. "So, make this quick."

She studies me for a few seconds, and the silence is daunting, but then she finally says, "Seems as if you grew some balls now that you're out of the house."

Her eyes are angry as she smiles at me, and it instantly brings up all those old feelings I have for her.

Disdain.

Distrust.

Disgust.

"Tell me what you want, or I'm leaving," I say shortly.

Rachel is two years younger than me and the apple of her wicked mother's eye. There was once a time that I truly believed that I couldn't blame my younger half-sister for how she treated me because she followed her mother's example. It was only later that I realized that she inherited her cruel streak from both her mother and our father.

"Dad won't like it when I tell him how you're talking to me." She taps her long, coffin-shaped nails on the table.

"Well, he can add that to the list of things that piss him off about me," I say harshly, trying not to betray the sudden fear of the threat.

As long as he gets money from me, I'm safe.

Rachel's smile slips.

"Maybe I should tell Daddy that he should pay you a visit now that I know where you live."

Normally, a threat like that would have me shaking in my boots, but it's been two years since I left my home. I walked out of that house, a shell of a human being, my hands stained with blood, *blood that I still can't wash off.* But a lot can change in two years.

"I don't have time for your fucked up games, Rachel." I stand to my feet. "Next time, don't message me trying to threaten me with the past. The past is where I left it, behind me."

I'm about to walk past her when she grabs my wrist, digging her sharp claws into the inner side of it. She looks up at me, and when I meet her gaze, for a short moment, I feel like I'm looking into my stepmother's eyes, those same cruel, soulless eyes.

"Don't think that just because you got away from the house, you can act so high and mighty with me." Her words are a vicious whisper. "You keep forgetting your fucking place."

My place.

A sharp strike on my back from a cane.

My place.

My face was forced down into a bowl of urine.

Memories that I continually keep trying to bury deep

inside of me force their way to the surface, and I snatch my hand away.

"Touch me again, Rachel, and I'll make sure you regret it. Stay the fuck away from me!"

My voice projects my warning loudly, and I can't help but notice as patrons of the cafe turn their heads in our direction. Rachel blushes with embarrassment and forces a smile on her face.

"You're overestimating your worth. All I have to do is go home and tell Dad that you hurt me and all the money in the world won't matter to him. If you think living at home was difficult, you'll just end up being somebody's bitch in prison."

I go still, fear of her very real threat sits bitterly in my mouth.

"Don't be ridiculous, Rachel. We're not kids anymore, and Dad isn't stupid."

The demon smiles broadly and I know that she can tell how she's managed to get under my skin. She was always better at this game than I ever was.

"I can call him right now and tell him how you're treating me today, or you can sit your fat ass back down and–"

"Megan?"

A deliciously cool voice calls to me from behind, and suddenly, the sense of relief that fills me almost makes me stagger. Hunter's hand is firm as he glides it across my waist, settling it on my hip.

"What're you doing here?" I ask with more gratitude than he'll ever understand.

I don't get a chance to say anything else because Rachel is on her feet, batting her false eyelashes at Hunter. It makes my stomach roll.

"Hi, I'm Rachel, Megan's sister."

The look in her eyes is so familiar that my palms grow sweaty. It's the same look she once had in her eyes when she saw me with a boy when I was seventeen. That desire to take what is mine has led to consequences that are now wrapped like chains around my arms and legs.

Hunter looks at her and then at me and his voice is his usual steady sound, "Hunter."

He doesn't look very interested, but of course, Rachel doesn't care. She steps closer to him, playing with a long strand of her hair, a coy look in her eyes.

"So, how do you know my sister?"

My insides are turning cold. I cover Hunter's hand with my own, a mixture of possessiveness and fear running side by side within me.

"We have to go," I say. "Come on, Hunter."

My tone is hard as I entwine my fingers with his, pulling him along, but Rachel steps in my path.

"What's your rush, sis'?" She stares at her hands and then back at me. "You just got here, and you haven't even introduced us properly."

Alone, Rachel's threats are quite effective because I fall back into my old emotional patterns, but with Hunter standing beside me, his presence serves as a massive security blanket. The fact that I know he has my back gives me the kind of confidence that I've never had before.

"That's because he's none of your business," I say sharply. "And I'm not sure how you found my phone number, but don't ever contact me again."

A shutter falls over Rachel's expression, and her eyes flash at me in a warning. "Don't be silly, Megan. We're sisters, and you're really hurting my feelings."

"That sounds like a personal problem." I bare my teeth at her. "Now get out of my way."

I pull an oddly compliant Hunter past her, and she calls out, "I'll call you later after I do a bit of sightseeing. I need a place to stay."

"The fuck you do," I hiss to myself, enraged and upset.

As soon as we exit the Café, Hunter says, "The car is there."

"I want to walk!" I basically bark as I take large strides along the pavement, my hand still holding onto his as if for dear life.

"Walk where?" he asks mildly.

"Anywhere," I mutter, wanting to get rid of this disgusting feeling inside of me. I feel tainted for some reason. A little bit of me feels like the old Megan.

"Megan."

Hunter pulls at my hand, abruptly yanking me to a stop and whirling me around in one heartbeat. I crash into his chest, and he looks down at me calmly. "Do you want to tell me what's going on?"

"No," I bury my face in his chest, struggling to draw in air, trying to get rid of this rage and frustration inside of me.

"What do you need?" His voice is a low whisper while also sounding quite commanding. "What can I do?"

"I want to set the world on fire." I hate how my voice breaks. "I want everything to burn to ashes."

"I can make that happen." He slowly lifts my chin and carefully pushes a few stray curls behind my ear. "I'll burn down whatever the fuck you want me to, Megan. Just say the word."

Chapter 4

You're My Weakness

Megan

The dark promise in Hunter's voice breaks through the suffocating cloud of unease surrounding me, and I shiver at the words that come out of his mouth next.

"You want me to take care of your sister for you? I promise she'll never bother you again."

"Stay away from her," I say with a tense expression. "If Rachel approaches you, just turn the other way. I don't want you two anywhere near each other."

When I look into Hunter's eyes, I can see a fury swirling inside of his pupils, even though his face is expressionless.

"What do you think would happen if she came near me?"

"I'm not saying anything would happen. I just don't want you two interacting with each other."

"I didn't take you for the possessive type, Megan." He cracks a small smile.

"I'm not." I can feel my face blush. "I just... I'm just saying don't let her get near you because now that she's seen you, she'll try."

"She'll try flirting with me or fucking me?" He grins down at me. "Are you saying that I'm that good-looking?"

"Oh, shut up."

Hunter pulls me in for an unexpected kiss. Public displays of affection are not really his thing, or mine really, but I welcome the warm comfort of his mouth demanding mine. It makes my whole body tingle.

After the kiss, I burrow my face in his chest again, finding it comforting, the familiar scent of his cologne relaxing me. The way he runs his fingers through my curls makes me calm down. If I could bottle up his methods of calming me down, I'd make a million dollars.

"If your sister makes you feel like this, then why did you agree to meet with her today?"

"Stop calling her that."

"Isn't that who she is?"

"Perhaps a DNA test would confirm that, but she's never been a real sister to me. And as for why I decided to meet with her today, it was a mistake," I admit somberly, on top of the fact that I was afraid of what she'd do if I didn't meet her. Rachel is so unpredictable.

"I won't go near her if just a mere discussion of the girl makes you this upset, but Megan, all your secrets are making my patience run thin."

There's a hard edge to his tone that I can feel vibrating through his chest, settling as a lump in my throat.

"I'm not good at swapping life stories," I explain. "But I'm trying to be a little more open, at least with you."

It's true.

The kind of baggage I carry is not something I can easily

just share with people. A part of me wants to tell Hunter and get everything off my chest, but it's hard to be vulnerable when you've grown up not trusting anyone.

How do I tell the man I'm dating that things were bad in my house–like Lifetime Movie bad? How do I admit to him that I was frequently physically assaulted by my parents and the horrible dynamic it created between me and Rachel? How do I reveal that my parents are monsters and that I was treated like a prisoner in my own home? What will he think about me then?

"You were wildly defiant when you were trying to evacuate that server from Table 21 when we first met," he reminisces. "But that is not the same girl I saw in the cafe just now."

"I know, and one day, I'll tell you everything," I assure him. "Just not today."

His hand tightens at the roots of my hair momentarily but then relaxes its hold. Hunter doesn't like to hear the word no, but that's all I can give him right now.

"I hope that day comes soon, Megan."

My childhood is my story to tell, and I'll share it when I'm ready. It's not like I know much about his past, either.

Once we arrive at the car and he gets into the driver's seat, something hits me. "Hunter, how did you know I was here?"

"I had Christian follow you," he says as if it's the most normal thing in the world to do. Then, he pushes the ignition button to start the car. "Also, next time, unless I tell you otherwise, don't let anybody into your apartment."

"They said you locked them out of the penthouse," I say with a slight attitude. "Plus, they're your friends. Why wouldn't I let them in?"

"I'm not talking about those two clowns," Hunter

growls. "I'm talking about the so-called plumber that you let in."

"I knew he felt a little suspicious."

Hunter swerves the car onto the street before shooting me a careful look.

"Then start following your intuition, Megan. I thought you didn't trust people? What if Vaughn and Christian didn't come by? What if that man was there to hurt you? Just because he had on a uniform doesn't make him any less dangerous."

"Okay," I exhale nervously.

"Listen," he tries calming his voice. "Being with me comes with its own set of risks. I'm not talking about the shooting in my apartment. I was the obvious target of that, but the longer you stay beside me, the more likely that you may become the target. If my enemies think they can use you against me or that you're my weakness, you'll be in danger."

He taps his palm in rapid succession against the steering wheel as he talks through what must feel unsettling for him.

"Hell, you probably already are a target. The moment I moved you into my building made you one. None of my employees can afford to live there. Any idiot can put that two and two together."

I pay little attention to whatever he's rambling on about because I'm still too focused on the phrase he used a few sentences ago, you're my weakness.

"Am I your weakness?" I ask, as my heart flutters just by the mere possibility of the answer being a yes.

Hunter shoots me a dark look before shifting the gear and turning his attention back to the road.

"Let's not find out."

There's a thrum of silence, and then he says in a voice

that lowers the temperature of the car by a few degrees, "Just be careful, Megan."

"I found out what you did for me," I say with a cautious voice, clumsily changing the subject. "Miss Maverick told me, but why didn't you?"

"I didn't want you to know."

"Don't blame her," I say, worried that he'll get Miss Maverick fired or worse. "I figured it out on my own, and she only confirmed it."

"It's fine, Megan. I wasn't planning on telling you, but I also wasn't going to just sit idly by and allow someone to steal away your chance to share your talent with the world."

"My talent?"

"Yes."

"You think I'm talented?"

"Obviously."

"You had her reassess the submissions, but what if she hadn't chosen my work?" I ask, turning to look at him. "What would you have done?"

"The department already selected you once and then stole the opportunity from you because of school politics. I knew she'd choose your work once she saw it. Your strong technique speaks for itself."

The confidence in his voice makes my heart full. Sometimes, when I talk to Hunter, the faith that he has in me and my abilities is staggering. I've never felt this kind of unwavering support from someone. I have to be careful, though. I could become dependent on that kind of blind faith, and I don't want to depend on anyone.

"Thank you," I whisper softly, sinking into the car seat. "For what you did at the university and for getting me out of the cafe today."

I can see his fingers flex on the steering wheel. He

wants to know more about Rachel, but he's trying to be respectful of my boundaries.

"Next time, if you find yourself in a situation like this, don't be afraid to walk away or make a scene. Remember the girl from Table 21. Do whatever you need to do, and don't worry about the consequences. There's no problem that I can't make go away for you. I will always have your back, Megan. Remember that."

His words and the frankness with which he says them stun me.

"Thank you, but–"

"Even if you kill somebody, I promise no one will touch you. Not while I'm around. Do you understand what I'm saying to you?"

His assurance should chill me to the bone, but there's a reason why Hunter makes me feel so safe, and it's because I understand what he's capable of.

"Yes, Hunter, I understand."

This is a dangerous man I work for and sleep with... and am falling for. I don't doubt for a second that he would move heaven and earth to protect me. In fact, I think he'd kill for me.

He's shown me in countless ways already that he will protect me and while I love he feels that way about me, I fear for what the future may hold.

Will falling for Hunter make me a target in his world as he mentioned, or worse... will it make people from my past his targets?

Do I even care if it does?

I sneak a peek at Hunter's beautiful face, rigid with worry about me, before I ask, "Do you think I'm a good person?"

"What kind of question is that?" he responds flatly. "Who cares if you're good."

"Never mind." I shrug, feeling silly that I even asked, especially to someone like him.

I stare out the car window at the Los Angeles skyline as the sun sets, and I can feel his eyes on me as he changes his mind about answering my question.

"The words 'good' or 'bad' are very subjective. There's always a gray area. I live in the gray areas of the world. I like it there. Do I think you're good or kind? Yes, and while I consider kindness a weakness, I think you carry it well."

I shift uncomfortably in my seat, reminded that Hunter Middleton doesn't really know me at all.

My weakness isn't my kindness. I wouldn't describe myself as a kind person.

My weakness is my fear.

I can only imagine where my life would be if I hadn't been so afraid to live it for so many years. I would have believed in my art when I was in high school and allowed my art teacher to help me apply to art schools in New York. I wouldn't have been bullied by a cunt like Ashley or treated like a whore by someone like Ricky when I finally made it to art school. And I wouldn't allow someone like my sister to still try to make my life a living hell.

Then I daydream for a moment about what it would look like if I took Hunter up on his offer. What would life look like if I swallowed my fear and asked him to blow some shit up for me?

Would I finally be free of the past?

It's a mighty tempting offer.

Chapter 5

Something Feels Off

Megan

I'm silent for the rest of the drive to the Blue Whiskey. Once we arrive at the club, I give Hunter a quick peck on the lips and thank him for the lift.

"You're in a rush," he notices.

"I don't want to be late for the interview."

"Is this the first person you've hired for the club?"

"I'm just a little worried about what's going to happen to the kitchen when Bobby leaves. We're known for our wings."

"I'm sure it'll be fine. You've got this."

"I'll see you later." I smile, kind of blowing off his encouragement. It's so strange having someone in my life who actually believes in me. I think it makes me uncomfortable.

I quickly change into the extra set of clothes I always store in my office closet and head to the kitchen to see if the girl I'm interviewing is here. The club hasn't opened yet, but the kitchen staff is in full preparation mode.

Billy sees me when I walk in and lifts a hand in greeting. "Megan, this is Lacy. This is the friend I was telling you about. She's here for the interview."

Lacy offers her hand. "Hi."

I study her for a moment, recalling the picture on her resume. She's definitely young, but there was clearly a filter on the picture I saw before because now that she's in front of me, I can tell that she's not as young or polished as I originally thought.

She doesn't have a head full of beach-worthy brunette waves, but instead, she has a lifeless box-dyed ponytail, and when I move even closer, I can see the soft curve of violet-colored contact lenses around her irises. I wonder what her actual eye color is. And I also wonder why she's trying so hard to look so different. Is it the pressure that social media seems to place on most of us nowadays, or is it something else?

I don't know.

I'm trying not to be too judgmental, but something feels off about her. But Billy looks so hopeful that his referral will work out. I try to let go of my initial doubts.

"Nice to meet you," I offer, extending my hand to meet hers.

The girl has a firm handshake, and despite her oddities, when she smiles, I have to resist the urge to smile back. She has one of those infectious smiles where the corners of her eyes crinkle.

"You're looking for full-time work, right?" I ask her.

"Yes, I am."

I raise an eyebrow. "And you've worked as a line cook before?"

"That's right."

"She's great," Billy adds eagerly, and it makes me

wonder for a moment if this is someone Billy has had a romantic relationship with. He's not known for being particularly loyal to his girlfriend.

"Okay, let's see what you can do. Billy is going to clear a counter for you, and you're going to make two items from the menu and one dish of your own creation. Obviously, we're a bar and grill, and we don't have very sophisticated offerings, but we want our simple fare to taste good."

She nods in understanding.

"Billy, bring the food to my office once it's ready."

"Gotcha." Billy swings his arm over the young woman in what actually seems like a brotherly manner. "Lemme show you the menu, Lacy."

I have some scheduling work to get done in my office, but when I walk in, Hunter is lounging on the couch, his phone to his ear.

"I see. Well, send me all those profiles, and I want you to drop by my office within the hour." He pauses and then adds cooly, "Or I can always come to you."

I quietly open my laptop, wincing at that tone. His words seem more like a threat than a casual offer.

When he ends the call, I ask, "What're you doing here?"

"You're always asking me that as if you want me to leave. It's impolite."

"We're at work, Mr. Middleton." I grin. "And we just saw each other. I'm just wondering if you need anything in particular. I was about to handle the schedule."

"I need a lot of things." He pats his leg as a signal for me to sit, and I narrow my eyes.

"No, thank you. The last time I sat in your lap, I had trouble walking the next day."

I can tell that he's about to say something dirty when I

add, "I met the girl that Billy recommended. I told her to make some dishes for me to sample, so if you're sticking around my office, you can try them, too."

"I'll stick around if you-"

"I'm not sitting on your lap, Hunter," I scowl. "I'm at work just as are you. Go do something."

He watches me from the couch, and when he doesn't say anything for a few long seconds, I wonder if I've finally managed to piss him off.

"You're giving me whiplash. One minute, you're shivering in my arms, and the next, you're bossing me around."

"I'm not bossing you around." I give him an indignant look. "And look who's talking! Talk about whiplash. Have you ever met you?"

"Yeah, but I *am* the boss."

"I wonder why that line comes out of your mouth whenever it's convenient for you?"

"It's not that I say it because it's convenient. I say it because it's facts."

I roll my eyes defiantly.

"Do you realize if you're nice to me, you might get a raise?" He smirks suggestively at me. "That's the perk of having a special relationship with the boss."

I give him a dirty look. "Thanks. That really validates the nature of our relationship."

He grins harder, loving the banter between us, and I must admit that I love being the one responsible for his smiling. It's the side of him that he only shows when we're alone, and somehow, that feels really special to me. I don't think he smiles this much with Vaughn and Christian. At least not that I've seen.

"By the way," I reach into my tote. "I wanted to ask you for something."

He immediately sits up, intrigued. "You want me to take you shopping?"

I run my tongue over my teeth before saying carefully, "No."

I walk over to him and hand him one of the tickets that I received for the exhibition. My voice is a little awkward, but I say the words anyway.

"Since we're dating now, I thought I would invite you on our official first date."

"Our first date was in Paris."

"That was not a first date," I tell him. "That was a seduction."

"And a damn good one," he agrees, smiling devilishly.

God, he's so handsome.

"So, now you want me to accompany you to the exhibition?" He questions. "I thought you were dead set against the idea."

"Well," I answer, fidgeting with my blouse. "This event is important to me, and you said we're dating."

"We *are* dating," Hunter confirms. "In public and in private, you are mine, Megan."

"Okay." I blush at the possessive look in his eyes. "Well, as I said, it's an important night for me, and I want you there, but only as my date. You're not coming as Hunter Middleton, the businessman or patron of the arts. No making deals on my behalf with rich people over drinks or anything. I can do that on my own. I just want you to be there next to me. You know... like arm candy," I tease.

"I see." He takes the ticket from me, and I see a strange emotion cloud his eyes, one I can't define.

"It'll be boring," I warn him, but he stands up, bowing his head to kiss me, almost achingly gentle.

"No, it won't. Thank you for the invitation."

I'm so used to his dominating behavior that this kind of gentle treatment flusters me.

"Don't make a big deal about it," I mumble, and he lets out a light chuckle.

"I'm not, but it's a first for me."

"To be invited to an exhibition?" I ask, unclear of what he means.

"No," He looks down at the ticket in his hands. "To be invited somewhere not because of what I can do for you, but because you simply want my company."

It never dawned on me that Hunter was wary of relationships with women for those reasons, but now that he mentions it, it makes sense that women probably try to use him for his money, especially the kinds of women that frequent the Blue Whiskey.

I find myself standing on my tiptoes to press a kiss on his cheek. "You'd better dress nice. Remember, you're my arm candy for the night and a reflection of me."

The next thing I know, I'm laying supine on the couch with a large hand under my blouse, freeing one of my breasts from my bra.

"You're going to be the death of me, Megan," he growls deliciously.

"That's Miss Taylor when we're in the office," I say as wetness quickly dampens my panties.

"Get on your knees and lean over the back of the couch, Miss Taylor," he growls possessively. "And spread those thighs wide."

I know we shouldn't do this. It's too early in the evening. Anyone could walk in and catch us, but I don't seem to care as I do what I'm told, anxiously awaiting the bliss that is about to push its way inside of me.

As I grip the edge of the sofa, Hunter pushes my skirt

up to my waist, slides the crotch of my panties to the side, and enters me swiftly. The sudden feeling of fullness leaves me utterly breathless.

"Your pussy is as dangerous as you are." He says as he strokes deeper inside of me.

"Hunter," I moan.

His punishing strokes grow faster and harder until he's pounding my pussy so hard that I can't even speak. There's nothing else I can call it but a claiming. Reminding me of who I belong to.

I come swiftly, and he follows right after me, grunting through his release. I flop over the back of the couch, totally spent, waiting for the stars flickering behind my eyes to dissipate.

Hunter hands me a few tissues to clean myself up, puts himself back together, then slaps one of my ass cheeks before exiting the office door.

"I can't wait for our date, Miss Taylor," he says, giving me an uncustomary wink of his eye. "I'll see you later."

I've just been fucked senseless on my work couch by my official new boyfriend and boss, and all I can do is grin from ear to ear.

As he exits my office, for once in my life, I'm not worried about a damn thing. It's incredibly refreshing.

Then there's a knock at the door.

Chapter 6

What's Up With Diana?

Megan

Gage is on the other side of the door, looking like a cat who just swallowed a canary.

"What?" I ask defensively, praying to God that my office doesn't smell like two people just had sex inside of it.

"It's none of my business," he says amiably, shrugging his shoulders and walking inside the room. The two of us have slowly been building a cordial working relationship but rarely discuss personal matters.

"What's none of your business?" I ask snidely.

He inspects me carefully as I adjust the seams of my skirt. "Do Lars and Parker know that the rumors about you are true?"

"The rumors aren't true," I say without even thinking. Then I remember that Hunter and I are about to go public in a very big way when I take him to my art exhibition. Why am I still hiding it from people at the club? They've already assumed that I've slept my way into this managerial position anyway, so what does it matter at this point?

"Okay." He throws both of his hands up in a motion of surrender. "As I said, it's none of my business."

"Walk me to the kitchen," I tell him, wanting to change the subject until I'm ready to talk about it. "I want to see how the new girl is doing. She's making some sample dishes."

"Sure."

I notice that the after-work crowd is starting to enter the club as we descend the staircase and walk through the main room. When I used to work on the floor, I'd get to know some of the regulars and I wave hello to a woman named Samantha who stops in for a drink most weekdays. She'd been in an abusive marriage for thirteen years when her husband choked on a chicken wing and died in an easy chair in their living room. I've never seen someone tell a story about the death of their husband with such glee, but in a very unfortunate way, I understand her. And I'm happy for her.

My smile fades when I notice Diana. She's still on probation and it ends in another week. I don't think she'll be continuing here. It's not that she isn't good at her job, but I'd bet a hundred dollars that most of the rumors floating around the club about me can all be traced back to her. A lot of shit goes down at The Blue Whiskey, and it must operate with loyal staff. I can't have one employee causing chaos.

Also, the way she looked at Hunter the other day, makes me want to punch her in one of her icy blue eyes.

There's also that.

I motion to Gage, and when he leans over, I ask in a quiet voice, "Did you do what I asked?"

"Yeah." He gives a slight nod. "There is something going on."

Since Gage is working side-by-side with Diana, he's the best person to observe her. It was Lars who suggested that I talk to him.

"Does she seem completely focused on her job, or does it seem that she's interested in other activities? I've found her roaming around in the upstairs staff area a few times."

Gage sticks his hands in his pockets, glancing over his shoulder at Diana before saying, "She's curious about you. About how you got promoted from bartender to manager and whether anyone can just get promoted."

"So, she wants my job."

"She's been getting close to the servers, trying to rearrange their schedules. I've caught her changing the schedule board a few times."

"Changes to my schedule?" I respond incredulously.

"Yeah, and she encourages the staff to come to her with their issues rather than you. Billy and the kitchen staff like you, so they don't do that, but most of the servers are young, and they seem a little resentful of you."

"Has she implied anything about how she might think I got this position?"

Gage's eyes crinkle in an easy grin. "You mean, did she ask me whether you slept with the boss or not?"

I narrow my eyes at him, and he shrugs. "She may have suggested it and I tried showing her that I was open to the idea of chatting about it."

"With any success?"

"She's ambitious but smart. She didn't reveal much because I think she's feeling me out, especially because I'm a man. She must be under some sort of impression that you have all the men in this club hypnotized."

"I see," I say, forcing myself to remain calm.

This has been a long-running theme in my life, and I swear I don't understand it. Most women despise me for wielding some imaginary power over the guys in my life. Little do they know that before I met Hunter, most of the men in my life chewed me up and spit me out. I have no power over anyone.

"Thanks for this."

Gage just shrugs before stopping at the entrance of the kitchen. "Mr. Middleton told me to make myself available to you, just not *too* available."

He's grinning at the last part as he walks away, leaving me to wonder about the exact nature of Gage's relationship with Hunter. As I stare after him, it occurs to me that Gage might not be the simple hire that I initially thought he was. I mean, if he was transferred from Chicago, who's to say that he doesn't work for Hunter in some other capacity the way Lars and Parker do?

I catch Diana side-eyeing me. I know she's going to try to grill Gage over what we talked about. If the man is smart, which I get the feeling he is, he won't say anything.

Before I walk through the double door entrance of the kitchen, I hear a familiar voice from behind me say, "Well, hello, Megan. I didn't know you worked here."

The voice makes my spinal cord stiffen, and I turn around to see Ashley standing there with a group of her friends from school, all of whom I recognize. Ricky is standing next to her quietly, his arm around her shoulders. Dimly, I wonder if they were dating the whole time he and I were involved as I absorb the shock of their sudden presence.

When I'm going to be done with this bitch?

"Aren't you going to welcome us?" Ashley sneers at me.

"I should've known that you'd be working as a waitress at a place like this. It suits you."

I blink, forcing myself out of my dazed state, before responding tightly, "I'm the manager here."

"The manager?" Ashley scoffs as the others snicker. "You don't have to lie to impress us, Megan. Now go get us a booth before I call over the *actual* manager."

I'm so close to reaching my limit with Ashley and her elitist nonsense. She's nothing but an insecure bully, but I won't cause a scene in my place of business, especially when the servers are looking for any excuse to justify their assumptions about me.

"Please get this group a private booth." I gesture towards Diana since she's doing her best to eavesdrop, anyway.

I'm about to walk away when Ashley's fingers suddenly wrap around my wrist. "I asked you to do it, bitch."

I whip my head around and give her a cold look.

I've had enough.

We aren't at school.

This is my turf, not hers.

"Watch your hands and your tone, or I'll get you tossed out on your bony little ass." I yank my hand away from her roughly, enjoying the way her eyes fill up with rage at my dismissive behavior.

"Do you know who I am?" Ashley steps into my face, her eyes sparking with anger.

"Hey, Ash'." Ricky attempts to stop her, but she swats him away, ignoring his interference.

"You're no one," I counter, lifting my brows, refusing to be intimidated.

"Is that right? Well, this isn't school." She points at me with one of her bony pointer fingers. "You work here, which means I'm the customer, and you have to serve me. Otherwise, you'll be out of a job that you so obviously need."

Diana snickers, and I give her a cool look. Instead of heeding my non-verbal warning, she adds her unwanted two cents. "She's not wrong, you know. If she wants you to secure her table, I don't see the harm in it."

"Diana." My tone is sharp. "I think it would be wise for you not to interfere and do your job."

"Let the girl talk," Ashley smirks. "At least she seems to have an ounce of sense."

Emboldened by Ashley's encouraging words, Diana adds, "The customer is always right. If they want you, it's only right."

"Diana," I warn. "If you don't want to be out of a job in the next five minutes, I'd suggest you stop talking."

It seems that being nice to the servers is pointless. I'm so busy trying to prove that I'm still one of the gang that no one on the club floor respects me, especially this one.

Diana pales. "You can't just fire me."

"I can and I will. Now, show this party to a booth or get out of the club."

With that, I turn on my heel and walk toward the bar, trying not to let my anger show at the blatant display of her insubordination. I'm too angry to deal with the interviewee in the kitchen, so I walk behind the bar and pretend as if I'm checking the register. I need a moment to cool off.

"What was happening over there?" Gage asks, eyeing the group as Diana guides them to a booth in the back of the club.

"Some students from my college," I grouse. "Here to make trouble for me."

"You go to college?"

"Art school."

"I didn't realize you were an artist. You never mentioned it."

"It never came up."

"Why does Diana look so pissed?"

"How do you have time to notice what's going on with me when you're supposed to be busy preparing drinks?" I demand, staring at him, and he grins.

Is he keeping a purposeful eye on me?

"I'm just that good." He begins preparing a cocktail for one of the customers. "So what gives?"

"Diana tried to undermine me in front of the group and I told her off," I turn and stand behind the counter, rolling up my sleeves since there is an unusual amount of customers today.

As I help out, Gage frowns. "That's not okay."

I shake the cocktail mixer a little too rough for the cosmopolitan I'm prepping.

"I'm going to have to do some re-staffing. Clearly, being nice to them isn't really working."

"You're the manager," Gage responds, pouring out a drink and sliding it down the bar. "It's not your job to be their friend."

"I know," I mutter, mostly to myself. "It's just that I've been in their shoes and thought that I could do things differently."

"It doesn't matter what you thought." Gage shakes his head. "You can't be the manager they get to walk all over. Being thoughtful doesn't equal being a doormat."

He's right. I've been so focused on being considerate that I stopped exerting my authority.

"Were you a manager back in Chicago?" I ask curiously. "You seem to have a lot of sage advice for a bartender."

"That's a long story."

Diana saunters over and shoots me a nasty look as she places the orders from Ashley's booth. I want to ignore both women, but it's no coincidence that someone as stuck up as Ashley would be slumming it at The Blue Whiskey. Either she plans to get me fired, or she plans to humiliate me. Knowing her, it's certainly both.

As I watch Diana take the drinks and walk away, I murmur to Gage, "I bet you twenty bucks that there's going to be trouble from that booth before the night is out."

Gage raises an amused eyebrow.

"The question is, trouble for who?"

Chapter 7

I Knew They Weren't Done With Me

Megan

I walk into the kitchen galley and observe a very proud Billy leaning over the shoulder of Lacy as she plates the appetizers that she's prepared. I arrived just in time. I can tell by simply eyeballing the plates that the food is tasty, but I don't want to reveal my thoughts just yet. I'm not one hundred percent sold on the fact that someone basically my age can lead a kitchen of our size.

I know.

I have a lot of nerve since I'm just as young and I'm the manager.

Yeah, I need to work on that.

"Are they ready to taste?" I ask them both.

"It's damn good," Billy boasts as Lacy hands me the first plate.

"What's your specialty dish?" I ask her.

"I made my famous smoked paprika wings. They're fast to make and packed with lots of flavors."

I take a bite of one of the wings and pause for a moment

as the mixture of garlic and smoke swirls around my mouth in a happy dance. After a few chews, I try a sample of the other dishes and am equally impressed.

"Well?" Billy asks.

"Set a plate aside for the boss," I say.

"Does he need to try the food before you make a decision?" Billy asks anxiously.

I consider the question for a moment. I haven't made many decisions around here without Hunter's input, but if I'm going to gain anyone's respect around here, I'm going to have to make some without always running every decision by him.

"Billy, you're still here for two more weeks, which I hope is enough time for you to run through the entire menu with Lacy."

He smiles. "It should be."

"And Lacy, I'll let you know what Mr. Middleton says, but you come highly recommended, and the food is delicious, so I think we should move forward. Did Billy discuss money with you?"

"Yes."

"Obviously, I can't pay you what he gets because he's been the lead cook for The Blue Whiskey for years."

"Just two and a half," Billy interjects.

"Which seems like a lifetime," I chuckle, teasing him. "But I can certainly pay you a competitive wage for the position."

"Okay," Lacy agrees. "I'm good with that."

"And you realize the only day off is Monday?"

"Yes, Billy explained the schedule. It's no problem. I like to keep busy."

I give Billy a silent look, which he can totally read. Out of everyone in the club, he's the person I've had the most conversations with. It's kind of nice that he knows what I'm thinking without me having to say a word. I'll kind of miss him when he leaves.

He offers me a knowing nod in return. "She's prepped and primed, boss lady. She understands the assignment and is ready to work."

"Okay then, let's try it."

I can see the huge relief in her eyes and I remember Billy telling me about her living situation. Lowering my voice so that only she can hear me, I ask her, "There's some paperwork I'm going to need you to fill out, but I just wanted to let you know that Billy already explained your situation. Do you have a place to stay for the next few weeks? One you can put on the tax documents."

She doesn't look embarrassed but simply shrugs. "There's a battered women's shelter I'm at, and we have to keep the location private for obvious reasons."

"Drop by my office after you finish up here," I tell her, my heart aching for her. "I'll see if I can arrange something more permanent for you."

I can tell that my offer just blindsided her, but I'm only paying my good fortune forward. I may not be able to set her up in a high-rent apartment in Hunter's building, but I definitely get paid enough money to help her find somewhere safe and clean to live.

"Thank you."

"Sure."

Billy chuckles as I grab another wing before exiting the kitchen. I can't help myself. They're damn good. As I'm chewing, my eyes catch a familiar figure in the dimly lit room and it takes me a second to place him. It's a man I'm pretty sure I once saw talking with Hunter.

I study him as he ascends the staircase to the second

floor of the club, and I realize he's headed toward one of the VIP booths. I notice that Lars and Parker are standing outside of the booth as well and deduce that Hunter must be sitting there as well.

Parker catches me staring and winks at me. Then Diana comes hurrying over with a smug look on her face.

"The Parillo party wants to see the manager."

It takes me a second to recognize the last name.

That's Ashley's group.

Gage owes me twenty bucks.

I knew they weren't done with me.

"What happened?" I ask her.

She shrugs indifferently, but I can see the sly look in her eyes. She's enjoying this.

"They said that something is wrong with their drinks."

"That's hardly something to call the manager for. Get them new drinks."

"I did, but they still want to see the manager." She gives me one of her judgmental looks as I stare her down with one of my own. "Just go and do your job."

My patience is running thin with this woman.

"Diana, once your shift is over, I want you to come to see me in my office. We need to have a talk."

"If you even have an office by the end of my shift," she mutters nastily under her breath.

I catch every word, and the nasty intent behind them, which is why I'm itching to scratch her eyes out, but losing my temper is not who I am. In fact, I'm pretty sure that the reason why I've gotten through so many awful times in my life is that I know how to keep my head down and my mouth shut.

The easiest solution to my Ashley problem is to just get this over with, so I make my way up to their booth, crossing paths with Lars and Parker. They shoot me a curious glance as I stand in front of the booth's privacy curtain, waiting to be acknowledged.

The second floor of The Blue Whiskey has a very different feel than the first floor. The first floor is animated and busy. There are dozens of patrons drinking and dancing, as you would see in most crowded LA clubs. But on the second floor, things are quieter. There are private booths that are luxurious, with soft lighting and plush couches. Sometimes, they're reserved for meetings by very dangerous men, and sometimes, they're reserved for groups of friends who can afford it.

"You may enter," Ashley announces in some sort of fake regal accent.

As I slide the luxe fabric curtain open, the first thing I see is Ashley sitting in Ricky's lap. On seeing me, she gives me a deliberate smile and then leans down and presses her mouth against Ricky's in an open-mouthed kiss. I look in disgust, wondering what exactly she plans to achieve out of this public display of affection. Now that I'm sleeping with a man like Hunter Middleton, I couldn't give two shits about these two sleeping together.

"Okay." I look around at the shot glasses on the table. "So, what seems to be the problem with the drinks?"

Ashley's eyes are open and fixed on mine as she continues to French Kiss Ricky. When she didn't get the reaction, she clearly expected to get out of me. She pulls away, wiping the sides of her mouth delicately with her thumb.

"I asked to see the manager."

"You're looking at her."

"The drinks are shit here."

The two other girls sitting on the opposite side of the booth snicker.

"I see." My eyes go to the tequila bottles and one empty bottle of wine. "Which is why you and your party consumed all of it?"

She doesn't get annoyed by my retort but instead surprises me with an offer.

"Why don't you join us? We've ordered some more drinks, crappy as they are."

"Join you?" I echo. "Now, why would I do something as stupid as that?"

She picks up her wineglass and rises from Ricky's lap, beaming at me. "I just think that we should try to get along."

"Unfortunately, I don't share that opinion, Ashley. And since it's obvious that the server is getting you another round of drinks to make up for whatever convoluted problem there was with the first round, I'm going to excuse myself. Some of us have work to do."

It's a physical struggle to be polite. I can feel a sickening feeling of fury moving through my veins like sludge. Choking me from the inside out.

Suddenly, Ashley moves closer toward me, and her two minions stand. One has the empty wine bottle in her hand as if she's ready to use it as a weapon.

Oh, fuck.

I don't get time to react as the three of them quickly surround me. The only one still seated and quiet is Ricky as if his irresponsible behavior isn't the source of Ashley's sick obsession with me.

The short girl with a menacing look on her face raises the bottle up high, and my arms quickly form a protective formation to defend myself. Ashley then shoves me back into the glass table with so much force that the table shatters under my weight.

"You fucking bitch!" She spits on me as I try to avoid the surrounding glass. "I'm sick of your ass. First, you try to steal my place in the exhibition, and then you make a sex tape with my boyfriend! You fucking slut!"

Stunned by what's just happened, I'm barely listening to her. All I can think about is how I'm going to get up and not stab myself with the large shards of glass sticking out from the table's edges. Enjoying my struggle, Ashley kicks at my leg, and I feel a sharp pain from my barely healed stitches.

"Crawl over the glass!" She jeers, and the girls surrounding me hoot in laughter.

Finally looking uncomfortable, Ricky stands and extends his hand to help me up until Ashley pushes it away.

"Don't you dare help her," she hisses at him.

"You've lost your fucking mind!" I snarl at her, wincing in pain. "This is a goddamn assault! Do you think I won't press charges? You think I won't tell them how you've practically been stalking me because your boyfriend couldn't keep it in his pants?"

"Assault?" Ashley sneers at me before looking around at her friends. "You saw the way she attacked me, right? I was just defending myself. Even that employee saw it!"

She points towards where Diana is standing, looking a little shaken by the amount of violence that she clearly hadn't expected.

"Right?" Ashley presses, her eyes narrowing, and Diana bobs her head up and down in frantic agreement.

I pull myself out of the broken table, ignoring the scratches on my legs, and I stand.

"You've royally fucked up this time," I warn her. "This was the worst place you could have attacked me."

"Is that right?" Ashley leans in to put her ugly snout in my face. "Did you think I would let you steal my position in the program and fuck my boyfriend?"

"I'm not interested in your pencil dick of a boyfriend, Ashley," I spit out before glowering at Ricky. "Is that what you told her? That I made a move on you? Why don't you tell her the truth, you dickless bastard? Why don't you ever speak up? You asked me out the moment I stepped onto campus and have been sniffing up my ass ever since."

"Don't be ridiculous," she sniffs. "Ricky would never actually be interested in a low-class slut like you."

"Really? Because I didn't force your boyfriend to put his dick in my mouth."

Both of her minions audibly gasp. "What did she say?"

"I knew you were trash." Ashley shoves me, practically snarling. "You tricked Ricky into whatever that was I saw on tape, and now you've resorted to using some withered old man to steal my spot in the exhibition."

I'm seeing red right now. For once, maybe I should react. Perhaps I just punch her perfect little nose and break it.

Fuck the consequences.

"Where's your old man now?" My hand curls into a fist as Ashley continues to taunt me. "Does he know you work in this dump, or is this where you met him?"

I think about the last time I hit someone out of blind fury. It was years ago, and it hurt like hell, but I swear it would make me feel so much better inside.

So, just as I'm about to lift my fist and punch the living daylights out of her, the curtain of the private booth is yanked clear from the metal pole it was hanging on, and a chilly voice with piercing grey eyes pins Ashley violently in place.

"Her *old man* knows every fucking thing about her."

Chapter 8

Malicious Intent

Hunter

There's a reason why the private booths in my club are not fully enclosed with walls and doors. A lot of very violent people tend to want privacy. Therefore, I need someone on my team to be within earshot of everything going on in this place. So, even with the heavy bass of the music thumping downstairs, I immediately heard the sound of glass shattering.

And the noise was enough for me to pause right in the middle of my meeting and send Parker and Lars to check out what was going on. Before he has a chance to speak, I already know that it has something to do with *her* once I see the look on Lars's face.

"Boss, it's Megan."

Of course, it is.

I don't hesitate.

"Excuse me a moment."

Now that I'm making my way down the hallway, I can hear some part of the conversation.

"Where's your old man now?"

"Does he know you work in this dump, or is this where you met him?"

It's the taunting voice of a woman, and I can only imagine who it is because it is clear that the words are targeted toward Megan.

My Megan.

"I've got this," I tell Parker and Lars, my veins turning icy. "Lars, please make sure my guests are still comfortable. Parker, you stay."

I yank open the curtain and make my presence known.

"Her *old man* knows every fucking thing about her. How can I help you?"

I can see the startled faces of the young women (and that damn little boy she used to play with) who are surrounding a furious Megan standing in the middle of a broken glass table. I can see that I've interrupted her in the middle of throwing a punch.

Too bad.

She has nicks and cuts all over her arms and legs, and as I stride toward her, I make a mental note to get rid of anything made of glass around this woman. I don't want any more injuries marring her beautiful, deeply melanated skin.

I shrug off my favorite Tom Ford blazer and wrap Megan's form in it as she glowers at me. I know she wants to be the one to settle this, but I cover the jacket around her tightly, my voice full of malice. "You had your chance. Now, it's mine."

I see a small figure try to dart out but Parker steps in the path of the female server.

"Now, who would like to explain what is happening here?" I ask pleasantly as Megan continues to breathe fire.

There are several familiar faces in this booth. I thought

college was a place of civility and higher learning, but clearly, it's also a place where elitism and bullying continue to thrive.

Besides the boy, I definitely recognize the young woman standing next to him. The same girl whose family tried to steal Megan's exhibition spot. She clearly has it out for Megan, but this nonsense stops tonight.

Her eyes gleam as they run over me in open appreciation. "And who are you to question us about what we're doing, *old man?*"

"I'm the owner of this club," I study her. "Care to explain what happened here?"

A look of understanding shadows her face, and I can see the malicious intent enter her eyes as she steps toward me.

"Your manager or girlfriend or whatever tried to assault me! She made an overt pass at my boyfriend, and when he rejected her, she attacked me. When my friends came to the rescue, she stumbled and fell through the table. I want her fired."

Megan is still under the crook of my arm and I can feel her breathing slowing as she calms herself down.

"It doesn't look like you were attacked," I comment. "However, it does look like my manager was assaulted."

"I'm sorry, sir, but–" The young woman flips her hair over her shoulder. "Do you know who I am? My father is the CEO of the Parillo Investment Group. I'm Ashley Parillo."

Her smile is more meaningful this time when she runs her eyes over me in a deliberate attempt to let me know she's checking me out.

How amusing.

"Why would somebody like me," Ashley continues haughtily, "lie about something like that?"

Megan starts to interrupt her, but I give her a quick squeeze. She's had enough of this girl's vitriol for a lifetime.

"Besides," Ashley points towards the server, trembling in front of Parker. "She saw the whole thing. Didn't you?"

I look at the girl who looks terrified, and I wonder if she's going to make the right decision.

"I – I saw it," she stammers. Her eyes focused on the ground. Whatever she's about to say is going to be a complete lie. That's clear as day. "Megan gave me a note to give to her boyfriend, and then she came up and tried to attack her."

I'm not completely unaware of the hostility amongst the staff when it comes to Megan and her new promotion. Gage mentioned a thing or two to me about it.

The only reason I haven't interfered with things so far is because this is a learning opportunity for her. Megan is talented, smart, and strong but some people have to learn from their mistakes a few more times than others. And she needs to learn the lesson of "threshold," also known as how much shit a person is going to take from another person regardless of who they are or who they know. However, I did not anticipate the amount of malicious intent aimed at her at school *and* at my place of business. Sometimes women can really be cruel to their own.

"I see," I respond to their server coolly. I can't even remember her name right now. "Parker, why don't you-"

"Hunter," Megan's voice is sharp and I meet her gaze, seeing the discreet shake of her head.

She wants to handle this one herself, and I don't blame her. It's obvious the server is lying through her teeth, and Megan is her supervisor. This is between them.

"Fine." I'm curious to see how she'll handle things.

"Take her downstairs and keep her in my office until Megan and I are finished up here," I tell Parker.

"What?" The server's eyes widen. "But I didn't do anything!"

"Let's go, Diana," Parker says, his voice unforgiving.

"But it's her fault!" she cries.

"I won't ask again," Parkers adds, and this time she complies.

Now that it's just us, I look at Ashley and her crew of college idiots. "You were saying?"

"Why did you send her away?" Ashley has an uneasy look on her face. "She was my witness."

Funny how she thinks she's entitled to some sort of fair justice in my building.

"How I handle my employees has nothing to do with you," I respond lightly.

"The hell it doesn't." She frowns. "She's our witness."

"She's not a very reliable witness." I smile at her. "She's not a very good server either. Maybe this isn't the place for her."

"It doesn't matter," Ashley says after an uncomfortable beat. "The fact of the matter remains that your employee came at us, harassed us, and we had to defend ourselves. She's crazy. We want her fired. Otherwise, we'll sue."

"All right." I tuck my free hand inside my pants pocket, watching her calmly.

"So, you're going to fire her then?" Her expression clears, and her lips curve.

She looks towards Megan, her voice dripping with smug satisfaction, "Let this be a lesson to you. Next time–"

"I'll contact my lawyers," I cut her off smoothly. "You or your daddy can deal directly with them. In the meantime, if you want to sue me, then I should at least give you a legitimate reason to do so."

I turn my attention towards the boy, Ricky. I'm just about sick of this bastard. If he wasn't someone that people would miss, I'd have put his ass underground a long time ago. He has no backbone and serves no purpose on this planet, as far as I'm concerned.

To some people, that might seem harsh, and I realize that most of my feelings may be influenced by the fact that once upon a time, his dick was in my Megan's mouth, but whatever.

"I thought you and I already had a talk about this?" I say to him.

"Just because you talked doesn't mean I listened," he responds, clearly impressing his entourage with his misguided bravado. Ashley and her minions smirk.

Does he think I won't do anything to him because there are people watching?

The gun tucked behind me in my waistband is in my hands within seconds, pointed at his puny chest, and he freezes.

"Senator Wyatt owes me plenty of favors. I'm sure he wouldn't mind if I teach his nephew a lesson."

"W-What?" Ricky's face drops. "You know Uncle Wyatt?"

"Oh my God, he has a gun," another girl murmurs.

"Oh shit, he's a gangster," the other one says.

"I warned you the other day not to put your hands on my woman ever again, didn't I?" I question him.

When he doesn't answer, sweating like a pig, I speak in a soft but menacing voice. "I believe I asked you a question."

"I was..." He stammers, his watery eyes darting toward Megan.

"Don't look at her," I say coldly. "How dare you look at her. I find it baffling how you would allow a woman you're fucking to come to Megan's place of business and harass her in this way. What kind of man are you?"

I can hear the sounds of the girls whimpering behind me, frightened at this sudden turn of events.

"What are you doing?" Ashley sputters. "You can't just shoot people in a public place. My father will have you put *under* the damn jail."

"Your father is trying to secure a contract with my company at this very moment," I glance toward her while my gun is still aimed at Ricky.

"That's a lie. What would my father want with a shitty nightclub?"

"This establishment serves as an office for my actual business and considering that your father's company is on the verge of bankruptcy, it's quite unfortunate that his daughter's actions are going to lose him that contract. I won't do business with a man who raised a bitch like you."

After my words, I can feel Megan's energy filling the room with newfound confidence. Good, she needs to understand that this isn't just about someone making a scene in my club but about me showing her that I will always protect her.

"W-What?" Ashley looks uncertain. "That's not true."

I glance at Ricky's crotch and can see that he's peed on himself. Sometimes I forget that Megan's life is filled with soft college students and not hardened criminals like mine. Pulling a gun on this asshat was probably overkill, but I still can't help but smile to myself. What a pussy.

"You might want to take care of that," I say to him as I lower my gun and place it back in my waistband.

"Call him," I return back to my conversation with

Ashley. "Ask him if he's trying to negotiate a contract with the Middleton Financial Group."

I triumphantly grin as the slow realization of my identity finally becomes apparent to her. I guess my reputation in this town precedes me.

"Wait, you're Hunter Middleton?" Her voice is almost faint.

"As I said, I'll have my lawyers contact you and your father," I inform her. "After all, you claim that my manager assaulted you, right?"

Cold satisfaction moves within me at seeing the horror in her eyes once she puts all the pieces together.

I am Hunter Middleton.

Of Middleton Financial.

I also own this club.

Where Megan is the manager.

And also my girlfriend.

Ashley is fucked.

"The video footage will be the proof we will provide. I make it a point to have both audio and video surveillance in all areas of the club," I say calmly.

I've known many women like Ashley, and now that she's cornered, I can see herself trying to figure out a way to bullshit her way out of this.

"Megan knows it was just a misunderstanding. Come on, Megan, tell him."

Megan shrugs, and then, to my utmost delight, she takes a step back and casually sits down on the couch behind her, tightening my coat around her shoulders. "Tell him what? My *boss* seems to be handling the situation just fine. Do what you want, Hunter." Her eyes give me a slight warning. "Just, well, you know, don't do *that*."

I smile at her.

No torture.

No shootings.

Got it.

"You heard her." I shrug. "It's time for you and your merry band of idiots to leave the premises."

"You bitch!" Ashley spits out, losing her temper. "I will make sure you never step foot on campus again."

I pull out my Glock again and shoot at a random spot on the painted concrete floor. I do it to make a point and because I already know that it's safe. The concrete will stop the bullet from traveling and hitting anyone below us.

The shot goes off near Ashley's feet, and she stumbles to the ground in shock and fear. Her companions burst into hysterical tears.

"That sounded like a threat," I say icily to her. "And no one threatens Megan. Not ever again."

I finally get an appropriate reaction from Ashley as one lone tear falls down her cheek.

"I only give warnings once," I tell the whole lot of them. "There's never a second time. Are we clear?"

"Listen, this wasn't my idea," Ricky says like the coward he is, but the time for excuses and explanations is over.

I don't let him finish his sentence, my gun now aiming at the ear over his right shoulder.

"Don't kill him!" Ashley pleads in a high-pitched voice of desperation. "We're leaving."

"Hunter," Megan says softly.

I can feel and hear every bit of warning in her, but the longer I stare at this piece of shit, the more I want to hurt him.

"Are you protecting him?" I ask angrily through clenched teeth, my eyes still entirely focused on his ear. If I shot him there, there'd be blood and a significant amount of pain, but he'd live another day.

It doesn't escape me how far down a dark path my conscience seems to be wandering. It's why I usually choose not to get close to women. I've seen men start wars over them and now I see why. I hate that this kid has touched her intimately, and I especially hate that she let him.

"No," she assures me calmly as she moves to stand next to me. "I'm protecting you."

Fuck me.

Is she protecting *me?*

I thought I was protecting her.

Ah, of course, I think to myself. She's protecting me in the same way she pushed me out of the way of the assassin's bullets in the penthouse. She is safeguarding me from the biggest threat of all – myself.

I reluctantly tuck my Glock back into my waistband and consider how I've allowed myself to be totally put in check by this art student.

Hell, if I know.

All I know for sure is that this beautiful creature is going to be the death of me, and now I have to find another way to appropriately punish everyone responsible for pushing her through a glass fucking table.

I will not let that shit stand.

And I don't care what Megan has to say about it, even if she says it in bed...and now my dick is hard.

This damn woman.

Chapter 9

A Special Kind Of Pain Reliever

Hunter

"This has been a tremendous waste of everyone's time," I say to the room as I reluctantly tuck the gun back inside my belt. "And tonight marks the end of whatever issues you have with Megan, Miss Parillo. In fact, it would be in your best interest for you and your ragtag band of misfits to cease making any kind of trouble for Megan ever again. Otherwise, I'll pay your father a house call to let him know what you've been up to and how it's affecting his bottom line. Not only will I not give him any funding for his failing business, but I'll make sure that no one in the United States gives him one red dime. You'll be penniless in less than a week."

Ashley's eyes water as the realization of my threat penetrates her thick skull and settles into her minuscule brain.

"Let's go, Ashley," Ricky says curtly as he and the rest of the group quickly scoop up their things to leave.

As the booth clears, Parker returns to check on us. "You all right, boss?"

"We're good, but this group needs an escort directly to the exit."

"Gladly."

"Is my guest okay?" I ask him about the business associate I have waiting in my office.

"Lars is taking good care of him," Parker assures me.

"And the girl?"

"Waiting in your office, as requested."

"Perfect."

Once it's just me and Megan left, Parking sliding the curtain closed behind him, I turn my attention to her and sigh heavily, "Were you always this drama prone, or is this a new thing?"

She looks down at her legs before looking up at me, her tone dry. "It was never this bad until I met you."

"Somehow, I doubt that."

It takes a lot to make me sad, to make me angry, or to make me feel just about anything, but I feel a mixture of all of those emotions as I walk over the shattered glass and crouch next to her.

"Are you okay, baby?"

It's almost as if my question gives her permission to finally lower the shield I figure she must have had up ever since these so-called classmates of hers walked into the club.

"I think so." Her eyes are wide, and there's a slight tremor in her hands as she holds onto the edges of my jacket and falls into my embrace. The murderous rage within me is calming down now that I have her in my arms. "I think I'm going to have to make a few staff adjustments." She lowers her head and leans it into the crook of my arm, her expression tired now. "I need a fucking vacation."

"Where do you want to go?"

"Just stop talking, Hunter," she mutters against my chest, and my hand comes up to settle on her head.

"Lars is going to see to your wounds."

"They're just shallow cuts." She lifts her head. "Thankfully, I don't need stitches again."

I inspect her wounds and am relieved that she's right.

"He'll still take a look at them. In the meantime, I can either have a word with that server myself or—"

"I'll come with you," Megan says sharply. "If she tells another lie about me or about her part in what happened tonight, I'm going to punch her in the mouth myself."

A small grin spreads across my face as I look down at her. "Is it just me, or are you getting a little bloodthirsty?"

"I wouldn't say I'm becoming bloodthirsty, but I'm sick of letting people take advantage of me all the time. It stops tonight, and it starts with her."

"I wish it would have started a little earlier. Then maybe you wouldn't have shards of glass in your beautiful legs."

"They were paying customers."

"They were here for one thing only, and that was to fuck with you. You should have never let them in. That's why you're the manager. I pay you to make those types of judgment calls."

"You're right. I'll do better."

She wiggles herself deeper inside my embrace, tightening her arms around my waist.

"And if there's anything I can do to make things better, you know I will," I tell her.

"Like shoot a few college kids in a nightclub?" She deadpans.

"I was only going to shoot one."

She leans her head back. "You can't go around shooting people and think that's okay."

"He could have put a stop to this a long time ago. He's a pussy."

Megan shakes her head in disbelief. "You're insane."

I've become helplessly entangled in Megan, and I'm level-headed enough to acknowledge that. If she can't bring herself to trust me all the way yet, then I can at least become the place she can lean against if it helps her stand firmer.

"About you." I caress her cheek before leaning down and kissing her deeply.

As always, her eyes flutter shut as she obediently opens her mouth, allowing me to force my tongue inside and taste the bitter coffee that's still fresh on her tongue.

My cock hardens almost instantly when she fists her hand in my shirt, trying to pull herself closer to me. My blood heats up from her submissive reaction whenever I put my hands on her. She may snarl and swipe at me during the day, but when I touch her, it's as if her body already knows that it belongs to me. When I pull away, I wonder when kissing her became so addicting.

I can see her trying to clear her head, and she glares at me. "Stop it; I've got glass in my legs."

"Does it sting?"

"A little."

"Let me fix that."

With my forehand, I sweep any remaining bits of glass on one of the velvet sofas and place her down on it.

"What are you doing?"

"Pain reliever."

"I thought you were going to have Lars handle it?"

"He can't handle this part."

I kneel on the floor before her, sliding her skirt high to her hips.

"Your knees," she comments, concerned that I may cut them.

"I don't care about that. I only care about this."

I slide the crotch of her panties to the side, bury my head between her legs, and inwardly groan at the hypnotic scent of her pussy.

It feels like a lifetime since I've tasted her.

"Hunter," she moans, then mews as I taste the delicious bud between her folds.

I slide her hips forward and gently place each leg on my shoulders so I can make her forget about the last fifteen minutes. Then I thrust my tongue inside of her as her head falls back in bliss.

"Yes, Hunter," she approves.

I continue working her pussy with my tongue as I feel her orgasm wind inside of her. She squeezes my head like a vise with her thighs, but it only makes my dick harder.

She tastes sweeter than I could have imagined. A honeyed sweetness, heady and thick, as if a field were flowering in my mouth.

Her hands grip my biceps, and her nails dig into my skin. I continue thrusting my tongue inside her cunt, and she cries out, pulling me deeper inside of her.

I stop for a moment and raise my head so I can look into her eyes. "I love you," I tell her with sincerity.

She smiles in response, then wraps her legs around my waist in an effort to pull me closer. "Come here, Mr. Middleton."

Our kiss is slow and gentle until I end it. Sliding back down to my position, but this time with both of my hands wrapped around each of her breasts. We both moan as I squeeze her nipples and slide my tongue back inside her wet pussy.

She starts to move her hips in time with my tongue, and I'm still holding onto her tits as her entire body becomes rigid with desire.

"Oh, god!" she cries out as her orgasm comes swift and hard and does exactly what I hoped it would. It replaces a horrible memory of what happened to her in this booth with a much better one.

"That was fantastic." She smiles.

I wipe my mouth with the back of my hand.

"I'm glad to have been of service."

She stares at the huge bulge behind my zipper.

"I can help you out, too."

"Not right now, Miss Taylor. We're still at work. But you can reciprocate after hours at my place."

"Is that right?" She grins seductively.

"You can reciprocate all fucking night if you want."

"We'll see how I'm feeling later," she giggles. "I mean, I have been injured on the job."

I love it when she's playful like this, so I slide open the curtain and pop my head outside, feeling totally playful myself.

"Lars, we need first aid pronto!"

Chapter 10

The Judge, Jury, and Executioner

Hunter

When Lars arrives a moment later with a first aid kit, I can tell that Megan is slightly horrified by the prospect that he's possibly heard what we've been up to behind the velvet curtain.

"Were you outside the whole time?" she asks Lars as I try holding back a laugh.

"Nah, but you're like a beacon for trouble. I knew when I heard glass breaking that you'd be in the middle of it," he tells Megan gruffly. "So here I am with a first aid kit... again."

"I guess I'm a little accident-prone," she admits.

Lars opens his kit and pulls out a few antiseptic packets as I quietly watch the interaction between them.

"You almost took the boss's head off when you were defending that server a few months back. Why don't you ever defend yourself like that?"

"Lars, I swear I was this close to stabbing her with one of the shards," Megan blusters, suddenly finding some fighting spirit. "You would have had my back if I had, right?"

"Without a second thought," he assures her as he carefully cleans her wounds.

I chuckle to myself at their budding friendship. Lars and Parker really seem to look at Megan as their new little sister, and I find something really comforting about that. At least I know that if I'm not around, one of them will always step up to protect her.

"Wasn't Lars babysitting one of your business associates?" Megan asks, reminding me of my horrible manners.

Before her, I would have never ditched a meeting, but after her — I find myself moving a little differently.

"You sent him home in a car?" I ask Lars, already knowing that he's handled business.

"With a bottle of his favorite cognac."

"Good and have someone clean this mess up, Lars. Megan and I need to handle something in my office."

"Will do."

"Thanks again, Lars," Megan says, gently tapping his shoulder.

"Yep," he gruffly responds, not quite comfortable with common niceties.

Since Megan is bandaged up, it's time to walk toward my office and deal with Diana.

"None of the guests seem to have noticed that World War Three was going on up here," she notices. It's business as usual on the first floor. Loud music, drunk patrons, and boisterous laughter.

I abruptly enter my office, and the server appears shaken, yet some of her bravado returns when Megan walks in right behind me.

I don't make it a habit of harming women or children, but in this instance, I'm tempted to break my own rules. I'm not sure how I didn't notice it before, but this girl is toxic, and I've clearly put a sweet lamb in charge of managing a rabid wolf. Women are truly complicated creatures.

"I don't see why I'm here," the girl says in a sulky tone. "I didn't do anything. Megan broke the table because she's just clumsy."

I unclench one of my fists, smooth my hands down the front of my slacks, stride over to my chair, and sit down. Megan prefers to stay standing with a hand on her hip by the office door.

"Slandering staff of the Blue Whiskey is a punishable offense, miss whatever your name is."

"Punishable?" she swallows nervously.

"Something you should be wary of because in this establishment, I'm the judge, jury, and executioner."

Her eyes anxiously dart toward Megan as if she's looking for help, but she still refuses to accept any responsibility.

"I didn't slander anybody." Her hand lifts, and she points a finger at Megan. "The group wanted Megan to make things right, and she wouldn't."

"That's Miss Taylor to you," I interrupt. Then I pull an electronic cigarette out of the middle drawer of my desk and blow a lazy puff of smoke in the air. "You seem to have forgotten that she's your superior, not your equal."

"Fine," she huffs. "The customers weren't happy with their drinks and asked to speak to a manager. *Miss Taylor* refused to do her job and appease them."

"Since when does a manager have to make things right with a bad drink order?" I ask lightly, then take another puff. "That sounds like a conversation between you and the bartender."

The server's jaw tightens but she continues with this line of reasoning because it's obvious that she can't accept when she's in the wrong.

"She may be the manager, but she didn't act like one tonight."

"How so?"

"Yeah, how so?" Megan chimes in angrily.

"Well, when I first brought them their first round of drinks, Miss Taylor gave me a note to pass to the man who was with the group. Then later, she had the audacity to insult me in front of the guests when all I was doing was trying to do was diffuse the situation she created."

I'm about to interrupt, but Megan gives me a discreet shake of her head, so I lean back, waiting.

"The man showed his girlfriend the note, and that's when she demanded that I call the manager, which I did."

"So it wasn't about the drinks?" Megan interjects. "Get your story straight, Diana."

The server rolls her eyes and continues the story. "Anyway, *Miss Taylor* arrived, and then she made a pass at the boyfriend again, and when his girlfriend told her off, your manager attacked her."

The server's little story ends on a smug note. She must have taken quite a bit of time to plan out her version of events in her head once I sent her down here.

I glance towards Megan, who is watching her with a thoughtful expression.

"What do you want to do?" I ask out loud, giving her a wide berth to give me whatever answer she wants, but it better end with *her being fired.*

Megan suddenly crosses the room, marches towards one

of the guest seats, and sits down in a graceful manner. She no longer looks angry. In fact, she's smirking as she takes her time crossing her bandaged legs as one finger taps against the exposed metal edge of the armrest.

"I need you to call down to the bar and ask Gage to come to the office, Mr. Middleton." I smile, and my dick gets hard as Megan gives me an order.

"This is Middleton," I call down to the bar. "Send up Gage."

The silence in the room is heavy and almost strategic and I can see the server's confidence begin to falter as she waits for someone to speak. On the other hand, Megan inspects her nails as if she hasn't a worry in the world. I love to see how her confidence has grown since I met her. She's become less passive-aggressive and more calculated...a trait which only benefits her if she's going to continue to be in my world.

When Gage finally arrives, Megan readjusts herself on the chair as if to make herself more comfortable. The server frowns at Gage's presence but doesn't say anything.

"Now," Megan starts calmly. "Gage, can you resolve a small dispute for us?"

Gage meets my eyes and I give him a small nod of approval before releasing another halo of sweet smoke in the air.

"When Diana came to place the order for Booth Four, who was in contact with the drinks, the tray, *and her?*"

Diana goes still and I watch with growing interest as Gage eyes her before saying calmly, "Nobody aside from me."

"And where was I?"

"You were preparing a cocktail next to me."

"Did I speak to Diana?"

"No."

"Did I touch that tray or put a piece of paper on it?"

"Absolutely not."

"Did I handle *any* part of that order?" Megan's voice is steady.

"No."

Megan then glares at a pale Diana. "Well, there you have it."

"Well, he's obviously lying!" The server blurts out.

I'm itching to step in but I can see that Megan's put the girl in a bind. What had probably started out as a malicious prank by some college kids to get Megan fired ended with the server in the crossfire. If she admits that she lied, she might lose her job. But if she manages to convince everyone that her version of events did in fact take place, then Megan takes the heat as if I'd ever let that shit happen.

"Why would I lie?" Gage looks between her and Megan with confusion. "What is even going on here? And what the hell happened to you, Megan?" Gage asks, noticing her bandages.

"He has a point." Megan shrugs, looking directly at the server. "Why would he lie?"

"Because maybe your manipulative ass is sleeping with him too."

I notice a small smile vanish from Megan's face when she addresses the server, "I beg your pardon?"

"Everybody knows that you're-"

"Are you sleeping with someone aside from me, Megan?" I ask casually, deciding to cut in before Diana says something else insulting and this conversation turns in a whole other direction.

Megan whirls around to face me, and while I know she's annoyed by the way I'm exposing our relationship in this situation, it's not like everyone in this room doesn't already know it.

I give her a flirtatious wink and watch as the anger fades away from her eyes. She presses her lips together before saying in a tight voice, "Don't be ridiculous. Of course, I'm not."

"Uh, and I'm offended too. I just got here," Gage says, feigning offense. "I'm not sleeping with anyone in this town yet."

"So, there you have it," Megan says. "Your entire story falls apart just like this. Why would I go after somebody like Ricky when I have Hunter? But more importantly, why are you so focused on fucking with me, Diana? Do you want Hunter for yourself? Is that it?"

She looks at me nervously. "No, of course not."

"And by the way, there's video footage of what happened in that booth as well. I just brought in Gage to simply prove a point."

The server is shaking now but says nothing. Her eyes dart between both me and Megan and she looks terrified. It was one thing assuming that there was a relationship out of pure spite, but to have it confirmed considering the accusations she's just made, she knows she's been caught.

"You're fired," Megan finally asserts.

"Wait, you can't fire me." She looks directly at me. "Can she?"

"She's the manager." I grin.

"Oh, hell no." The server tries to jump out of her seat but Gage places a hand on her shoulder, holding her in place.

"Calm down, Diana," he advises as she struggles against his hold, her eyes wet with tears of panic.

"I had no choice but to tell the story they wanted me to. They threatened me!"

"Who threatened you?" Megan asks rhetorically. "A bunch of college kids? Please. I want you to get your things out of the break room and never show your face here again. I've had enough."

"And I'll be making sure you don't get a service job anywhere in Los Angeles," I add lightly. "Guess it's time for you to change careers or change cities."

She glares at Megan with a lethal look. "The only reason you can do this is because you're fucking his brains out."

"Watch your tone," I warn, ready for this drama to be over. When I fire people, I toss them out literally on their asses. There's never this much talking.

"I'm not like you, Diana." Megan stands, giving her a dark smile. "Unlike you, I don't have to sleep with my supervisor to get more hours."

When the girl's eyes widen in shock, Megan continues. "Did you really think I didn't know? Did you think I didn't notice how you would leave Steve's office with your buttons misaligned and your lipstick smeared? I notice everything in this club, but I stayed out of it because it didn't affect my check, and frankly, it was none of my business."

"I didn't—"

"And I would have ignored your petty jealousy after my promotion had you not gotten involved with those customers tonight. They were rude, and they assaulted me, and you did everything you could to help them. The fact is, whether you like it or not, is that I'm the manager and I have the right to make staff decisions. So I repeat, you're fired. Now get out before I have security toss you out."

Megan has never appeared more fuckable than she does

right at this moment. She was already sexy and can suck a mean dick, but now that she's coming into her own power — I want to fuck her senseless right now.

"Remember what I told you earlier, Diana? The judge and jury have spoken, and I suggest you follow directions if you don't want the executioner to get involved. I do not give out lenient sentences," I threaten.

"I'm leaving!"

Finally.

"I'll walk you out," Gage offers as he escorts her out of the office.

"I don't need you to walk me anywhere!" She screams at the top of her lungs.

"I'm doing it anyway."

When the room clears, I look hungrily at Megan and consider how selfish of me it would be if I fucked her for the second time tonight.

Her legs are bruised.

She just fired her first employee.

But all I can think about is spreading her limbs from east to west and fucking her silly on top of my desk.

Chapter 11

I'm Off My Game

Hunter

"You handled that well," I say once the room clears.

"Yes, well," Megan sinks deeper into the chair across from me. "I feel like shit."

"Why?"

She doesn't meet my gaze, as she explains.

"The only reason Diana took this job was so that she could help pay her younger brother's medical bills, and I'm pretty sure that this was the highest-paying job she's ever had."

I study the beautiful but complicated creature in front of me, wondering why it baffles me that despite everything she's been through and still goes through, that she still manages to feel empathy for someone who was trying to ruin her. That kind of compassion is not part of my DNA.

"Kindness may just be your biggest weakness, Megan," I tell her, hoping she comprehends what I'm saying as a warning.

She's a part of my life now, and there's no room for weakness in my world. I've learned that the hard way a million times over. Of course, look at me calling the damn kettle black.

Megan *is* my weakness.

"I know she doesn't deserve it," she mutters regretfully. "But I still feel bad."

When I don't say anything else in response, she looks up at me. The gleam in her doe-like eyes makes me narrow mine because I already know what she's thinking.

"Absolutely not," I say firmly.

"Oh, come on," she pleads in a soft, beseeching voice that I've never heard her use before. "It's not fair that nobody else has to pay the consequences of what they did today, but Diana does."

Jesus, I've got to toughen this woman up.

"No."

"Hunter." She crosses the room toward me, and I give her a hard look.

Watching her limp over to me with bandages on her legs isn't helping her case. All I can think about is the reason why she's injured. Somebody pushed her through a goddamn table. If those brats had been anybody else, I would have gladly put at least one of them in the hospital and left another lying in the alleyway.

"Don't even bother, Megan. It's not happening. That server was complicit in a series of events designed to harm you tonight, and it looks like she succeeded," I say, pointing to her injuries. "And what's the deal? You were ready to knock her out fifteen minutes ago."

"I know." She locks the door and then seats herself carefully in my lap. My hands instinctively rise to steady her. "I wanted to hate her, but this isn't about her. It's about her little brother. I won't be able to sleep at night if she can't find another job."

"Then you should sleep with me tonight," I say seductively as my hand lowers to caress her ass. "I'm sure I can help with that."

"Well, what about after tonight?" she adds flirtatiously. Her expression morphs into a pout. "Please, Hunter."

It's quite obvious that she's trying to manipulate me, but I can't help but enjoy the attempt.

"Stop it," I tell her half-heartedly.

Her mouth settles on my cheek, close to my ear, and she presses a sweet kiss to it. "Stop what?"

I tighten my jaw, my voice holding a hint of warning, "Megan."

"I know she can't come back here, but I also know that you're Hunter Middleton, and you have connections all over the city. You can find her another job."

"And why would I do that?"

"Think about her poor brother. It'll be a good deed."

My dick swells as I allow her to continue to pepper my face with kisses. "I'm afraid that all the good deeds in the world won't balance out my karma."

"You don't know that," she whispers, stealing an arousing kiss from my lips, prompting me to actually consider her request. It's stupid, I know, but clearly, Megan has been a bad influence on me.

"There is one place," I finally relent. "There's a chain of bars that I've recently invested in. The one I'm thinking about is kind of far from downtown, but I guess it would work."

"That sounds perfect," Megan says quickly.

"You think you've accomplished something," I scowl at

her, tightening my hold on her hips and pulling them forward. "But I don't like this, Megan. I'm not pleased."

"You seem pleased," she teases as she motions her hips in circles on top of me.

"Don't let my dick fool you," I tell her. "I'm not happy."

"Aww, but you're doing it for me." She presses another kiss to my mouth. "The woman you *love*, remember?"

"Oh, you heard when I said that, did you?" I smirk.

"Of course, I heard."

"I wasn't sure."

"Well, you have to admit that I was a bit distracted. You were in between my legs doing what you do best."

"That's not all I do best."

I lean into a second kiss, but she deftly slips out of my hold.

"What's the name of the bar? I wonder if I can catch her before she leaves."

"Megan!" I growl. "Get your little ass back here!"

But she just winks at me and rushes out the door, leaving me with a perpetual hard-on.

I let out a frustrated groan.

Megan heard me tell her that I loved her, but she craftily avoided giving me a response.

With all that's going on, I'm starting to question why I've let this woman distract me from everything that's supposed to matter to me.

I have feelings for her.

Deep feelings.

But this has got to stop.

I call Parker's cell to let him know that Megan is on some sort of misguided mission to save Diana and to keep an eye on her while I catch up on some work. But after an hour of mindlessly shuffling files across my desk, I decide to get a change of scenery and walk the club floor. I've got a lot of things to think about.

My earlier meeting before Megan's incident proved to be fruitless. While I did have to cut it short, the man showed me pictures of a few young women but none of them had been Lena. It had been easy to identify their lack of common characteristics with my sister. It was the small things: the shape of their noses, their eyes, their lips. It's been years since I've seen her face, but I'd be able to spot it in a crowd of a million.

But I'm off my game.

Distracted.

And I'm starting to wonder if I've thrown myself into a wild goose chase of Jonathan's making. The violent hit on me at my apartment is not how I thought he would come at me. It was well executed, and if it hadn't been for Megan, I'd be dead. I don't think that's his style. If indeed he's coming for me, I think he'd try to play with my head. Like a cat batting around a mouse before the kill.

Weeks have passed, and even with all the feelers I've thrown out, I'm coming up empty-handed. Vaughn's information network runs deep, and I'm getting daily reports from his team, but it's almost as if Johnathan doesn't exist and my sister didn't survive. I'm coming up short on leads for both of them, and it's beyond frustrating.

What if Jonathan laid a trail of breadcrumbs that lead to nowhere? What if he used Steve to get into my head to distract me from whatever his real goal is? Perhaps he did hire the shooter to come to my apartment that night, but only to scare me, not kill me. What assassin shoots that many rounds and misses?

We actually tracked down the shooter a few days later, but he managed to kill himself before the interrogation (torture) could begin. On a street level, I have to respect someone who wanted to leave this earth on his own terms. However, the few clues he left behind are enough to tell me that the person behind this attempt on my life is a new player in my world who's been hiding in the shadows.

I still don't know yet if this new player and Jonathon are working together or whether both of them have their own individual goals to steal what's mine. Whoever they are, ultimately, they are both rivals who must be eliminated. And the hope that has slowly begun to build up inside of me at possibly finding Lena alive must take a backseat. It would be a happy accident if I find her, but I can't forget that my number one priority is staying alive and staying on top.

Everything else, even Megan, is secondary.

Speaking of Megan, I don't see her on the club floor observing servers or by the bartender's station yapping with Gage, so I assume she's in her office. I find myself hoping that she didn't catch up with Diana and has rethought her attempt at being a Good Samaritan.

Still contemplating everything I need to handle, I open the door to Megan's office and see that she's not alone.

Another young woman stands across from her with a cup of water in her hands as she inspects something on the desktop.

"This is just for the initial two-week training period. I'll talk to Mr. Middleton about–" Megan looks up when I enter. "Oh, you're here."

"I wanted to discuss something with you, but I see you're busy. I can come back."

"Actually, this is great timing. Lacy, this is Mr. Middleton."

The woman turns around, and I blink. There's a dullness to her eyes, but there's something vaguely familiar about her features.

"Mr. Middleton, Lacy is the new kitchen hire I told you about–Billy's referral. Today was her trial run in the kitchen. I tried some of the food earlier before all of the drama, but I have to say, I think it's quite good. I was hoping you'd agree if we signed her on for a two-week probationary period and, if all goes well, a full hire."

I nod at Megan as the woman doesn't make direct eye contact with me but at least extends her hand. "Hi, sir; thank you for the chance."

I look down at her hand, and as I grasp it, I see something on the edge of her inner wrist. Without thinking, I turn her hand over, and suddenly, it feels like I've been punched, and all the air has left my body.

Holy hell.

There's a faded leaf-shaped mark on her wrist.

Chapter 12

Do You Trust Me?

Hunter

Lacy's voice fades as she stares at the grip I have on her hand. "Is everything okay?"

When she pulls her hand away, I raise my eyes to hers. "Um, what did you say your name was?"

"Lacy." She pulls her wrist towards her chest warily. "It's Lacy."

"What's your last name?" I look at her face, trying to discern whether I'm actually seeing what I hope for or if I'm just imagining things. "Who are your parents?"

"I don't have parents."

The young woman is beginning to look exceedingly uncomfortable, and she looks over her shoulder at Megan, who justifiably looks just as confused.

"I was raised in foster care," she finally adds, only increasing my curiosity about her.

"I see."

"Hunter, can I have a word?" Megan gives me a sharp

look, and I follow after her without any pushback because I'm a little off-kilter.

Closing the door behind her, she studies me and then whispers, "What's going on? Who is she?"

I stare at her blankly, not knowing what to say. What I'm thinking sounds improbable and frankly a little desperate.

"Hunter?"

"Hire her," I finally tell her. "I need her bio-data."

"Hunter." The sudden fear on Megan's face snaps me out of my shocked state. "Is there something I should know?" She hesitates, and I can see a flash of pain in her eyes before her face becomes hardened. "I told you that I would step back if you found–"

My heart almost goes still at the words she's forcing out, so I stop her before she continues. "Wait, it's not like that," I promise her. "Don't be ridiculous. Don't even think of trying to get rid of me."

I can see her trying to search my eyes for truth, and finally, her stiffened face starts to relax. "Okay then, what's going on? Who is she? You clearly seem to know her."

I'm silent for a moment, and then I ask, "Do you trust me?"

She meets my gaze and gives me a dim smile. "That kind of goes without saying at this point, doesn't it?"

"If that girl doesn't have a place to stay, bring her home with you. You told me she was practically homeless and that Naomi is always over at her new boyfriend's house, right?"

"Yes, but–"

"So don't let her out of your sight for the next two days."

"Hunter."

"Trust me."

Megan gives me a doubtful look before closing her eyes and pinching the bridge of her nose.

"I just think it's weird for me to hire her one day and have her live with me the next."

"Some would say it was weird for me to move you into my apartment building when you needed a safe place to stay."

"Are you throwing that in my face?"

"No, I'm just making a point, Megan. There was something about you that made me want to take action, to protect you."

"And so you're saying you feel the same way about Lacy?" She raises an eyebrow.

"Again, it's not the same. This is different, but you're just going to have to trust me. Have I ever lied to you?"

"Fine." She lets out a heavy sigh. "But she seems like a sweet girl, and she can cook her ass off. You'd better not have anything heinous planned for her."

"I don't," I assure her. "I just need to confirm something, but I need to keep her somewhere safe until I do."

Megan studies me and then nods slowly. "It's still weird, but she can stay with me for a bit. I'll give her my room, and I can sleep in the living room. Even though she's never home, Naomi still pays rent, and I wouldn't want to invade her space."

"Okay."

"That's if Lacy even agrees to it."

"You can be very persuasive when you want to be." I smile, leaning down to give her a chaste kiss on her pouty lips.

"And so can you, Mr. Middleton."

An hour later, I tell Lars and Parker to drive both Megan and Lacy to the apartment.

"Stay with them," I order both men. "Keep your guard up."

Neither of them probably understands why I'd want my two best men to transport and guard two women who are not an imminent threat, but it's not a requirement for my security team to understand my orders. The only thing I require is for them to execute them, and Lars and Parker do that without fail.

In the meantime, I'm going to send in the drinking glass that Lacy was using in Megan's office, along with a strand of my hair, to a local lab that Vaughn has connections with.

"Are you sure?" he asks me, his face grim.

"I have to check, Vaughn. She was wearing colored contact lenses, and her hair was definitely dyed."

"So you think she's purposely disguising herself?"

"I'm not sure what's going on."

"That's unlike you."

"Tell me about it."

"It's going to take me at least two days to get the results," Vaughn says.

"You can't rush things? I own a piece of the lab."

"Just because you are an investor in a bio lab doesn't make science magically work faster for you. It's fucking science."

Christian is in my office with us as well, lounging on the couch, working on something on his laptop, when he suddenly looks at me. "What's with the obsession with the new girl?"

"It's a long story," I say, not wanting to explain my whole theory about Lacy.

"Listen, man, I know you have a lot going on, but I actually came by the club to tell you that I found out something about that nurse, Rose Grant."

"Jonathan's ex?"

Damn, I almost forgot about the nurse.

"It seems that someone did list her as a missing person, and even after all this time, there's still an active search. According to the detective I talked to, every few months, someone whom he assumed was her brother calls him to ask for updates."

Christian sets his laptop aside, interested in this new piece of news. "I wonder why Jonathan would risk exposing himself by looking for her?"

"Assuming it's him," I say.

"Oh, it's definitely him," Vaughn adds. "I've done a deep dive into the nurse's background, and I guarantee you that there's no one else alive who would care enough to keep checking on her whereabouts."

"But if Jonathan's looking for her, that means she isn't with him, which could mean that she's in some serious danger."

"That could also be a possibility," I muse.

"Right, he could still be the rich boyfriend her coworkers mentioned Rose having, but they also could have had a falling out once she realized how demented Jonathan is."

"Another possibility," I agree. "But we just don't know enough yet to draw any definitive conclusions. Are there any other concrete leads, Vaughn?"

"A woman matching her description was seen around a few homeless shelters." He frowns. "The only reason she stood out to those who were questioned is that she traded her clean clothes with those of a homeless person who was in a nearby tent community. The woman remembered her because she thought it was odd."

"So, Rose was actively trying to avoid detection," I say. "What else do we know?"

"I'm the best in the city." Vaughn shakes his head. "But you know how long these things take. The wider the information network, the longer it takes. This Rose person is determined to hide, which means she could literally be anywhere right now. I need more time."

"I'm losing patience, Vaughn. If it was indeed Jonathan who tried to kill me, he needs to be neutralized sooner than later. I can't have the streets thinking I'm weak."

"I know, and I'm on it, but there's one more thing I didn't tell you. Rose's mother stopped showing up to work a few months after Rose disappeared. When the police found her body, she had been tortured, and the dead body was fresh. My suspicion is that Jonathon was trying to draw Rose in by using her mother, and that failed."

Something churns inside of my stomach upon hearing that. Torturing and killing an innocent woman to use as bait? I know I've done some very illegal things myself, but there are limits to what I will do, and if this is true, Jonathan's gone too far.

"Find him, Vaughn," I tell him, frustrated with our lack of progress in finding one damn man.

"I'm on it."

After Vaughn leaves, Christian looks at me warily. "There's something else you should know."

"What the hell else?" I explode.

"Don't shoot the messenger, man."

"Just say whatever it is you're going to say."

"Chinatown is completely being taken over," he says grimly. "Some of our contacts there were attacked by an unknown group of gang members. Three are three fatalities, but one managed to escape. The Eastside Riders and Blood Nation both said that they have nothing to do with it, but our man who escaped said differently. He says it was a joint effort from both gangs."

"What's our guy's name?"

"Pike."

"Is he being protected?"

"He is now."

My eyes darken. "Contact the presidents of both gangs and arrange a meeting tomorrow night. Maybe I've been too lax."

"This is all just a little too convenient." Christian stretches his legs, looking thoughtfully at his laptop. "There's definitely somebody behind the scenes who's pulling the strings. Just a few days ago, one of my contacts told me that there's been some unusual activity between those two gangs."

"Like what?"

"Both gang leaders have been meeting someone for the past couple of weeks. The meetings are held in private, and she's been trying to find out who it is, but now that three of our allies are dead, she's keeping a low profile for now."

"She?"

"She's the old lady of the sergeant-in-arms of Blood Nation."

"And you trust her?"

"As much as I trust anyone who's a part of a biker gang. Remember, I'm a lawyer."

"Did she see anything else?"

"She keeps hearing a name that is being tossed around in the club. She said they call him the Executioner."

I digest this new information and lean back in my seat.

"We've heard that name before, and it's coming up far too often for my liking. Keep looking into it."

"Both Vaughn and I are on it, but if Jonathan is this Executioner person, I still don't understand why he sent a shooter to your penthouse. The attack was unsuccessful."

"He was sending a message," I say plainly. "The assassination attempt was well planned out, but I don't think he wanted or expected it to work. He just wanted me to know that he could get to me, especially in the place where I feel safest: my home. Whoever this is, I've underestimated him, but I'm not going to do it again."

"Coward," Christian hisses.

"His approach is quite smart, actually." My smile is cold. "He's trying to garner support and allies by overriding my previous alliances."

"Alliances?" Christian echoes. "I'd hardly call the relationship you have with those gang bangers *alliances*."

I tap my fingers on the desk and consider the last few months of my life. I've been lax. I've been distracted. I've been worried about protecting one woman when the whole underworld network I've built is falling apart around me.

"Point taken, but that's why I think it's time to remind these people why I'm at the top of the food chain."

"Now that's what I'm talking about." Christian grins with approval. "I look forward to refreshing some memories out there."

I smile in return, but instead of sharing Christian's enthusiasm, Megan's beautiful face pops into my head, and for the first time in my life, I feel the impulse to hesitate.

I'm not out here playing a kid's game. This is a dangerous and deadly world. And I have to wonder... is all of this really worth the chance that I could lose *her*?

Chapter 13

What A Dick

Hunter

The next morning, I wake up to a full house. Lars is waiting for me in the kitchen as usual, watching the morning news, and Vaughn is still here, half asleep on the couch. I don't know why the man just doesn't sleep in my spare bedroom. It's not until I walk by the bedroom on my way to my home office that I understand why. Christian is here, snoring under the blankets like a newborn baby.

"Why can't they just get hotel rooms?" I mutter under my breath. I even tried changing the locks, and they still manage to find a way inside.

Homeless bastards.

Preparing a cup of coffee, I take a seat at my kitchen island and give Lars a look.

"Well?"

I feel like I'm juggling multiple volatile scenarios in my life, and I need clarity on how to handle them all. I've got Vaughn and Christian looking for any leads on my sister, keeping the peace with the local gangs, and keeping their ears close to the ground about this so-called Executioner, but there's still another question I need answered. Who else (other than those spoiled college kids and maybe myself) do I need to protect Megan from so that I can finally get a good night's sleep?

The only way to answer that is to find out everything I can about my new lady love, especially the things she's reluctant to share.

Lars hands me a thin paper file because I prefer to do things old school and not leave a digital trail. "I looked into the half-sister like you requested."

I open the folder and look down at the face of the girl I met a few weeks ago. Her full name is Rachel Taylor and while they look nothing alike, she is indeed Megan's younger half-sister.

"Is she still around?"

"She is."

"Megan hasn't mentioned seeing her again."

"I don't think Megan has seen her. The girl is just lurking." Lars accepts the cup of coffee I handed him. "And unless Megan told her where she lives, the sister has managed to track her down here. I saw her waiting outside across the street the other day, staring up at the top floor of the building as if she's imagining what floor Megan lives on."

"So she was just outside, staring at the building?"

"Yes."

"But she never tried to come inside?"

"The front desk said they never saw anyone matching her description come in."

"Where is a kid like that staying?"

"Local motel near the club."

I skim through the rest of the flimsy file, which is just basic information I could have found with a basic Google search.

"The information in this file doesn't tell me anything new, Lars," I huff as I now use the folder as a coaster for my coffee mug.

"There are a few things that didn't make the report." Lars gives me an uncertain look.

"You've been holding back?" I meet his gaze. "Do tell."

"I had to be certain before I shared this information," he says, letting out a deep breath. "I think I am. The story is that Megan's birth mother ran off and left her with her father when she was just a kid."

"And is that not the case?"

"Not exactly; I actually think her mother lived about five miles from her the entire time."

"That's a shitty thing for her to do."

"Yeah, but she didn't run off and just leave her. No one from the old neighborhood seems to know the exact details anymore, but they say she was a beautiful woman who got mixed up with some bad people and fell victim to a local human trafficking ring."

"A trafficking ring? Can we find her and pull her out?"

"No, boss, she died a few years later."

I go still and look up at him. "Does Megan know?"

"I doubt she knows any of it." Lars shakes his head.

"So the father had to raise her."

"Yeah, and apparently hated every minute of it. He believed the mother stepped out on him, so he was angry and took out a lot of that shit on Megan. He raised her along with his girlfriend, Veronica, who was a registered nurse practitioner. She is who Rachel's mother is. The two are still together."

"Wait, the timeline doesn't make sense. Megan and her sister are only five years apart. If her mother left when she was nine years old–"

"Yeah, the father had obviously been cheating on Megan's mother with the nurse for years. So when her mother left, he just moved them both into his house."

What a dick.

"Do you think he had something to do with what happened to Megan's mother? Maybe he wanted her gone so he could move in his second family."

"The father, Samuel, is definitely a douchebag, but I don't think he's capable of something like that. He's too much of a chickenshit."

A trafficking ring.

That's ruthless.

While I may make my money dabbling in very gray areas of the law, I find sex trafficking vile and inhumane. It's one area of the underworld I stay completely away from so I can sleep at night.

"Is there anything else?"

Lars finally takes a sip of his coffee. "I knew there was something about her that I could recognize in myself."

"What else, Lars?"

"Child protective services were called several times by one of Megan's teachers. I think it was her art teacher. They didn't find enough evidence to prove abuse, but they were suspicious."

"Of what exactly?" I study Lars.

Lars has a disturbed look on his face as he continues. "According to the caseworker's files, there was a dog food bowl with Megan's name on it and there was a chain attached to the kitchen table's leg. The Taylors claimed that it was for their dog, who supposedly happened to be named

Megan, but the neighbors I talked to said they never owned a dog."

My blood is growing cold at this revelation, and I recall something I overheard Megan say once.

"My dad threw me into the street and made me beg on my knees. His wife liked making me eat scraps off the ground. Kinky bitch."

At that point, while I had been curious about Megan, I wasn't trying to get too involved, so I pocketed the statement in the back of my mind to address it another time. But it's putting a lot of things into perspective for me right now.

"The dog bowl and chain were damning information. I can't believe CPS didn't act on those findings. What the hell else did they need as proof? Did they need to actually walk in and see her chained to the damn table? As if any abuser being investigated would ever be that stupid."

"You know how the system is," Lars says angrily. "I had one of our people locate the old caseworker and get the information out of her. She's retired now, but she was forthcoming. She said she needed her job and followed things by the book back then. She said she knew there was something wrong in that house, and she tried to get Megan to confide in her, but Megan wouldn't say anything."

"She was probably scared to death. Was there anything else?"

"The caseworker admitted that another sign of something being off was that the girls' bedroom didn't seem like it was being shared by them. It felt like it was only for the younger child."

"So why didn't she do anything?!" I explode, wishing desperately I could do something to go back in time and protect little Megan.

"There were two beds in the room. One was an ornate

sleigh bed with clean, girly bedding, and the other was a cot with a thin sheet and no pillow. Unfortunately, the condition of the bedroom only proved favoritism, not abuse."

The picture forming in my head is sickening, and I'm beginning to realize why Megan is always so sure that I'll throw her away.

After all, *everybody else did.*

"So, they tortured her?" I ask rhetorically, my hand slowly tightening around the mug. "What about the younger daughter?"

"She was a normal, happy kid. Raised like any other child except for the fact that her parents are psychopathic abusers, and she witnessed their abuse of Megan."

I've known Lars a long time and I can tell that he's furious, not that he'll let it show in any obvious way.

"I see."

The look on Megan's face from the other day is still imprinted on my mind. She appeared both angry and terrified of her younger sister. Based on this new information Lars has given me, it's quite likely that her sister also grew up playing a hand in the abuse.

"When did Megan leave that house?"

"Things are a little tricky here. From what I found out from their neighbors, Megan had a boyfriend who was murdered during a break-in at their house. After the police closed the case, she left. She's never been back since."

"Did the police find the killer?"

"They suspected a local gang in the area, but nothing was ever proven. One of their neighbors said that Megan left in the middle of the night with just a bag and no money. This neighbor had been living next to their house for years, and, according to her, she guessed that they were abusing her. When she saw Megan sneaking out, instead of informing her parents, she gave her some cash and bought her a bus ticket to LA."

"Get me the name of that neighbor," I murmur.

Some good deeds need to be repaid.

"Yep, I have it in my notes."

"I'm not sure what the devil's spawn is up to, but make sure Rachel doesn't get anywhere near Megan again. Either give her a security team, or you watch after her. Parker can be my security detail. I don't need both of you, and I don't want Megan going anywhere alone. Also, get me the case file of that break-in at the house. Something seems off. If they hated her so much, why would they allow her to bring a boyfriend over?"

"I'll arrange that," comes a lazy voice from the couch as Vaughn stretches and then huddles deeper into his blanket. "Write down the details and leave them on the table."

Well, at least he's good for something, I muse.

When Lars leaves, Vaughn sits up, the blanket wrapped around him. "You're really serious about Megan, aren't you?"

"Mind your own business."

"You are my business." He drags the blanket on the floor as he comes to sit at the kitchen's island counter. "I've just never seen you like this around any woman."

I don't respond and he continues talking. "Is this going to be a long-term thing?"

I shrug. "We'll see."

"You can be vague as much as you like, but you're obsessed with this girl. You never go out of your way for anybody else like this. Not even us."

"That's a lie."

"You think so?" Vaughn scoffs before pouring himself a

cup of coffee and adding, "You are well on your way to falling in love with this girl if you aren't already."

My eyes narrow at him. "Don't be ridiculous."

I realize I've already professed my feelings for Megan in a moment of weakness or perhaps a moment of strength, but there's no need for everyone to know my truth.

"Then what is it?" He pokes at me with his words, lifting his brows. "She's just going to be a fuck buddy for a few months, and then you both find somebody else?"

"Stop talking, Vaughn, or I'll rip your tongue out," I warn him as he almost spits a mouth full of coffee out laughing at me.

"It's too early in the morning for this sort of violence," Christian comes sauntering out of the guest bedroom, his voice sleepy. "Can't you both keep it down?"

"I told Hunter that he's falling in love with Megan, and he threw a temper tantrum."

Christian sits down next to him as I contemplate the mechanics of actually ripping out Vaughn's tongue.

"He's not wrong." Christian grabs the jug of water on the counter. "You're crazy about her."

"Both of you, get out of my house," I growl, taking my cup of coffee and retreating into my bedroom to change. "The Four Seasons has rooms available."

As I close the door of my bedroom behind me, my eyes go to the framed sketch on the wall.

I'm falling in love with Megan.

Hell, who am I kidding?

I'm already there.

I don't have to admit it to Vaughn or Christian because they can already see it. The fact that I want to kill every person who has ever hurt her tells them everything they need to know.

Finishing my coffee and feeling more reassured that I know more about Megan's difficult past, I shower and change into a suit, then make my way downstairs.

"Are you ever going to tell me about the girl staying with Megan? What's her story?" Christian asks.

For the first time in years, my hands feel clammy. I've been restless ever since I sent the new hire to stay with Megan. I wanted her close, though, because I just want to see her again with my own eyes and maybe check out that scar again. I want to hear her voice and look into her eyes. A part of me is wary, but I have to know.

This is why when I knock on the door a few floors below me and a short, stocky woman with long braids opens it, I blink.

"Is Megan here?"

Chapter 14

I Knew You'd Be Wet

Hunter

The girl who answers is dressed in a pair of pink pajamas with slices of pepperoni pizza all over them, and while we haven't met before, I know exactly who it is.

All the sleep vanishes from her eyes as she takes me in head to toe before saying slowly, "I know you. You are Mr. Middleton."

"And you're Megan's roommate Naomi."

"Look, man." She immediately gives me a look of warning. "I don't weigh that much, so I might not be able to physically fight you, but if you break Megan's heart, I promise you I will write out your number in every public bathroom in Los Angeles. Ooh, and I'll also write shitty Yelp reviews about all of your businesses. And–"

"Hush." A hand quickly clasps over her mouth and Megan appears from behind her, scowling. "We talked about this, Naomi."

Megan is wearing a thin, white, cropped tank top and a

pair of loose black sweatpants as she pushes her Naomi behind her. "Go check on breakfast."

"Whatever," she huffs as she stomps away.

"Is everything okay?" Megan asks with a slight grin, probably because I can't keep my eyes off her breasts.

The tank top does little to hide her pert nipples and the heavy shape of her breasts, so it takes me a second to conjure up my legendary self-control.

"I wanted to check up on your houseguest."

"Lacy?" Megan looks over her shoulder, and I follow her gaze to see Lacy cooking something on the stove. "She's settled in nicely. I gave her my room and she said she slept well."

I notice a comforter and pillow on Megan's sofa. She must have slept there. I hate that I'm inconveniencing her, but it can't be helped. This is too important.

"I need one more day. Maybe two. I'm trying to find out something."

It's clear that Megan wants to say something, but then she just snaps her mouth shut. "Fine, I get it. Do you want to come in? You look like you kind of want to."

When I meet her gaze, there's a small hint of sadness in her eyes, but she's smiling.

"I can read you pretty well now," she says, backing up so I can fully enter the apartment. However, I'm distracted by a sad look in her eyes.

My hand comes up to rub her cheek with my thumb. "What's with that look?"

"What look?"

"Like I've done something terrible to you."

Her smile falters and I realize what she's thinking when she looks over her shoulder toward Lacy.

"Whatever you're thinking, I promise you that's not it," I try assuring her.

She shifts in her spot and I see the uncertainty in her eyes. While a part of me likes that she's even capable of having jealous feelings for me, I know that they make her sad, not angry.

As I look at her, I'm reminded of what Lars told me about her past just a while ago and my blood heats up in anger. Despite everything she's been through, she's still managed to stay sane. Many a person I know would have become twisted inside.

Sadness is not an option. All I want is to make Megan happy.

I cup her face, forcing her to look at me, and then lower my head to press my lips against hers. She lets out a quiet gasp and then leans into my touch.

"Get a room!" Comes a shout from behind us and I break the kiss, frowning over at Naomi who sneers at me.

"I thought she was missing in action?" I whisper into Megan's ear.

"She showed up out of the blue last night, and I didn't ask any questions."

Megan takes my hand and pulls me over to the kitchen. "I invited Hunter to stay for breakfast."

The quiet young woman looks over at me with a timid glance and gives me a weird smile. She's probably remembering the way I flipped over her wrist yesterday like a lunatic. Naomi just shoots me a narrow-eyed look, which I return.

Breakfast is simple, consisting of bacon, eggs, and toast with coffee, but whatever veggies and spices Lacy seasoned the eggs with make them some of the best scrambled eggs I've ever had.

It seems that in a matter of fewer than twenty-four hours, Lacy has made herself quite comfortable and seems to get along with both Megan and Naomi.

"So, what's with the bad hair job?" Naomi asks Lacy, and I focus my eyes on them, waiting with bated breath for an answer.

"I – I just wanted a change," Lacy answers, stuttering through her soft explanation.

She's clearly lying.

After hundreds of interrogations, I know how to spot the body language of a liar. Her eyes focus down and then dart away to the right. Her smile is forced, and her answer is basic.

Now, why would somebody lie about that?

"Well, if I'm around the next time you want a change. I can color your hair for you. I'm a cosmetologist. We could do something cool, like give you purple highlights."

"Thank you. I'll remember to ask." She turns to Megan. "Is it okay for me to use the shower first?"

"Sure, if you need an extra towel, just let me know."

Once Lacy retreats into the bathroom, Naomi and Megan start clearing the breakfast dishes.

"Do you work as a cosmetologist in LA?" I suddenly ask Naomi, who appears startled that I've addressed her at all.

"Yes, I do."

"Oh, you've been MIA for a while, so I wasn't sure what the deal was."

"The deal is that I was visiting my folks. I'm close to my parents. I miss the old fuckers like crazy. I bet you and my dad would have a lot in common."

"Naomi!" Megan exclaims in horror at the clear-cut jab to our age difference.

"I doubt your father is in his thirties."

"Oh, I didn't realize." She smiles. "You give off an even older vibe."

I chuckle.

This girl has spunk and a whole hell of a lot of nerve.

"Is this how you talk to all of your landlords?" I say, reminding her that she is staying in this overpriced apartment because of Megan...and because of me.

"No, she doesn't. She's forgotten her manners," Megan interjects. "Can I talk to you for a moment, Naomi?"

Naomi squints her eyes suspiciously at me as she walks back to her bedroom. It bothers me that the roommate despises me for no reason at all but that's nothing new. I should be used to it. It's just that for whatever asinine reason, I want whatever friends Megan has to like me.

"I'm sorry about that. She's a little territorial and may have a few trust issues."

"Did you two grow up together?"

"No, I met her when I left home. She was the first friend I made here in the city."

"So, I need to get my day started, but I didn't want to leave without letting you know that I'm attaching a security team to you for a while."

She blinks at me. "Come again?"

"I just don't want you to be startled if you see two men following you," I explain. "They'll stay out of your hair for the most part, and I'll make sure that Parker or Lars introduce you."

"Wait, I don't understand." She grabs my hand. "Why do I need a security team?"

I stare into her gorgeous eyes and know that if I tell her that I looked into her family situation, it will not go over well. What I deem as looking after her might come off as prying, especially when it comes to her family. The fact that her sister is practically stalking her and that I'm pretty sure it has something to do with her father worries the hell out of me. And with everything I've got going on, the last thing I need is to be concerned about Megan's dysfunctional family hurting her. So, instead, I decide to give her an alternate but completely valid reason.

"There are some things going on with me and the club, and I just want to make sure that nobody looks at you and sees a vulnerable target."

"Oh." She releases her hold on me, frowning. "That makes sense, but can't Lars or Parker do it?"

"They need to be with me since I'm the one in the real trouble." I try smiling to diffuse the tension between us.

As I head to the door, she says, "I told Diana about the new job yesterday, so you'll make the necessary calls, right?"

"I had Parker take care of it, but I still don't approve," I tell her. "Did she thank you at least?"

"Not really." She shrugs. "She didn't say much of anything to me when I told her, but she looked relieved. It's fine. I didn't really expect a thank you. She's learned her lesson, and I doubt she'll try to pull something like this again. Plus, this whole incident has put the rest of the servers on alert. I'm doing a reevaluation of everyone on staff, and then I'm going to do a round of new hires. Just because we serve some questionable customers at the Blue Whiskey doesn't mean we should have questionable service."

"Very funny. My club serves an elite clientele."

"Whom have all served time."

My lips twitch, and I walk over to kiss the tip of her nose.

"Keep up that attitude, and I might fuck you right here on your kitchen counter."

She blushes at the thought, and I make a mental note of it. *Megan wants to be fucked on the kitchen counter.*

"People are here. You need to behave." She scowls at me. "Just go."

"You sure?" I tease. "I could finger fuck you real quick and make you come. Neither one of them will know."

"What is wrong with you?" She laughs hysterically. "You seriously have a problem."

"I've had a problem with that shirt you're wearing the entire time I've been in this apartment."

I walk her back against the wall next to the front door. Her butt hits the wall first as she stares up at me in wonderment. I slide my hand down the front of her loose sweatpants and into her panties.

"I knew you'd be wet," I say in guttural tones.

Her head tilts back against the wall. "Hunter, don't do this."

I steal a kiss from her delicious lips as I work two of my fingers slowly through her folds. I know I have her right where I want her when she grasps the sides of my jacket because her legs are quivering like noodles.

When the shower water cuts off, I know I need to end this. Anyone could walk out and see us, and while I'm down for people to watch me pleasure my woman, I don't really think that's Megan's thing.

I finish the kiss and then pull my hand from her pussy, gently sliding the finger in my mouth so that she can watch me taste her. Her eyes sparkle as I savor the sweet taste of her pleasure.

"I'll see you later tonight, Miss Taylor."

When she finally closes the door with a smile, I linger for a few seconds, wondering when Megan will open up to me about the abuse she faced in her childhood home.

There's only so far I can dig into her past without her finding out, but I want to have a better understanding of how deep her wounds cut. I have not forgotten the phone call that I interrupted the other day. The man on the other end had been threatening her, demanding money, and deductive reasoning leads me to only one explanation, which is that it was her father on the other line.

A man whose acquaintance I can't wait to meet.

Yeah, there's a lot of mystery surrounding Megan. She holds her secrets close to her heart. A break-in, a murder, and a midnight escape. Combine that with the demand for money and her sister's threatening arrival, there's a lot that Megan is hiding from me.

I have no problem letting her keep her secrets and waiting her out. However, I need to make sure that the secrets aren't ultimately going to destroy her.

If her sister has discovered where she lives, it won't take long for the rest of them to figure out that Megan might be a little better off than she led on.

And if they are who I think they are, then they'll come for her.

But I'll be ready for them.

Chapter 15

You're Not Making Sense

Megan

"Okay, you gotta stop following me around like this, guys." I look over my shoulder at the two funny-looking men who have glued themselves to my side. "Nothing is going to happen to me here. We're in the club, I'm surrounded by people, and I've got work to do."

The two oversized oafs exchange a look, and finally, the meatier one of the two responds in a rough voice, "Miss, it literally is our job to follow you around."

I notice Lars sitting in Hunter's empty office, reading something on his computer screen, and I give him a pleading look. "Please, do something about this. I can't have them breathing down my neck. I'll stab someone at this rate!"

Lars appears amused and shakes his head at the security team assigned to me. "Take a thirty-minute break. She'll be fine."

Watching their retreat to the kitchen, I let out a heavy breath. "Thank God."

"Who were you planning to stab?" I can tell that Lars is trying not to laugh.

"Myself," I say darkly.

"The boss is just trying to be careful."

"He's too careful."

Lars gives me a questioning look. "If he were his usual *careful*, there wouldn't be so much activity around his penthouse. People aren't supposed to even know where he lives."

Ah, yes, he's talking about the shooting, and while I completely understand why that would rattle everyone, it had nothing to do with me. Why am I the one who needs the extra protection? But I'm not going to argue with Lars because we seem to be forging a mutually respectful relationship, and he's one of the few allies I've got in this place.

I retreat to my office to pick up the day's schedule before making my way to the bar where Gage is.

"When you have time," I tell him. "Take a look at these. I'm sure Hunter briefed you already."

He makes a cheeky clicking sound with his tongue as he gives me a two-fingered salute, "Got it, boss lady."

Two of the servers are side-eyeing us and I sigh to myself. I still haven't talked to them collectively since the incident with Diana, and now they're walking around me on eggshells. I'm both anticipating and dreading that team meeting.

Lacy is working with Billy, and as I pour myself a cup of coffee from the machine, I ask her, "Have you taken a break yet?"

She looks towards Billy, who says, "She'll take one in ten. We just have to finish this up."

"I'll be outside then," I tell them. "Taking my break."

Grabbing a sandwich from the refrigerator, coffee in hand, I go outside, grateful to breathe in the fresh air. It's cold out but my lungs feel good, away from the stale atmosphere of the Blue Whiskey.

It's been two days since Lacy came to stay with us. The girl is relatively quiet, and despite her circumstances, she seems to have a positive outlook on life, which I like about her, but I still can't figure out why Hunter is so interested in her.

I'd be lying if I said that it doesn't bother me. I've seen the way he looks at her. There's confusion in his eyes and a hint of sadness that I've never seen before. And the strangest thing of all is that he avoids interacting with her. I don't see his normal swagger or confidence when he looks at her.

That scares me.

Hunter is not a liar, and I have no reason not to trust him, but he's also the first man that I've allowed myself to be vulnerable with. While I almost convinced myself that our age difference is what makes this thing between us so different. So safe. I am quickly realizing that the trust between us is fragile.

As I perch on the steps, I look down at my coffee, sighing helplessly. I'm dating Hunter Middleton, the billionaire and the philanthropist. I'm also dating his alter ego, the ruthless club owner and underworld negotiator. He's been so preoccupied with work lately that aside from a few stolen kisses, I've not really managed to spend any quality time with him. Normally, that wouldn't be the worst thing to happen, but my body is half-starved for him.

For someone who wasn't exactly getting laid, I am addicted to his touch, and I miss it. He knew exactly what he was doing when he basically turned me out by flying me to Paris and seducing me in that hotel room (or maybe I seduced him). Now I want him all of the time. I bet if I go into his office right now, he'll put everything aside and fuck me so deeply that I'll lose my mind.

My vagina twitches as if she's itching to follow through on my dirty thoughts, but I force myself to stay still and take another gulp of coffee. This can't be about me and my raging hormones.

It's obvious that Hunter is busy and much more stressed than normal. I wish I could just go up to him and ask him to talk to me. Make him talk to me. I kind of want to. But if I do that, I'm going to be throwing myself deeper into this tangled mess of feelings and trust that is growing like a bunch of angry weeds.

I'm sitting in the back of the club but hear footsteps approaching the alleyway. I'm expecting to see my new security detail, but instead, it's Diana.

"Hey," she greets me casually as if we're old friends.

It's a little awkward that she's approached me after everything we've been through in the last 48 hours, so I stand up, sipping my coffee.

"Do you need something?"

"No." She shakes her head. "Not from you, anyway."

I frown at that but don't comment on it. She has a weird expression on her face, almost anticipatory.

"Okay," I say, biting into my sandwich but keeping a close eye on her. "Did Parker give you the details about your new job?"

She doesn't say anything for a few moments, just watching me with this strange gleam in her eyes.

"You want me to thank Hunter or you for that, bitch?"

"I beg your pardon?" I ask, nearly choking on the sandwich, not even fully grasping that she called Hunter by his first name.

"I don't need any piece of shit job you ask your fuck buddy to give me." She smiles at me, the expression almost twisted. "I only stayed here as long as I did because I needed to see how precious you were to him."

The hairs on the back of my neck are rising as I study Diana. Her statement is confusing to me, and then I hear something shuffle in the background at the opening of the alley, which makes me jump. I quickly turn my head, only to see a cat.

"What is that supposed to mean?" I ask. "You're not making sense," I say, wondering if Diana may be high on something.

"You'll find out," she murmurs. "I never expected Hunter Middleton to reveal his weakness so readily."

Okay, now I know something's wrong and that I've unwittingly found myself in a possibly dangerous situation. It doesn't take a genius to figure out that Diana has an ulterior motive here. She's a different person.

She looks different, she's dressed differently, and she's referring to Hunter and his supposed weaknesses in some super creepy way.

I'm in deep shit right now.

"I don't know what you're smoking, Diana, but I'm not that important to Hunter." I try to keep my tone casual. "Girls like me are a dime a dozen to a man like him."

Diana smiles at me, cocking her head in an unnatural manner. "I'm not that easy to fool. I've been watching you way before you hired me."

"What?" Now I feel really confused. "Why?"

"You probably never recognized me because every time I came in, I made sure never to interact with you. Plus, I was always wearing different wigs. This is my real hair, by the way. I'm a natural blonde. Do you like it?"

Oh, my god.

Suddenly, I remember why she looked so familiar when I hired her. It had been a fleeting thought. An improbable connection. One I should have evidently done a little more digging into.

Steve.

Chapter 16

A Good Bargaining Chip

Megan

In the flashing neon lights of the club, it's always difficult to recognize somebody unless you see them on a daily basis. However, Steve would often meet up with different women. I didn't think much of it then because he was single and he was the manager of the club. I once caught a glimpse of a woman talking intensely with him. Her face was done up with heavy makeup. Yet now, as I look at fresh-faced Diana, I can see the strong similarities in their features. I can't believe that she was the woman who often came to visit Steve and never mentioned it when I hired her.

A sinister feeling crawls up my spine.

Why wouldn't she drop his name in her interview with me? That would have been an obvious way to get hired. And why didn't I ever notice this before?

She walks toward me slowly, almost as if in slow motion. "It seems you realize the situation that you're in now."

I hear another sound from behind me, and this time, my instincts tell me it's not a cat.

"Why wouldn't you mention that you knew Steve?" I ask her, my voice cautious, my hand steady as I hold the hot coffee, ready to use it as a weapon if I have to. "What was the big secret?"

"Don't take it personally." Diana shrugs. "I needed access into the club and thought my way in the door was going to be Steve, and then he conveniently disappeared." She tilts her head to the side as if waiting for a reaction from me. "Then I thought I'd move on to bigger fish and thought I might be able to get your job if I slept with the big boss. But then I realized that it wasn't just the sex for him. Hunter Middleton is quite invested in you. I mean, the way he protects you. The other day, he nearly lost his mind when your classmates showed up and made a scene. He's rather unpredictable thought, so I realize it's just a gamble at this point, but I'm pretty sure that he wouldn't want anything to happen to you, which makes you such a good bargaining chip."

My blood chills at the words, bargaining chip, and even the way she's saying them. Diana is much more well-spoken and confident than she portrays herself to be at work. Who is this woman?

I can feel the presence of somebody else coming, but I force myself to calm down. Diana still hasn't managed to make a move on me, and I'm not going down without a fight.

"You're really overestimating my value to him," I try convincing her, but a disbelieving laugh tells me that she's not buying it.

I never gave it much thought until this very moment, but I do believe that Hunter would be angry if Diana did something to hurt me. A man doesn't just give a woman a security detail and not care if something happens. However, at the same time, he's only known me for less than two months. He's not going to sacrifice his entire – I can only call it empire – for a girl, he's...simply fucking.

Diana is standing at the bottom of the steps now, and I feel the door behind me slowly move open and then stop. The only person I was expecting to come outside was Lacy. The fact that she doesn't open the door completely and just remains standing there inside makes me hope that she knows that something is wrong.

"That's up to us to decide," Diana sneers.

I move my shoulders in a delicate shrug. "Well, I guess you gotta do what you gotta do."

I can feel the breath of a man standing right behind me, and I know that it's now or never.

Even as Diana frowns at my casual statement, I'm whirling around, tossing my coffee in the face of the man standing right behind me. As he howls in shock and pain, I catch a glimpse of his face and, to my utter shock, it's the plumber from that day in my apartment.

"You bitch!"

Diana rushes forward, but before she can do anything, I hear a thud, and then her face goes blank, and she slumps to the ground. A quivering Lacy is standing behind her, holding a cast iron pan in her hand.

As much as I want to congratulate her on her fast thinking, we're still not out of danger yet. I can see another man rushing towards the alley, and I scream, "Get inside!"

Lacy rushes towards the door, but the plumber has a firm grip on my ankle, and I stumble forward. I don't hesitate to kick his face with my shoe. "Let go, you creepy fuck!"

He grunts in anger and then tightens his hold on me. However, my fight and flight response is in full mode right now, and I shove his hand away with my other heel before scrambling away from him.

Lacy is already at the door, but I know that I won't be able to reach her since the man running toward us is nearly upon me. Then it'll be two against one. I won't stand a chance.

However, the door is thrown open before Lacy can reach it, and a bullet whizzes past my face, making me freeze.

Hunter is standing there, and he pulls Lacy up by the wrist, throwing her inside, behind him. His eyes are on me, and as Lacy disappears, Parker and Lars suddenly appear in the doorway, both of them armed.

"Come here, Megan." Hunter holds out his hand, and I realize that my attackers behind me are frozen.

I hobble towards Hunter, and he wraps his arm around my waist, yanking me into him, and I collide against his hard chest.

"Why don't you introduce yourselves?" Hunter says coolly to the men.

Nobody says anything, but from my peripheral vision, I can see the plumber rise to his feet.

"You haven't changed," Hunter says to him.

"But you certainly have Jonathan," Hunter's chest rumbles. "You got facial reconstruction or something? That jawline of yours is a lot more angular than the last time I saw you."

What the hell?

Who is Johnathan?

"You think you're so smart, don't you?"

"Smarter than you. You thought you could bring me down by sending a woman into my club to do your job for you? Did you really think I wouldn't investigate anything about her? I conduct deep background checks on all of my employees. Did you actually think I was going to fuck her?"

Deep background checks?

A sliver of alarm flows through me.

I wonder what Hunter has found out about me?

I don't get much time to worry about this particular line of thought because Parker angrily aims his gun at Johnathan's head. "You're a dead man."

"You think this is it?" Jonathon just laughs. "This is only the beginning. I just wanted to figure out how attached you truly were to this little girl, and you've just proved my suspicions. Word of advice, Hunter. Keeping a weakness around you makes you a susceptible target. I thought you learned that lesson all those years ago. If you really cherish this girl, put a bullet in her head right now. Otherwise, she'll be your downfall."

I can't contain myself any longer, and I struggle in Hunter's arms, shouting, "Hey! Fuck you, dickhead!"

"She's a feisty one. I can see why you like her."

Jonathan's taunting words make me see red, and Hunter's arm tightens around my waist, and he murmurs in my ear, "Behave yourself."

"He just told you to shoot me!" I hiss at him.

"You're not escaping me that easily, so calm down," he responds dryly, his eyes still focused on Jonathan. "Parker. Lars."

There's a finality to Hunter's tone that chills me to the bone as he turns me around and pushes me back inside the club door. Then, just as I hear the deafening sound of a shower of bullets, he closes the door behind him, and my insides grow icy cold.

"*Oh my God.*"

My stomach drops.

Why did he lock himself outside with them?

The man I love is going to get himself killed.

Chapter 17

DNA Revelations

Megan

"**M**egan, are you okay?" Lacy asks, crouching next to me.

I look over to see the kitchen staff huddled in a corner, and then a few men in suits guide both me and Lacy away from the kitchen to Hunter's office.

"Wait!" I try turning back in panic. "Hunter's out there! We can't just leave him out there."

"You can," comes Christian's firm voice as he nods at the men. "He knows what he's doing. He'll be fine."

"But-" Involuntary tears rush to my eyes, and Christian looks startled.

"Hey, there." He hugs me, whispering fiercely, "Hunt will be fine. Don't cry."

"I'm not crying," I sniffle, rubbing my eyes but finding comfort in his hug. "I'm just worried, and I've got allergies."

When Christian gives me a disbelieving look, I avoid his eyes. "Allergies from all that bullet dust? That's not even a thing," he chuckles, and I glare at him like he's got one screw loose.

"There's nothing funny about this right now. I was almost kidnapped, and now he's out there in a hail of bullets. What is wrong with you? What kind of friend are you? Go help him!"

"Yeah, so that he can shoot me as well?" Christian scoffs. "Not fucking likely. You two stay here."

Lacy is clasping my hand and I'm pleasantly surprised at how kind this usually very quiet girl is. "He'll be fine. You'll see," she says with a hope I'm not sure I totally share.

"You have more faith in him than I do," I mumble to myself.

A few minutes later, true to Lacy's words, the door to the office opens, and Hunter strides in, talking out loud to no one in particular. "Fuck, he got away, but I've put men on his trail. And you!"

He rounds his eyes on me with a look so angry that I nearly shrink into my chair.

"What did I do?"

"I gave you a security detail for a fucking reason!"

He looks really mad right now, and I press my lips together, my voice quivering with guilt. "They were following me around in the club and hindering my ability to work."

"There is only a certain amount of recklessness I can tolerate, Miss Taylor. If you want to behave like this, put yourself at risk like this, then I'll just lock you up somewhere!"

The mixture of adrenaline and the fear of being kidnapped, mixed in with Hunter shouting at me, makes tears rush back to my eyes, and this time, there's no pretending.

"Don't talk to her like that," Lacy says, sticking up for me. "You have no idea how upset she was for you! Why can't you be nicer?"

My heart nearly stops in my chest, and I wonder if I'll have to throw myself across this brave girl who might be the next person shot for standing up to Hunter, although he does claim to have a no-hurting women policy.

I see his eyes turn towards Lacy, and then, to my surprise, his expression softens. "You go wait outside. Christian, help her."

Christian gets to his feet, and when he approaches Lacy, she looks uncertain, either for me or for herself. "Megan?"

"I'll be fine," I say to assure her because, of course, she doesn't know that I just had this man's dick in my mouth not too long ago. He's not going to hurt me. If anything, I'm probably about to get an ear full of a Hunter Middleton lecture.

Lacy still looks reluctant but allows Christian to lead her outside. Since Lars and Parker appear to be on the hunt for Johnathan (or at least I hope they are), now there's just me and Hunter left behind.

We stare quietly at each other for a moment, each of us visually inspecting the other for wounds and perhaps for words.

"I'm –" I begin, but he cuts me off.

"Are you hurt?"

"No, not really."

He moves closer to me, brushing the back of his hand down the side of my face. It's a tender move that he usually reserves when it's just the two of us alone in his penthouse, but I welcome it right now. It calms me.

"I realize that you've been through some tough shit in your life, Megan, but you don't have to pretend for me."

"I knew the risks when I took this job," I try saying casually. "The Blue Whiskey has a reputation for a reason."

"This wasn't about the club. This was about way more than that."

I don't respond to that because there's nothing I can really say. I realize that Hunter and I still have a lot to learn about each other and that we have very different struggles to contend with. His are way bigger than mine could ever be.

"I didn't mean to make you cry." Hunter turns back to me, looking uncomfortable.

"I wasn't crying," I say, knowing that I sound completely ridiculous. Of course, I'm crying. That was some scary shit that just happened.

"I gave you security for a reason."

"And I apologize for that. I didn't understand the seriousness of the situation."

Hunter shakes his head at me before taking the seat next to me. "He got away," he finally says, reaching into his pocket and taking out a pack of cigarettes. He tucks one in between his teeth but doesn't light it.

"What about that bitch?" Diana was unconscious during most of the melee. There's no way she could have made it out of there. "Is she still out there on the ground?"

"They had smoke bombs and a getaway car prepared. They managed to get Diana out as well."

"What?"

"Those fuckers came prepared."

I listen to Hunter, watching him chew the end of the cigarette, his eyes tight.

"Maybe we should call the police, Hunter?" I ask, thinking that at this point, he may be in over his head.

Smoke bombs sound like some next-level stuff, like they're ex-military or something.

"The police?" He scoffs. "What the hell are they going to do that five of my best security guys couldn't get done?"

"Are Lars and Parker in trouble?" I suddenly think of my new work friends, and I hope they're not in trouble because of my part in this.

"Don't worry about them."

"They had no idea I was going to shake the security team."

"Obviously."

"And what was all of that with Lacy?"

"All of what?"

"You read me the riot act, but when she gives you some attitude, your tone completely softens."

Hunter sighs, then hands me a manilla envelope off his desk. "Read this."

I open the contents and blink. A blood test reveals that Jane Doe shares 50% DNA with one Hunter Middleton.

"I'm sorry, but is this a DNA test?"

"Yes."

"Do you have a love child you're trying to tell me about?"

"No, Megan," he says as if I'm exasperating him.

"Then what is this?" I say, shaking the envelope in front of his face.

As I meet his piercing gray eyes, it finally hits me.

"Lacy?"

Chapter 18

Try Not To Look So Offended

Megan

"Lena," Hunter corrects me. "Her real name is Lena Middleton, and she's my younger sister."

"You have a younger sister?" I'm so lost right now, but to be fair, Hunter doesn't know much about my family either, so I quiet myself and just listen.

"I didn't know she was alive until a few weeks ago, and even then, it was only a suspicion. A hope. Some enemies of mine figured out that she was still alive, and they were looking for her to use against me."

"That's why you asked me to let her stay with me," I say, slowly understanding. "Does she know?"

"I doubt it," Hunter looks perplexed. "She doesn't seem to recognize me, even a little bit, and I haven't figured out how to tell her."

"I'm assuming there's a long story as to why you didn't know if your sister was alive or not but this is probably not the time for it?"

"I'll explain later."

I look at his tortured face and then walk slowly toward him. Taking out the cigarette clenched between his teeth, I say bluntly, "While you should have told me the whole story before today, luckily, I don't hold a grudge against men who save my life."

"If it wasn't for me, your life wouldn't have been in danger, to begin with, Megan."

I can see that my brush with kidnapping and possible death hit Hunter harder than I first thought. He was angry that I left my security detail, but now I think that he was more scared than anything, which only makes me love him more.

"I can help you tell Lacy. If I'm there with you, it might be easier."

He meets my gaze, and I can see him searching for something in my eyes. He sighs and lowers his forehead on my shoulder.

"I mean Lena. I can help you tell Lena." My hand automatically comes to rest on the nape of his neck, hoping to comfort him. "Are you okay?"

"I'm tired," he simply confesses something which is so unlike him. "I'm tired of all of this."

"I can see that." My heart feels tight in my chest. Sometimes, it's easy to forget that my bigger-than-life lover is also just a man of flesh and bone. He has feelings, hopes, and desires like any other human being. "Want me to call *Laa-Lena* in?"

"You want to do this now?"

"Sure, why not?"

Hunter takes a deep breath and then raises his head, fixing his expression. "All right then, let's try it your way."

I walk over to the door and open it to see Lacy and

Christian sitting at one of the club's extra small round tables having a drink.

"Lacy, can you come in?" I ask her.

"Are you okay, Megan?" she asks cautiously.

"I'm fine. I just want to talk with you for a moment."

"You and Mr. Middleton?"

"Yes."

She seems hesitant to come back into the kitchen with me but when she walks in, I close the door behind her and then ask her a delicate question as Hunter sits in the corner silently and watches.

"This is going to sound like a very intrusive question, Lacy, but are you sure you have no family?"

She still looks shaken from the recent events (and rightly so), but at my question, she shakes her head, looking confused. "I told you, I was in foster care ever since I can remember. I don't have any family. I never did."

I look towards Hunter to say something at this point since I've opened the door to questioning. Finally, he does.

"Can you tell me why you're wearing contact lenses and why you've recently dyed your hair?"

"I've been hired as a cook, not a server." She flinches at the questions. "Is there a problem with how I dress or something?"

"There's a good reason he's asking that," I tell her, understanding her defensiveness. "He isn't criticizing."

"There is a reason." She looks between us both anxiously. "When I turned eighteen, I left my foster home. I did a few odd jobs, and I don't know why, but I learned later that some men showed up at one of my former jobs looking for someone with my description. It freaked me out, so I decided that it was safer to hide my most notable features."

"Well, that was smart," Hunter finally says. "You led us all on a very long goose chase."

Lacy freezes, and I see the panic on her face. "Wait, are you one of the men looking for me?"

"Not in that way!" I say quickly, waving her thoughts away with my hand. "Hunter has a legitimate reason."

"Do I look at all familiar to you?" Hunter asks, studying her carefully.

Lacy frowns. "Should you?"

He pauses, and I see the flash of hurt in his eyes at her almost careless answer. Seeing this unflappable man express that brief emotion breaks my heart, so I step in. "Lacy, it seems that you actually do have some family alive."

"What?" She turns towards me, rightfully confused. "I don't understand how you would know that or why you would care?"

Hunter walks over to her now, holding out the test results. "Fifteen years ago, there was a fire in my apartment where I lived with my mother and younger sister. My sister was three years old at the time, and her name was Lena. I thought she died in that fire, but I recently discovered that she may have been alive all this time. The birthmark on your wrist is the same as hers."

"No one ever made mention of me being orphaned in a fire," she says with almost pity for Hunter. "That's terrible what happened to your sister, but it isn't me."

Hunter looks at me for what I think is permission to continue. He's done some questionable things in the time since Lacy has arrived at the Blue Whiskey and I'm sure she won't like them, but I give him a head nod of approval anyway.

"So... I took some of your DNA and compared it with mine. I also reached out to the hospital where both of us were born and got a copy of your birth certificate. Your real name is Lena Ray Middleton, and you are indeed my younger sister."

"You took my DNA without my consent?"

"I've done much worse," he says, not fully understanding how that statement doesn't make things any better. Lacy doesn't understand his invasive personality yet, not like I do.

"His methods are questionable, to say the least," I admit to her. "But just read the results. They were conducted in a reputable lab."

Lacy's expression changes as she stares down at the test results, reading and re-reading the summary. She seems so shell-shocked that I lower her into a nearby chair. I'm not big on comforting people and am quite awkward at it, but I try patting her shoulder. "Look, I know this might be a lot to take in."

"I have a family?" Her eyes pop up and over to Hunter. "*You're* my family?"

The tone and the look she shoots Hunter has me wincing and I whisper by her ear, "Um, try not to look so offended."

"Sorry, it's just...you're *you*. I just– this isn't some sick sort of joke, is it?"

I can see her trying to grasp this new reality and I kind of feel sorry for her, actually for them both.

"I know it's a lot of information to take in," I say.

She cuts me off, looking directly at Hunter. "Why is she doing all the talking? Why aren't you saying anything?"

"I just told you everything," Hunter replies, standing to his feet.

"What does this mean for me?"

Hunter is quiet for a moment and then says, "Well, first

of all, we're going to straighten out your status as a living, breathing member of the Middleton family. We'll change your social security number, your ID, birth certificate, and any other important records. I'm also going to make sure you get a nice place to live, your college degree, and any further education that you can. Dangerous as that all is, it all needs to happen if we are to establish you as my next of kin."

"College? Dangerous?" Lacy is just repeating words at this point, completely lost. I'm a bit out of sorts myself. That story about what happened to Hunter's family in the fire? That sounds incredibly traumatic. I can't believe he's been carrying that quietly for most of his life...or actually, I can believe it.

"My line of work outside of the club is a little delicate," he says, clearing his throat.

"Maybe I should leave you two to speak alone," I say, feeling as if I've done enough to break the ice.

"No!" comes a simultaneous order from them both.

Lacy grabs my hands and pulls me into the seat next to her. "You have to stay with me. I have no idea what's going on."

Hunter just gives me a sharp look as if he's daring me to step outside the office.

So, I just settle in.

The conversation between them is a little stilted and almost rusty from Hunter's side. It's as if he's trying to figure out how to communicate with her but his words aren't really siding with him. His tone is a little rough and commanding, and I can tell that Lacy isn't really appreciating any of it.

"Okay," I cut Hunter off in the middle of something he's saying that sounds more like an order than a question. "I think what Hunter is trying to say is that it would be helpful for you to stay with him for a while and get to know him. You've both lost all of this precious time with each other."

Lacy darts a suspicious look at us both. "That's not what it sounded like to me. Didn't he just threaten to lock me in his apartment with a security detail if I didn't quit this job? A job, which, by the way, is in *his* club."

"Of course not." I glare at Hunter who just looks away. "He wouldn't be so stupid as to say something like that. It's just that you've had a difficult life so far, so maybe it wouldn't be such a bad idea for you not to have to worry about where your next paycheck comes from. Take some time and get to know your brother. But if you still want to work, maybe–"

"I want to work," she quickly cuts me off, facing Hunter. "I know you're my brother because that piece of paper says we are, but this is all new to me. I have to protect myself and earn my own money just in case you decide–"

She doesn't finish that sentence, and she doesn't have to. I think we both know what she means. In some ways, there are similarities between Lacy and me, and I think that I understand her reasoning.

We've both had a rough time of it growing up. She probably moved from foster home to foster home, never really building any lasting relationships with anyone. She's only had herself to depend on. Only herself to trust. Everything Hunter is throwing at her right now probably sounds like a fairytale she wished for many years ago, and now that it seems to be coming true, it feels too good to be true.

Yeah, I totally get that.

Chapter 19

Start At The Beginning

Megan

I rest my hand on Hunter's knee, only imagining how difficult this conversation must be for him. He's the kind of man who likes to have control over everything, and Lacy must feel like a wild card right now.

"I'm just saying that it's better for you to get the college thing out of the way now," he says to Lacy in a tone I don't recognize. "Work will always be there."

I close my eyes in silent exasperation. He's known her as his sister for all of five seconds, and now he wants to plan out her entire life. Typical Hunter. He's going to scare her off before they have a chance to get to know each other.

"You know," I interrupt, trying to keep some semblance of peace. "Instead of making all these decisions right now, why don't you two just wait? Spend some time with each other, get to know each other, and of course, you can keep coming here and working, Lacy. We certainly need you if we'll ever serve a decent chicken wing after Billy leaves."

I sneak a peek at the thunderous expression on Hunter's

face and wince. I guess I've overstepped, but I'm doing this as much for him as I am for Lacy.

"I mean, that's my suggestion," I say, trying to clean things up. "I'm certainly not firing you, especially if this job gives you the stability you need while you two maneuver this um...new situation. I'm sure Mr. Middleton would agree."

I enunciate each word of my last sentence, hoping that it breaks through Hunter's primal urge to control and protect. That's not what Lacy needs right now.

"This is a lot to process," Lacy says, her face turning a shade of pasty grey.

I haven't known her for that long, but my chest suddenly feels tight with emotion for her. Imagine finding out your brand new boss is actually your brother. This is all kinds of reality show crazy.

"You're right, Lacy, this is a lot. But maybe you could look at it from this point of view as well. You don't remember Hunter, but he definitely remembers you. You've just been reunited with your older brother. These things don't just happen every day. You're no longer alone in this world," I tell her almost wistfully. "You're one of the lucky ones, Lacy."

It's noticeable when my words finally register with her. She rubs her swollen eyes and says, "Yeah, that's true."

"You can stay with me tonight, and then I can help you move into Hunter's place tomorrow." I wrap my arm around her shoulders. "Is that okay?"

"I have to live with you?" She looks warily at Hunter.

"You don't have to do any of this, but it would be a good idea if you did," he tells her in a steady voice. "I will get you your own apartment, maybe in our building if you like it, but for now, it's safer that you stay with me until things settle down. I have a guest room that will be perfect."

"What do I call you?" she softly questions, and I see that the realization of who she is now may be starting to sink in. It may not be a full understanding because who can actually grasp the fact that they're the baby sister of one of the most dangerous men in Los Angeles in ten minutes?

"Hunter, you can call me Hunter."

"Why don't you go wait in my office?" I suggest to her when it seems that the conversation has fizzled out. Both she and Hunter seem to be struggling to find anything more to say, and we've all had a harrowing night. God knows I need a good shower and maybe a shot of something from the bar. "When I'm finished up for the night, we can go home together."

Christian is still waiting outside, and I realize that Hunter has basically assigned his friend to shadow Lacy for the time being.

"How are things on the floor?" he asks Christian, referring to the club, which surprisingly is still open for business. It's as if nothing in the back of the building ever happened.

"Normal."

"How could things be normal when there was just a series of gunshots in the back?" I ask, dumbfounded.

"The main walls of the club are soundproofed to meet the requirements of city ordinances. Between that and the decibel level of the music, no one could hear a thing that happened outside," Christian explains.

Incredible.

No wonder so many crimes go unnoticed around here.

"Take care of her," Hunter tells Christian.

"Like a newborn baby." He smiles.

I realize that we've monopolized the kitchen for far too

long, and the staff needs to get back in here if we're going to serve food tonight, so Hunter and I finish talking in his office. When it's finally just the two of us, I ask him cautiously, "Are you okay?"

"I'm fine," he mutters, but his expression is anything but fine.

I don't like assuming what other people are feeling but I also cannot just turn a blind eye toward Hunter. I care about him, and without knowing much about his childhood, I know that his finding Lacy has had a tremendous effect on him. He's moved in a way that I've never seen. A way that I thought him incapable of feeling.

Hoping that he won't snub me, I say, "You probably expected this to go in a completely different way, but you have to keep in mind that she doesn't remember her life before foster care at all. Not many people remember things from the age of three or four years old. You basically just informed her that not only does she have a brother but that she is also no longer broke and that she now has opportunities in front of her that she never expected to get. Living in a plush Los Angeles apartment and going to college were probably never things she ever considered. Give her some time to adjust to it."

I step towards him, and he wraps his arms around me as if seeking my warmth. I do the same, wrapping my arms around his waist and tilting my head up to meet his stormy grey eyes.

"You can be pretty smart sometimes," he says with a smile.

"I have my moments."

"I don't want her to have to work. Have you looked into her eyes, Megan? She looks so tired, and she's not even thirty yet."

"Don't try and control her that much. Give her some breathing space, or she'll just resent you. You can watch over her from a distance and let her cover that distance herself."

"I wasn't always rich." I feel the sigh that leaves Hunter. "When I was just graduating high school, my mother had Lena with some inconsequential man she met at a bar. She couldn't afford to feed us both, so I did what I could to keep the lights on and food in the fridge. I became a man on the streets of LA, but the way the streets are set up, it was destined for me to lose my family."

Hunter mindlessly plays in my hair as he continues a story that I know must be difficult for him to share.

"I got involved with a gang, and I was framed for something I didn't do. Nobody cared about the truth; they just needed to prove a point so they wouldn't look weak, so they dragged me to my house and made me watch as they set it on fire. They told me stories of all the horrific things they'd supposedly done to my baby sister and my mother and then held me back from rushing inside to save them."

Hunter's words are soft as he walks through memories of his past, and I listen with bated breath. I want to cry.

"A part of me died as I watched the flames of that fire. The protective son and brother disappeared, but out of those ashes rose a Phoenix. It took me years, but once I consolidated power and made something of myself, I tracked down all of those who were still alive and killed them slowly, one by one. Of course, it never brought my family back to me."

My eyes feel like they're burning. "You have Lena back."

"She doesn't even remember me," he says, and I hear the trace of thick grief in his voice. "It's interesting how not one of those assholes ever mentioned that Lena was alive as I sent them on their way to hell. Someone had to know. How did she end up in foster care?"

"Maybe it's a blessing in disguise that you don't have all the answers," I look up at him. "Now you get to be the big brother and protect her, and she has a chance to get to know you without experiencing the grief of missing you all those years."

"Maybe," Hunter meets my gaze.

"There's no maybe." I give him a firm nod. "Once she falls into the younger sister role, you're going to have your hands full. Besides, it's nice to have somebody in your life who puts you first. I remember, when I was little, I would often wish that some unknown relative would come swooping in like some sort of superhero and whisk me away from everything."

Hunter studies me. "Your childhood was that bad?"

"Like you didn't do your in-depth research into me." I give him a wry smile.

"I know some of it but I didn't want to totally pry." He shrugs. "I would rather you come tell me your secrets yourself."

"Is that why you told me this one about your sister?" I ask.

"I involved you because I trust you and because I wanted you to know. You belong to me now, Megan, and there shouldn't be anything we can't share with each other. I would move heaven and earth to keep you safe and happy, and in time, I'm hoping you'll feel the same way about me."

His words make something quiver inside my chest, and I try to breathe past it. "You don't play fair."

"That's because I'm not playing," he says thickly.

"Of course, I feel the same way about you. I'm just not as eloquent with my words."

He buries his face in my neck. "When I'm inside you, your body says everything I need it to say."

"Now you're just being fresh," I chuckle, my heart racing at his words even as I try to remain unaffected.

He just smiles against my skin as his hands slide around and caress the cheeks of my butt, but I think he's using physical intimacy as a defensive tactic to avoid the topic. Maybe he always has, and I never noticed.

I pull back and stare into his eyes. "Does it really bother you that I haven't shared everything about my past with you?"

Hunter gives me a steady look. "I've shared more with you than I have with any other woman, so yeah, maybe it bothers me a little."

"There's nothing I can tell you that you can't find out yourself."

"Is that the kind of relationship you want the two of us to have? Because it can be that, but I don't want you to resent me for it a year from now."

"A year from now?" I echo back.

"Unless you plan on going somewhere," he says through tight lips.

I sigh and wander over to the couch, pulling my legs up under me. He follows me, sitting beside me and pulling me into his chest.

This was supposed to be a physical relationship, something fun, and then he decided to give a name to it. I honestly never thought that Hunter would ever want to be involved in something serious with me. I'm a college student. I'm a starving artist. I work for him. I'm so much younger than him. I could go on and on about all the differences between us and all the reasons why the two of us don't make any sense at all, but the respect he shows me, the care, I've never experienced anything like it before. It makes me want to share some part of the pain that still lives inside of me, especially after what I've seen happen between him and Lacy today.

So, for the first time ever...I decide to trust someone, and I start at the beginning.

"My parents were inhumane monsters."

Chapter 20

What Did They Do To You?

Megan

I sit up straighter, pulling my knees to my chest and wrapping my arms around them. I haven't told this story in a very long time, partly because I'd hoped that I'd never have to.

"Ever since I can remember, I knew my father didn't love me like other dads loved their kids, and I knew the reasons were deeply connected to his feelings for my mother. He wanted to punish me for whatever crimes he believed my mother committed, and my stepmother wanted me to pay the price for being the child of the man she loved."

Hunter is listening intently, so I continue. "Before I was old enough to understand that, though, I naively thought that they were somehow just different people, incapable of human feelings, until I noticed how differently they treated me versus Rachel. They loved her.

"At first, I would blame myself. Maybe if I was a better daughter who cleaned her room or got A's in school, they'd treat me better. But later, I realized that they'd abused me so much that they stopped seeing me as a human being."

"What did they do to you?" he asks, his face distorted with wrath.

"I try not to think about the things they did to me because when I start thinking about them, I can't sleep. There was a time in my life when I never slept."

I notice Hunter's left eye twitching. Our conversation is making him uncomfortable, and he probably wants to stop listening and just go hurt somebody, but this is my story to tell and I need him to hear it, so I keep going.

"You asked me why I don't care about the kinds of things you do?" I meet his gaze, my own hard. "It's because I'm pretty sure most of the people you hurt deserve it and also because I simply don't care."

"You don't care about the things I'm capable of, Megan? That's not normal."

"Actually, it is because not caring about much is how I protect myself. Maybe it's selfish of me, but I have no problem being selfish. Hell, I have a right to be selfish after dealing with my family."

"You're right." He nods, lightly playing with a few of my stray curls. "You have every right."

"I think that's part of the reason why I'm still here. With you, I mean. You make me feel like I matter when I've never mattered to anyone before."

Hunter is silent for a few moments and then asks, "Are you still involved with any of them?"

My face stiffens.

"No."

"The man you were arguing with on the phone a while back? Was that your father?"

"I'm not sure what you heard–"

"I heard just fine." He moves closer to me. "Why are you sending him money every month? And what pictures was he talking about?"

"I swear." I glare at Hunter. "I give you an inch, and you just take a fucking mile, don't you?"

"I can't protect you if I don't know everything."

"I never asked you to protect me." I try standing to my feet, suddenly feeling anxious about how intrusive he's being, but he yanks me back into his lap.

"You don't have to ask me for something so basic. It's well within my right to want to keep you safe."

"I hate to tell you this, Mr. Middleton, but you're not doing the best job of keeping me out of harm's way," I say sarcastically. "I've been shot at and damn near kidnapped since I met you."

"That's not funny, Megan."

"You really need to learn how to take a joke."

"There's nothing funny about what almost happened to you in my apartment or this club, an issue I'm trying to remedy as we speak. But I need you to stop changing the subject. Right now, we're talking about your baggage, not mine, and I can track your piece-of-shit father down and beat the story out of him, or you can just tell me everything now," he glares down at me, and I glower at him.

"Is privacy a word in your dictionary?" I demand furiously.

"Not when it comes to you."

I hate how calm he sounds while I'm having a mini breakdown inside.

"What good will come from you knowing everything?"

"You know my one advantage with the drama going on in my business right now? It's that I know who my enemy is and if I do my best to think like him, I might just be able to beat him at his own game. So, while you can be angry with me all you want, I need to know more about your past, especially your father, because I don't intend on that man taking any more advantage of you than he already has."

My jaw tenses.

Logic dictates that if I tell Hunter the entire truth, he will believe me, and it will be a burden off my shoulders. But some part of me doesn't want to. I don't want to alter his perception of me. I don't want him to look at me and see the blood staining my hands, even if his are also dripping with it.

I'm not ready to talk about something that I've held onto for two years.

"Do what you need to do," I say coldly. "But you're not going to force me to spill every single detail of my life to you, Hunter. Even sharing this much doesn't come easy to me."

His expression turns thoughtful. "And if I were to investigate your past behind your back?"

"I can't stop you."

"What if I talked to your sister? What would she tell me?"

"My sister?"

"She's still in town, you know."

Shit, I didn't know that.

"At the end of the day, I'm very aware of the power balance between us." I stand to my feet. "Either you can wait and trust me to tell you when I'm ready, or you can just go and satisfy your curiosity like you normally do. I can't stop you either way."

His expression turns dark. "I'm not trying to hurt you, Megan. There's no need to get so defensive."

"Whatever," I shrug. "It's your call."

From the look on his face, it's obvious that he's angry. He stands as well and I feel an anxious churning in my stomach as he walks past me without so much as a glance.

Yeah, he's not angry, he's furious.

The silence in the room now is deafening, and I stand in the middle of his office, frozen in place, wondering if I've finally managed to piss him off for good.

Maybe he thinks I'm not worth the effort anymore. Or just maybe he realizes... that I never really was.

Chapter 21

To Shoot What?

Megan

All the insecurities that I've always kept locked inside me are rising to the surface. My eyes are shut, and I curl my hands into fists to keep them from shaking until I realize that Hunter hasn't actually left the room.

He's still here.

He didn't leave.

I hear a strange clicking sound and then my lover's unmistakable voice behind me.

"Here, take this."

I turn around and see that Hunter is holding a small black gun. A weapon so tiny that, for a moment, I doubt whether it's real.

"Is that real?"

"You just have to point and aim," he responds tightly. "Make sure to shoot at a body part that is wide so that you can inflict damage, like in the gut."

"You're giving me a gun?" I look from the gun to him. "To shoot what?"

"Until I get this mess under control, what happened today might happen again, especially if you decide to randomly ditch your security again." He puts the gun in my hand. "Carry this with you everywhere. Don't second guess when someone comes at you. Just shoot. I'll deal with any consequences afterward."

"Like if I mistakingly shoot an innocent person?"

"Mistakes happen," he says nonchalantly.

"I know you're pissed, Hunter, but–" I hesitate before looking up at him. "I promise never to dismiss the security detail again. I've learned my lesson. I don't need this."

I try handing him back the gun.

"Maybe you have," Hunter says with little effect, perhaps still annoyed with my lack of willingness to share everything about my past with him. "But I want you to be armed as well."

"Are you angry with me right now?" I swallow, suddenly feeling uncertain.

"Giving you a weapon to protect yourself is not a punishment, Megan."

"Are you angry that I don't want to talk about my father with you?" I ask again, not backing down.

"Yeah, I guess I am, but I'll get over it." He crosses his arms over his chest, watching me. "I want you to open up to me yourself. Forcing your secrets out of you against your will isn't what I want."

"I do trust you," I admit slowly. "It's just that I must do things in my own time."

He emits a quiet sigh and then crooks his finger in my direction, and I walk over toward him. He pulls me into his taut body, and the heat from his body relaxes me in the very delicious way it has the power to do.

"I can give you the whole world, Megan. You just have to let me."

"I don't want the whole world."

I just want you.

But I can't voice that last part. I'm just too afraid to actually allow myself to have what I want.

"Then what do you want?" He presses.

I sink my teeth into my lower lip, remembering a brief moment in time when I could completely let go of the pressures of school and work and my past and just live in the moment.

"I want Paris again."

His smile is slow, and my breath catches. "You liked it there that much?"

"I definitely enjoyed the experience, but I especially loved it because I went there with you. You made Paris unforgettable."

It's difficult to be this vulnerable with Hunter, or with anyone for that matter, but the look in his eyes is worth the effort.

"So, it's me then?" Hunter leans his forehead against mine. "I'm what you want."

"You've just been shot at *again* and reunited with your baby sister, and this is what you want to talk about?" I playfully push at his chest and his chuckle is deep and throaty, and I feel it deep in my core. "What I want?"

"Always, Megan."

His kiss on my mouth is fierce, as if he's starving for me, and I don't want it to stop. Now that the adrenaline from today's events is starting to dissipate, there is a sudden craving I'm having for Hunter to fuck me senseless. I know if he does, it will wash away all the violence of today, as well as celebrate his reunion with Lacy... I mean Lena.

Damn, I forgot about Lena.

"Your sister is waiting in my office." I place my palm on his chest. His heart feels as if it's going to thump through his breastbone. "We need to finish this later."

"No, she isn't."

"What do you mean?"

"She's at that bar with Christian having a drink."

"A drink?" I ask with concern. She may be Hunter's sister, but she's still underaged.

"A Pepsi, not an alcoholic drink."

"Oh."

"Gage texted me that she seemed to finally be relaxing. She's fine for now."

"Oh." I smile.

"So may I proceed, Miss Taylor?"

"Have your way with me, Mr. Middleton," I say in the sexiest voice I can muster.

Hunter grins as his hand fidgets with the buttons of my blouse. But just as things are about to heat up, there's a knock on the door. "Boss, you have a visitor."

"I couldn't make this shit up if I tried," Hunter says in sexual frustration.

"Yeah, but you can't ignore him," I say with disappointment that we've been interrupted as well.

"If I don't fuck you soon, I'm going to kill someone," he growls, and my panties dampen. God knows I want him, too, as I stare at the large bulge in his crotch.

"Later."

His eyes are hungry as they run over my clothed body, and a shiver of desire passes through me. I've never been wanted with such intensity by any man. It's one of the traits

I find so attractive about Hunter. I'm utterly addicted to the way this man wants me. Who wouldn't be?

"Sorry, boss."

It's Parker's voice on the other side of the door, and both of us know that if he's interrupting us, there must be a good reason.

Hunter adjusts my blouse, tucking it back into my skirt, and says darkly, "I'm going to come up with a reason to shoot him today."

"He might have saved your life today."

"It's his job to keep me alive."

"Don't shoot him. I like him."

Hunter just gives me a dirty look before telling Parker to enter.

"I need to handle a few things anyway before I leave for the night," I add.

"Wait for me to drive you and Lena back to the apartment," Hunter orders sharply. "And don't forget your gun."

I close the door behind me, stare at the piece of deadly metal in my hand, and pray that I never have to use it.

I might not survive that.

Chapter 22

The Elephant In The Room

Megan

"Are you coming home tonight?" I call Naomi and ask her.

The distance between me and my friend and roommate has only grown, although I'm trying my best to hold on to it. Outside of Hunter, she may be the only other person on the planet I "sort of" trust.

Between a few breakfasts and early dinners before our shifts, Hunter has been spending more time in my apartment than he ever has.

I like it.

Naomi doesn't.

She's a little wary of Hunter, and I think the feeling may be mutual.

"I'm braiding this girl's hair out in Laguna Beach. Her father is some sort of a hotshot actor from a medical drama or something," she says excitedly. "They said I could stay in their guesthouse if I get tired and need to finish up her hair tomorrow, which I probably will, so I'll catch up with you in the am."

"It's going to take you all night to do a kid's braids?"

"She doesn't know what style she wants yet. You know how that goes. I'll probably have to go to the beauty supply store to buy the hair and all that jazz. She'll probably want hot pink braids or something. Ooh, maybe blue ones."

"So…you're going to stay at some random actor's house tonight?"

"Guest house."

"That doesn't sound like the smartest idea, Naomi."

"It'll be fine, roomy. I'll drop you a pin when I arrive so you know where I am."

"But Naomi–"

"Hey, I'm not trying to be an ass about this, Megan, but I'm not always in the mood for hanging out with gangsters and mobsters. I could move back to my old neighborhood for that shit. I'll be fine tonight. You're the one that needs to be careful."

"Wow."

"Oops, was that too bitchy?"

"You know it was."

"Aww, I'm sorry. I'm just hungry. Seriously, girl, that was my stomach talking," she says, trying to make light out of her frank words. Words that I know she actually means.

Naomi has been giving me excuse after excuse about why she comes home late or not at all. For the past few weeks, it's been the elephant in the room between us.

I'm still quiet on the phone, affected by the jab she made about Hunter when she asks about Lena.

"So…is the new sister staying over again?"

"Yeah."

After a talk over a long night of watching back-to-back

Harry Potter movies, I've learned that Lena is actually a pretty cool girl. After a hot shower and fifteen minutes of self-meditation, she's less tense. Get a Pepsi and a few slices of gourmet pizza in her, and she's actually got a lot to talk about.

She's also someone who seems to stick to her guns once she's made a decision, which is pretty impressive for someone eighteen years old. I'm not that much older than her, and I feel like I change my mind about a ton of things every single day. Lena has decided that while she will continue working at the Blue Whiskey, she is not comfortable moving into Hunter's penthouse, so she's been staying at my place.

I totally get it. She's only known Hunter for a nanosecond; plus, if I'm being honest, he's a man who takes some getting used to, especially with his cool demeanor. The man I'm falling in love with, or I suppose who I'm already in love with and who I've begun to think of as perfect, seems to have a serious communication problem with his younger sister.

It's his one flaw.

And it's difficult to watch.

It's been a week since the trouble at the club, and while I can tell that he is desperately trying to get closer to Lena, he doesn't seem to understand that ordering her around isn't the right way to go about it. The pushier he gets, the more she pulls away. And while it's entertaining to watch them fumble their way toward a meaningful relationship, this past week has been taxing on me.

For some reason, the two of them have put me in the middle of their sibling struggle, and I don't know what to do. Okay, maybe my getting involved was my bright idea, but I messed up by getting involved. Getting in the middle of the most domineering man I've ever met and his sister was just plain stupid.

"I'm just saying." Lena grabs the groceries from the car. "He treats me like I'm a five-year-old who is incapable of making my own decisions."

"I think the last time he saw you alive, you were about five, so I guess that makes some sort of sense."

"Not for me. It's unbelievable that I and that man share the same DNA."

"Come on, Lena," I wave off the men from our security detail who want to help with the groceries. "You may have a point, but you don't have to put it like that."

"Tell me you haven't wondered how the two of us came from the same mother."

"Okay, maybe I've wondered a little." I pick up the oranges that have escaped from their bags into the car. "But... he's trying in his own way. I mean, the man shows up to the apartment for breakfast every day. That's dedication."

"Let's be honest." Lena makes a doubtful face. "He comes over to suck your face every morning, not to see me."

"Sucking my face, as you so eloquently put it, is a nice side benefit for me, but he mostly wants to get to know you, plus he's showing interest in your cooking skills. He's trying to meet you where you're at."

"It's hard to tell when all he seems to do is grunt through the entire meal," Lena says. "But I suppose he's trying."

"Exactly." I tuck everything into the paper bag, and we start walking toward the elevator in the parking lot.

The security detail enters with us into the elevator when Lena blinks. "Oh, damn, my phone. I think I left it in the car."

She places her bags down and quickly backs out of the

elevator. If there's another thing I've noticed is that Lena does not like to be parted from her cell phone.

"Stay with her." I give the two men a curt order. "There's nobody in the parking lot."

"What about you, Miss Taylor?"

"I'm fine. I'll head up first. I don't want the ice cream to melt."

The security team sees me as an extension of Hunter, per his instructions, so they do as they're told. After they exit the elevator, I notice a familiar car in the lot and figure Hunter is back early from the club. I wonder if he's planning to have dinner with us.

The elevator doors close and I press the number for my floor. Living with Lena is turning out to be a good deal for me. She's a great cook and I've never been this well-fed in my life. If Naomi keeps on shutting me out like this, I've got an idea to move Lena into her bedroom and move Naomi to the couch.

Getting off the elevator, I approach my door. I'm about to insert my key into the lock when I notice something odd. There are slight scratches around the edges of the lock, and I'm about to take a closer look when the door swings open. My eyes lock on a man with a malicious expression, and all the blood drains from my face as a rippling fear overtakes me.

Chapter 23

Full Blown Terror

Megan

"You sure took your sweet time," Samuel says before reaching out and grabbing me by the hair. He pulls me inside and then throws me down hard as I gasp in pain amid the dropped groceries scattered across my living room floor.

"You should have had the courtesy to tell your parents that you changed your address," comes another voice, which escalates my fear into full-blown terror.

The woman who strolls out of my bedroom is a pear-shaped beauty with an ugly expression on her face, which is full of fillers, my stepmother Veronica. It's only then that I notice Rachel sitting at the island counter, swinging her legs back and forth lazily. I was so shaken by Samuel that I totally missed she was in the room. She gives me a casual smile as she eats some red grapes out of a bowl.

My favorite damn bowl.

"Why the fuck are you here?" I hiss at my father, who

narrows his eyes at me. "And how the hell did you break into my apartment?"

"Rachel was right. You've grown pretty bold in these last two years, and you've got a nasty mouth on you now."

How did they even get in? I think frantically as I try to get to my feet.

"Answer my question!" I spit out.

I don't want to be scared. I don't want to be frightened. I spent the last two years rebuilding myself from the ground up, and I'm not going to let it go to waste because they've decided they want to pop back into my life.

I have to stand my ground, terrified as I am.

And I have to buy time.

Because Lena and the security team will be here any minute to help me, I just have to hold my own.

This time, the person who grabs my hair is my stepmother, and she yanks my head back in a vicious manner, making me scream.

"Ouch!"

"Remember who you're talking to, girl. It seems as if you've forgotten yourself speaking to your father like that."

"She still screams the same, though," Rachel says as she casually pops another grape in her mouth.

That bitch.

"This is my house!" It takes everything within me to stand back on my feet and push Veronica as I glare into her wicked face. "So get the hell out."

I enjoy the look of shock on my stepmother's face as she stumbles back, almost falling on her ass. She doesn't expect me to fight back. None of them do.

"Look at you getting all spunky," Samuel taunts as he takes off his belt. I know what's coming, and even though it would be in my best interest for the security team to save the day, a part of me hopes that they don't come. If they interfere with my family's ambush, they're going to be required to tell Hunter about it, and the last thing I want is for my present to clash with my past.

"But guess what?" Samuel continues. "We're not going anywhere. You think you can whore yourself out and not pay your due?" He cracks the belt, making me flinch. "Looks like you've been holding out on us." He gives me a venomous look. "I know how much a place like this costs. I checked. So where's the money you've been holding back from me? V checked the bedroom, and we didn't find anything there. Where is it?"

"There's no money!" I shout, jumping back when he tries to lash me with the belt.

The messenger bag I still have on across my body bumps into my hip, and I can feel the outline of the small gun that Hunter gave me last week. After everything that's happened, I decided to take his advice and carry it with me for protection.

I try slipping my hand inside the flap for it, but suddenly, Veronica slaps me across the face with an open palm, making my ears ring.

Whack!

Taking advantage of my momentary dizziness, she grabs me by my arms, locking them behind my back, and forces me to face my father, who cracks the belt once more like he has a million times before.

"You think you can deny your sister a place to live or food in her belly?" she hisses into my ear, and my frantic eyes fall on Rachel, who waves her fork in my direction.

"Mom, the guy she's dating is hot. He's definitely where she's getting her money from. Maybe I should just steal him from you since he likes 'em young or maybe after what happened last time, you can just give him to me."

My father raises his belt again but I'm not going to be beaten.

Not in my own home.

Using Veronica's hold on my arms as leverage, I push back against her, lifting my legs in the air and kicking Samuel in the stomach as hard as I can. He stumbles back and falls onto the ground, not having expected it.

Now that he's down, I don't hesitate, twisting around and pulling Veronica's hair and shoving her onto the ground as well.

"You bitch!" Rachel is on her feet, rushing towards me, her hands curled into claws, but I've already taken out the gun from my bag and then point it in her direction, my hands shaking.

"One more step, and I'll fucking shoot you! Don't make the mistake of thinking that I won't."

My voice is bordering on hysteria as my heart crashes against my ribcage as if it's trying to get out.

"You wouldn't do that." Rachel gives me an uneasy look, her hands up in a surrender position. "I'm your sister."

"You're no sister of mine," I tell her.

"Put that damn gun down!" Veronica snarls at me, getting up off her butt.

Slowly, I back away against the window of my living room, and there are three targets I'm keeping my eyes on. Samuel is struggling to stand up, and from the look on his face, if he gets a hold of me, I'll live to regret it.

"Have you finally lost the little bit of sense you ever had?" Veronica questions. "I *said* put that gun down."

"Have I lost it?" I let out a shaky laugh, and my eyes narrow at her. "This might be the smartest thing I've ever done! You all have always treated me like an animal. No, actually *worse* than an animal. All three of you. My supposed family.

"It doesn't matter where I go. You're never going to leave me alone, are you? You always want more money, and you'll never allow me to find some sort of peace in this fucked up world, so why shouldn't I just kill all three of you?"

I glare at each of them over the barrel of my gun.

"Killing you will definitely give me peace."

Chapter 24

It's Not Me

Megan

"There's no peace in prison, you weak little cunt," Samuel hisses. "You won't survive it."

"I'll survive," I promise him, with my finger still firmly on the trigger of the gun. "Trust me. Prison will be a cakewalk compared to the life I led in your house of horrors."

"Megan–" Rachel suddenly tries to reason with me.

"Quiet!" I hiss. "You two, sit on the floor next to Samuel."

Adrenaline is pumping through my veins, and my brain is working on overdrive. I know I need to calm down and search for reason, but the more I glare at each of their ugly faces, the more I realize that I don't want a reasonable ending to this.

I want them to suffer.

Running away from my horrible family was never the answer. If being with Hunter has taught me anything, it's that. They'll never be better people. The only thing they understand is pain, which is why they need to go through everything I have and worse.

"You're crazy, just like your mother," Samuel says.

"I told you that you should have made her have an abortion," Veronica says in an *I told you* kind of voice.

"Shut up!" I point the gun at her forehead. "This one is for making me drink your piss *when I was four!*"

The memory of a terrified child retching in horror is playing in my head like a clip from an old television show.

Suddenly, the gun goes off, but I'm not sure if I'm the one who made the shot or if it was someone else. I'm having something tantamount to an out-of-body experience.

Veronica's scream barely registers to my ears as she stumbles to the ground, clutching her knee. I'm confused. I know I had the gun pointed at her head, but why is her knee bleeding?

My eyes are wet, and I'm shaking, but when Samuel lunges for me, I suddenly get clear as hell and aim the gun directly at his balls.

"Stop right there!"

He freezes in place as I ignore Veronica's painful howls and Rachel's frightened cries.

"You were supposed to protect me," I tell Samuel. Spit flies out of my mouth as I curse at him. "You were my fucking father."

He doesn't flinch, his hatred for me simmering like a stew in his eyes.

"You deserved it," he says. "You deserved worse."

"Why?" I can't hide the agony in my voice as I try to steady my hold on the gun, tears streaming down my face.

"Your drug addict of a mother was fooling herself and

thought she could trap me. She actually believed she could be my wife," he scoffs.

"You should have helped her."

"I told her I didn't want a baby. I told her that she should get rid of you. I even made her an appointment at the clinic, which she purposely missed, and then saddled me with a baby. I didn't want to keep us together." Spittle is flying out of his mouth, his eyes crazed. "But nobody controls me! So I told her that she'd live to regret it, and as you know, Megan, I don't make any promises that I don't keep. I promised her that I was going to sell you off as soon as you got your period, the same way I sold her delusional ass off. But since child protective services had their eyes on me, I had to adjust my plan and keep you around longer."

His words are laced with pure evil, and they penetrate something soft inside of me. He's never explained his hatred for me with words before, only with physical force. No matter how much I hated Samuel, for some reason, I always thought that he was cruel because of some defect of mine. But now I understand...it's not me... it's him. It's them.

It's not me.

"I see," I say firmly, thinking about how he probably pawned my mother off to some other drug addict for a hundred bucks. "Then your death will be me doing the world a fucking favor. I mean, I've already killed once, right? What's a few more times?"

I remember Hunter's words and aim the gun at the largest part of Samuel's body, his middle-aged gut. I'm debating whether or not to pull the trigger when, out of nowhere, I hear Hunter's voice, "I think that's enough, Megan. Put the gun down."

My eyes dart over to where he's standing in the room.

Lars and Parker flank either side of him. I look from him to Lars, remembering what the older man had once told me in the bathroom as he had tried to comfort me. He had spoken of his daughter so lovingly.

My eyes flicker back to Samuel, who's looking over his shoulder at them.

Why did I come into the world in such an ugly way? Why couldn't I be loved like that? Why couldn't someone love me like that?

My insides feel numb as I stare at Lars, feeling an irrational jealousy of the daughter he lost. I don't realize that I'm crying until I feel the wetness on my cheeks.

It hurts so much.

It's like someone is ripping my heart to shreds, and I can't stand it.

Hunter moves toward me, and Samuel says in a grateful tone, "Thank God someone is here. She's lost her mind. She was trying to kill-"

Hunter silences Samuel by punching him in the mouth, making him stumble back.

"Dad!" Rachel screams, then turns to Hunter. "What are you doing? She's the one who attacked us!"

"Get her out of here," Hunter orders Parker while Lars wraps his arm around my shoulders, taking the gun from me.

"I want to see." I struggle with him, my tears still falling. "I want them to die!"

Hunter cups my face roughly, forcing me to meet his gaze. "That's what you want?"

"Yes!" I plead.

He moves even closer, and I can smell his whiskey-laden breath as he speaks again.

"I will always give you want, Megan, but after what I

heard, I think death is too easy. It's the easy way out. If you trust me, then trust that I'll make them suffer. They'll answer for every tear they forced from you and for every bit of humiliation. I swear to you. Leave them to me, and I'll get your revenge for you."

Hunter and I have spent many erotic nights together, but the words he's just said to me might just be the sexiest thing he's ever said. While I may never have a father's love, I've got something way better.

Hunter *wonderful-ass* Middleton.

"All three?"

"All of them, baby."

"She's a murderer!" Samuel pleads for mercy in a high-pitched voice. "Don't listen to her lies. She killed her own boyfriend in cold blood!"

"Good for her." Hunter looks down at him before kicking him swiftly in the groin. "Take her to my place, Lars, and make sure you and Parker secure this floor."

Samuel's story of what he did to my mother keeps spinning around in my head. He's a monster, and I don't want to leave until I see him being carried out of here in a body bag.

"Come on," Lars says quietly. "I'll take you upstairs."

On our way to the elevator, we pass by Parker, who isn't wearing his normal smile, as I exit the apartment.

"Where are you going?" Rachel screams after me. "Get back here, you bitch!"

Parker quickly wraps his hand around Rachel's throat and forcibly seats her on her ass in the hallway. "Quiet."

"Hand me my gloves, Parker," I hear Hunter request icily, and just as the elevator doors close, I take one last look inside the open door of my apartment and see a look of panic spread across Samuel and Veronica's faces.

For once, in our toxic dynamic, they are the ones in fear for their lives.

Not me.

And as diabolical as I know it is, there's something about seeing them that way that sits well with my soul.

And finally, I exhale.

Chapter 25

Check His Pulse

Hunter

I make enough money now that I need to allow the people who work for me to handle the dirtier parts of the business.

But that's always been hard for me.

Plus, this is personal.

Parker watches warily as I strip off my bloodied gloves and hand them to him. Megan's living room is a mess, and the dirtbag lying in front of me is twitching with blood gurgling out of his mouth. He's probably going to live, but he's going to hate every minute of it.

"Check his pulse," I say to Parker with a tinge of disgust in my voice.

It feels as if I've been waiting forever for Megan to share anything about the man lying helplessly in front of me, but now I see for myself why she was so reluctant to do so. Samuel is pure evil and nothing good will come from her rehashing all the horrible things I can only imagine happened to her in a home void of any love or respect for her.

Suddenly, I understand why so many Hollywood types make time-travel movies. What a fantasy. If I possessed that superpower, I'd find a way to change Megan's entire childhood. Why does she have to pay for the sins of her parents?

My eyes dart toward the other two members of Megan's family. I didn't harm the stepmom even though she one hundred percent deserves it. Instead, I gave her a few threatening promises because I don't hit women. It's fine. I'll leave that for the people I plan on sending these monsters to.

Clearly, the little sister doesn't have the stomach for torture when it doesn't involve Megan because she's rocking back and forth on the floor, her fist stuffed in her mouth, seemingly totally checked out. I can sleep at night knowing that she'll never forget the day of reckoning for all that her father's done and because she never stood up for her big sister. Not once. And I can never forgive her for that. I don't care that she was a child herself. A good person, no matter the age, instinctively knows right from wrong.

"Call the cleaners and get this scene cleared," I order Parker. "And call Dante DeAngelo and tell him I'm sending him a gift."

I may not indulge in the trafficking business, but I can always send this sadistic family to someone who does.

"Are you sure, boss?" Parker questions as he hesitantly looks over at the sister. I know what he's thinking. I've never sent DeAngelo a *gift*, not like this. But all I can think about is what would have happened in this apartment if I hadn't arrived when I did. I believe that Megan would have shot one of them, if not all three, and then where would we be?

"They get to live," I tell him. "That's more than they deserve."

"I can make this right," the stepmother pleads through mascara-streaked eyes. "I can make you feel really good."

I'm unable to hold back the chuckle from deep in my throat. "Are you propositioning me?" I ask in disbelief.

"I'll do whatever you want, whenever you want."

"Your husband is choking on his own blood, and your daughter looks like she's visiting the planet Mars, but you're ready to find the next warm dick to suck on?"

"I'm a smart woman. I always have been," she says proudly. "I know a real man when I see one."

"I don't like them long in the tooth," I tell her, figuring that crushing her vanity is probably the best way to get under her skin. "You're too old for my tastes."

"I understand, boss," Parker says out of the blue. "I'll call DeAngelo now. It's the only way."

"Wait!" she begs. "Then take Rachel. She's younger than Megan and much more obedient. Please!"

"Look at you being a mother now," I say sarcastically. "But unfortunately for you, not for the right kid."

"I was always a mother to Megan."

"Not much of one."

"Where are you sending us? Who is this DeAngelo person?"

"A man who is going to make sure that you live the rest of your days out in the manner you deserve. You're going to love it. It's right up your alley. Dicks everywhere."

I make my way up to the penthouse, some of my anger

relieved. When I enter, the first person I see is Lars, and I start barking out demands.

"Find out how a family of three got weaseled their way into this building and Megan's apartment. I selected this building for security, which there seems to be little of these days. Handle that."

Lars knows exactly what I mean when I tell him to handle it.

He hesitates for a moment as he passes by me and then says, "She went to your room, and she won't leave. Lena tried to get in to talk to her, but she's not even letting her in."

"Thanks." I nod. "I'll handle it."

Seeing my sister on the couch, looking miserable, I stop by her first. This is not the way I wanted a reunion with her to be full of drama at every turn.

"Megan is going to be fine," I promise her.

"What happened?" Lena looks terrified. "She was fine before I left to go back to the car."

I look towards my bedroom door and decide not to lie. Lena's not much younger than Megan and she's an adult. I have to start treating her like one.

"Her family broke in and tried to hurt her. She's upset. I'll deal with it."

"I'll..." She looks around. "I'll make some dessert or something. Something cold. It'll help. It might help."

She seems desperate to do something to help, which may just be a biological trait we both share, so I nod. "I don't have much in the fridge, so order whatever you need from a delivery service. I'll be inside talking to Megan."

When I enter the bedroom, Megan is lying on her side in the fetal position on a corner of my bed, the silk duvet around her.

I sit down next to her. "You okay?"

"No," comes the small voice, almost childlike.

"Well..." I tuck the duvet a bit tighter around her, and she lets me. "I paid your father back in blood if it makes you feel better."

She pops her head from under the covers but doesn't say anything just yet. She simply watches me as I lean back against the headboard of the bed. I motion for her to come to me with my hands, and when she complies, I adjust her so that she's sitting between my legs.

"I don't hit women, Megan, so I didn't physically hurt his wife or your sister, but I have made arrangements to make sure that they will feel the same amount of suffering you did."

"Does it make me a bad person to want that?" she asks in a teary voice. "Do you think I'm awful?"

"No." I wrap my arms around her from behind. "It doesn't. Some crimes you can forgive or let the wheels of justice handle. But some crimes have to be punished, and this will be their punishment."

Megan is silent, and I can feel her small body move with soft sobs. I hate the sound of her silent cries. Each time her shoulders heave, it feels like something is clawing at my chest.

"Megan," I murmur her name. "Can you live with my decision? There's time for me to adjust the plan."

She just cries harder.

My Megan is not usually a crier, but I can understand that she's all torn up inside right now, so I just hold her tightly and let her get it out of her system.

I don't know how long it takes for her to finally relax in my arms, but when she does, she begins to talk and tell me a story that I'm not completely sure I am ready to hear.

Chapter 26

It's Time I Tell You

Hunter

"There was a brief moment when I really believed that things would work out for me," Megan starts her story as if she's humiliated with herself.

"What do you mean?" I ask.

"In that house, with *them*."

"You thought things would work with those three?" I say in disbelief.

"I know. I was delusional, but the tide seemed to be turning when I turned seventeen."

"How so?"

"They hired a new art teacher at my school who encouraged me to paint just when I was thinking about abandoning my art. Then I got my first real job at a department store that paid me more money than I'd ever seen before," she explains, wiping her nose with a clean tissue. I hand her another one in silence and wait for her to continue. "Samuel didn't believe in giving us allowance."

I stay quiet, her voice in pain each time she utters his name like a shard of glass cutting me inside.

"But going to work after school also afforded me some independence, something else that Samuel rarely gave me. Honestly, it was a miracle that he allowed me to take the job, but I soon realized it was because he wanted me to contribute to the house bills. They were always awful with money, but I wanted to keep mine, so I had to make sure that I never told them what I really made there."

I try not to react in an audible way, but I can feel the imaginary shard of glass shredding me from the inside out. While this story is basically nothing compared to many of the other horrible ways those people treated her, I'm angered that Megan was a child who was treated like this, and nobody caught it.

"And how did you manage to keep the money from them?" I ask with a slight edge to my voice.

"The other thing that happened when I was seventeen was that I met my boyfriend, Peter."

"Peter?" My voice sounds gruff. I have no interest in hearing about Megan's past romantic relationships.

"He worked at the store too, and the best part was he didn't know anything about my home life and how fucked up it was. He helped me."

"What did he do?"

"I would cash my paycheck during lunchtime at the local cash checking place near my high school. I'd bring the money to work and ask Peter to hold on to some of the money for me."

"Didn't he ask why?"

"He did, but I never told him any specifics about my home environment. I just told him that it wasn't good. I never even told him about Rachel."

"And he didn't push you for any details?"

Megan turns her head to look at me. "He was a teenage boy, Hunter. He wasn't going to push for answers about my parents. All he cared about was getting in my pants."

If I could go back in time, I'd slap that teenage boy and tell him to pay attention to his girl. How the hell was she able to keep the crazy going on in her home from him?

He wasn't paying attention.

That's how.

"Got it," I reply. "Go ahead and finish your story."

"Well...my birthday was coming up," Megan lets out a shuddering breath as she continues. "I was planning on taking a day off from work to go to the carnival in town. Actually, I'm not sure how much of a carnival it is. I think most people from Los Angeles would call it a fair because it was a small event with rides and games sponsored by the local Rotary Club. I thought it would be romantic and something different to do because Peter and I would only see each other at work."

I didn't know that listening to Megan reflect somewhat wistfully on romantic dates with her teenage ex would make me feel so uncomfortable.

"I guess I was entirely too excited about the date because it wasn't long before Rachel noticed, and that was trouble."

"Even when she was younger?"

"Rachel was young, but Samuel and my stepmother brainwashed her early."

"So she hated you as a kid and probably didn't even know why."

"Yeah, I guess that's true."

"So, go ahead."

"Well, two weeks before my birthday, she dropped by

the store with a few of her little friends to spy on me and, unfortunately, found what she was looking for. Peter just happened to be in my section, talking to me, and Rachel soon figured out at least one of the reasons why I was so happy."

"What did she say?"

"I remember dread washing completely over me, and I froze in place as Rachel introduced herself to Peter as my sister. Remember, I never talked about my family, so I could tell he was shocked, but he did what any normal guy would do and was polite about it. He introduced himself as my boyfriend, but that was his biggest mistake, and of course, it was mine for not warning him."

Megan's hands clutch the duvet as she takes a second to breathe and finish her story.

"We don't have to talk about this now," I tell her.

"No, it's fine. I just haven't talked about it in a long time. A few of the memories leave me with feelings that are a bit raw."

"Understood. Take your time."

"Peter was not like the boys in my neighborhood or at my high school. While he wasn't the most attractive guy I ever met, he was sweet, and he was kind, which is why I liked him. He gave me the space I needed and did not pressure me to talk about my family. But after that meeting, my two worlds collided, and I was helpless to stop it."

"What happened?"

"Rachel happened. She decided to make it her life's mission to discover the source of my happiness and then declare war on it. First, she went home and told them I had a boyfriend, and I was punished. My parents were always creative when it came to punishments because after child protective services were called, they were careful not to hit me in places where I would be inspected. So they found other ways to hurt me."

"Did anyone ever realize how you were being treated at home?"

"Everyone knew."

Her voice is flat as she speaks, almost empty as if she's trying to disassociate from the memories of her past.

"I thought Samuel would tell me to stop working there, but they needed the money I was bringing in."

"So you didn't give your entire check to your...your boyfriend?"

"No, that would have obviously raised suspicions. I had to give them some money and prayed that they wouldn't ask to see a check stub."

"And what was your punishment for having a boyfriend?" I'm almost afraid to ask.

"I had to sleep on the kitchen floor for a week, but worse than that, I was told to break things off with Peter. At the time, that seemed like a death sentence. Peter was the only person I had in my life who seemed to care about me."

"So what did you do?"

"I didn't do it, of course. Instead, I told him that we should hide our relationship because my parents were strict and didn't approve of me having a boyfriend at my age."

"He agreed?"

"He agreed, but he was also determined to prove to my parents that he was worthy of me. He thought a good way to show that was to get an "in" with my little sister."

"Uh oh."

"Exactly." She nods her head. "I told him not to talk to Rachel, but he didn't listen. It was hard for him to understand why when I wasn't telling him the entire truth. But Rachel continued coming to the mall on the days I worked and would drop by the store to chat with him. I didn't know this at the time. But Peter confided in her that the two of us were still seeing each other, and as my birthday drew nearer, he started discussing my birthday plans with her."

Megan pauses and then pushes up against me as if seeking the comfort of my body heat and I hold her tighter, wondering why this story is so hard for her to share. *Was she in love with this kid?*

"You don't have to share the rest if it's too hard," I tell her, although I'm hoping that she does. However this story ends, it is big enough that those asshats held it over her head for years, even to the extent of extorting money from her. It's probably best if I know everything because it's the only way I can protect her moving forward.

So I wait with bated breath for her response.

"No, it's time I tell you, Hunter."

Chapter 27

Like A Bad Movie

Hunter

"I may leave some details out because I've banked this time of my life away, somewhere in the recesses of my memory," Megan says, her hands twisting together in her lap.

"That's fine. Just tell me what you remember."

"Rachel convinced Peter to change the plan and come to our house for my birthday."

"Your house?"

"Of course, I didn't know anything about it because she convinced him that it was going to be a pleasant surprise and one that our parents would be fine with."

"I thought this Peter person already knew that you wouldn't be comfortable with him getting to know your family?"

"Honestly, I don't know what Rachel said to him to convince him not to tell me she was coming by the store and that coming to my house would be a good idea. I guess he believed that getting in good with my family would somehow make him closer to me."

Sounds like a familiar strategy.

"He was wrong. All it did was set off a series of events that turned my life into even more of a shit show than it already was. When he showed up at the house to surprise me, Rachel made some sort of advance toward him, which, of course, he rejected."

"A romantic advance?"

"I don't know if she had a crush on him or if she simply wanted him because he wanted me, but when I came home, Peter was in the living room pale as a ghost, and she was in the other room crying to her mother."

"Dare I ask what happened next?"

"After the initial shock of seeing Peter sitting in my living room, literally ten steps from where I slept on the floor the night before, I tried to convince him to leave. I could tell he was hurt and confused, but I didn't have time to explain. I just wanted him out."

"Makes sense."

"But then, like some kind of bad movie, Rachel tore out of the bedroom and had one of Samuel's hunting knives in her hand. God, it happened so fast. She ran toward him, without uttering a single sound, and stabbed him twice."

"Damn."

"I know."

"Where was that bitch Veronica?"

"Standing in the doorway of the bedroom, staring at us. She didn't move. She didn't talk. She wouldn't help. She just watched."

Megan starts rocking back and forth, her hands still wringing in front of her. This is bringing up a type of pain that I've never seen her exhibit before, but I allow her to continue.

I allow her to feel it all.

She needs this.

"I tried to protect him. I swear I did, but he was bleeding out so quickly, and I didn't know what to do."

"Was he dead?"

"No, it might have been better if he were. His eyes were open, full of fright, and staring pleadingly at mine. He was just a kid, just like me, and he was scared."

"What about Samuel? Where was he?"

"He'd been in the garage, working on one of his cars, and walked in on us. It was the first time in a long time I looked to the monster of my life for help, but I remember feeling so desperate."

"Help me," I begged him. *"He's bleeding so much."*

"What the fuck happened?" I remember he asked all three of us. *"Who's this bleeding out on my floor?"*

"Megan's boyfriend," Veronica said cooly. *"He tried to hurt Rachel."*

"That's a lie!" I remember screaming. "She stabbed him for no reason. Tell him, Rachel!"

"I will never forget what happened next. Without even flinching, Samuel grabbed the knife out of Rachel's hand, wiped the handle on his jeans, placed it in my hand, and told me to finish the job, or he'll kill me."

Tears are rolling down her cheeks, and she's talking fast, forcing the words out as if she's desperate to get it over with.

"Megan–"

"I begged them to let me send him to the hospital, but Samuel smacked me hard with an open palm and told me he'd stab me with the same knife if I didn't do it. He said he wasn't going to let his favorite daughter go to jail, that he'd like nothing more than to be done with a whore like me, and that all I ever did was to cause him problems."

This is not the direction I thought this story would go. While I remember the asshole referring to some supposed murder Megan committed, I never gave the reality of that any real consideration. Now I see, I underestimated just how evil that man really is.

"I believed him, Hunter. I believed that he was looking for an excuse to be rid of me once and for all, and I wasn't ready to die, so I pushed the knife into Peter's stomach as he lay dying, hoping that I was finally ending his pain."

I push my face into the top of her head and close my eyes. I can't believe my Megan had to endure such a horrific event. I hate that I can't turn back time and fix this for her. Fuck, I hate how powerless I feel right now.

"Is there any more?" I ask softly.

"And then I saw the flash as Veronica took pictures of me stabbing him with her phone. And–"

Her voice is faint, and I say firmly, "Finish it. Get it out."

"Someone in the house behind us heard the screams, knocked on our door, and told us they called the police. This is where things get blurry. I'm not sure if I'm remembering things the way or in the order they happened."

"You were in shock at that point. That's perfectly normal. What do you think happened?"

"Rachel and my father trashed the place, and I think Veronica was the one who forced me to wash my hands. I don't know why they didn't turn me in. Probably because they changed their mind and thought that I might tell the whole truth to the police. I'm not sure."

"So Samuel said it was a robbery?"

"Peter was still alive when the ambulance came, and the

police believed Samuel's ridiculous story about us inadvertently being in the middle of a drug deal gone bad."

"Drug deal?"

"Peter was a teenage boy from the wrong side of our nowhere town. It was easy for Samuel to weave a lie about his daughter getting mixed up with the wrong kind of kid."

"Understood."

"For appearances, Veronica took me to the hospital. We waited for four hours in the waiting room, but Peter died of blood loss and fatal injuries. She kept whispering in my ear that whole time that I was responsible. That I killed him. And then something in me broke. I walked out of that hospital waiting area that night with a plan to never come back."

"So, how did we get from that night to where we are today?"

"Samuel found me six months later. He showed up at my job, making a scene and getting me fired. At first, he threatened to drag me back home, but then he decided it was even better if I stayed away but paid him for the privilege."

"And why would you ever agree to that?"

"Because of the pictures," she whispers.

"*Fuckkkk*," I mutter. "The pictures."

Megan's head falls back against my chest, and she feels almost weak.

"But I deserve to be blackmailed by those monsters. I killed my boyfriend, an innocent boy. His family doesn't even know the truth about what happened to him. I deserve worse," she laments.

"Yet somehow you got me."

Chapter 28

In Deep Shit

Hunter

I make a mental note to myself to inform Dante not to be too lenient when he plans for the future for the three individuals I've sent him. Nobody deserves the kind of hell that Megan's been through, so I want them to pay...even the sister.

"I understand why you feel that you're responsible for your friend's death." I stroke her hair back from her forehead and press a kiss to her temple. "But none of this was your fault. I promise you. Unfortunately, your friend was in the wrong place at the wrong time."

"I don't know how you can say that. I was the last one to stab him. I remember how it felt to pierce his flesh and then press the knife in deeper. I remember the look on his face." She presses the heels of her hands to her eyes, her voice choking. "I know that Rachel started it, but I'm the one who finished it. Peter died in the hospital because of me. I'm sure of it."

"No," I say sternly. "He died because he thought he

knew better than you. He died because he chose not to listen to you. He should've never started a secret dialogue with Rachel. If you tell a person not to stand in front of an oncoming train, and they still do it, their death isn't on you."

"But I'm not sure he understood that Rachel was as dangerous as an oncoming train. I never told him the truth about my family or my home life. He didn't know how bad it was for me. How awful they were. Maybe if I had been more forthcoming, he would have stayed away."

"That's a lot of maybes and wishful thinking. The reality is you did what you had to do because you were in survival mode. You stabbed him because you weren't given a reasonable choice. It was either you or him. And I'm glad you picked yourself, Megan."

"I guess."

"Be honest with yourself. There was no way Samuel was going to let Rachel take the wrap for stabbing your friend."

"You're right. Samuel despises me. They all do." She sounds like a wounded bear, and I wonder to myself if she'll ever recover from the evil she endured under that man's roof.

"Turn around and face me, Megan," I tell her. She's finally been so forthright with me. It's time I confess what I know to her. I've been holding onto it too long. "I want to share something with you."

"What is it?"

"It's no secret that once we began an intimate relationship, I felt the need to have you investigated. My life and business choices dictate a certain amount of control on my part. I need to know as much as I can about any of the variables in my life."

"And I'm a variable?"

"Yes, baby. You are very much a variable." I smile.

"And why are you admitting what I already suspected?"

"An investigation can only reveal a limited amount of information. There was no way for me to know everything you endured growing up in your house, especially because your abuse was never documented, but I did learn about the stabbing."

"You knew?" Her eyes lock on mine in a hardened way.

"Okay, you're wondering how I could hold on to a piece of important information like this, aren't you?"

"Um, yeah, Hunter. We're fucking."

"Megan," I warn, but she ignores me.

"Plus, I pay Samuel money so that no one will ever find out my part in Peter's murder. But you're saying it's information that can be easily found out?"

"I didn't say it was easy."

"You found out, didn't you?"

"Listen to me, Megan. I'm telling you all this because what you clearly don't know is that it wasn't you who killed Peter, and I can't have you walking around in agony about it any longer."

"What the hell are you talking about, Hunter? I just told you the whole story. I was there. You weren't."

"Most of what I know is simply through a police report made after the incident that my investigators were able to get access to. There was information in the report about the break-in, possible gang activity, and the cause of death of the suspect. The cause of death in the report was not from the knife wounds."

"What?"

"You didn't kill him. His blood isn't on your hands."

Megan takes a few seconds to calm herself and then

asks in a relatively quieter voice, "That's what you read in the report?"

"Peter was recovering in the hospital. Neither you nor Rachel hit any major arteries or organs when you stabbed him. They were flesh wounds. He would have been fine."

"Then what the hell happened? I don't understand."

"There was a mix-up with his IV medication at the hospital, and he went into cardiac arrest."

"A hospital error?" she says in disbelief.

"That's why there wasn't an additional investigation of the case and why you weren't questioned again. The case was closed."

"Why didn't I know any of this?"

"Because Samuel didn't want you to know. How could he hold those pictures over your head if you knew the truth?"

Megan lets out a shuddering breath. "I see."

"I want you to know that you don't have to worry about any of this anymore. You won't ever have to see those people again, and you certainly don't have to pay Samuel another red cent. Those days are behind you."

"And the pictures?"

"Are either in their phones, their cloud drives, or their computers. Vaughn will find them and permanently delete them."

She looks up at me, and I see the puffiness around her eyes. "Vaughn knows about this?"

She sounds defeated, and I hate it. I don't think she's fully comprehended what I've revealed to her about Peter's death.

I gently pull her into my arms. "Yes, that's what Vaughn does for a living. He knows all of my secrets and I trust him with my life. Do you trust me with yours?"

I see the tears well up in her eyes, and this time, I hold her to my chest, doing something I never imagined myself to be doing.

I comfort her.

"You didn't do anything wrong, Megan," I tell her in hushed tones. "You never did anything wrong."

It's easy to be gentle around her, and as I run my fingers through her hair, I look down at her and see a reflection of myself in her eyes that I almost don't recognize.

She's changed me.

"Is this hell really over?" she asks.

"It's definitely over and I'm glad they're going to get what they deserve," I murmur as I stroke her hair as she just rests her head on my chest.

She quietly snuggles into me, and I don't mind this position as we lay there in silence. It's only when I look down a half hour later that I realize she's fallen asleep on me.

I slide my phone out of my pocket and try sending a text carefully so I won't wake her.

Me: I need you to do a clean digital sweep of Dante's new guests. Everything. I want it to appear as if they never existed.

Vaughn: On it.

I could make Megan more comfortable and move, but I don't want to. Her weight on top of me is soft, and I just want her to hold her like this for as long as I can.

"I don't know what you've done to me," I whisper against her hair. "But I don't want to let you go."

Suddenly, I realize what Vaughn and Christian have been alluding to for weeks.

I'm in deep shit with this girl.

Chapter 29

Do You Need Me?

Megan

I don't know how long I've been asleep, but when I wake, the room is pitch black, and I'm still enveloped in a set of powerful arms.

Shirtless but still in slacks, Hunter is sleeping, but you can barely tell.

His breathing is quiet.

Face at rest with zero expression.

Gun on the nightstand.

There's no weird eye twitching or snoring, as most men do. It's almost as if he never fully falls into a deep sleep because he's waiting for the other shoe to drop.

My stomach growls, and I realize that I probably haven't eaten anything in at least twelve hours, and even then, I only had a few Blue Whiskey wings. I try my best to slide myself out of his embrace so that I won't wake him, but it's no use. Just the slight movement of my left arm wakes him right up.

He tightens his grip around my waist.

"And where are you going?" he asks with a luscious, low voice that makes my stomach stir.

"To eat. I'm starving."

"There's nothing in that kitchen worth eating. Why do you think I always come down to your place for breakfast? I'll take you somewhere."

"Where are we going to go at this time of night?"

"There's an all-night restaurant fifteen minutes from here. They serve pretty decent Asian-American fusion food. They usually keep a table open for me."

"Of course they do."

I reach my arms around his neck as the last few hours of my life hit me hard like a ton of bricks. I never have to worry about Samuel, Veronica, or Rachel again. I don't have to pay them. I never have to see them again. I don't even have to think about them.

"Did I ever say thank you?" I ask him.

"I'm not sure. Those aren't words that I'd ever need or expect from you."

"Well, thank you anyway."

I stare for a moment into Hunter's eyes and am in awe at the way he protected me today.

How he always protects me.

"Don't think about it anymore."

"I think the words you were looking for were *you're welcome*."

"Go brush your teeth so we can get going."

"Why?" I crawl the length of his body and straddle his hips. "Does my breath smell?" I blow in his face.

"What are you doing, Megan?"

"What do you mean? I think it's pretty obvious what I'm doing."

I can feel him hardening in between my legs.

"You need a proper meal. You've been through hell."

"I'm hungry for a lot of things."

I trace my hand down the right side of his chest as I lean into the left.

"Is this your way of thanking me?" he asks cooly as he stoically tries to ignore my advances.

"This is the way I show you how much I want you," I say, kissing the side of his neck.

Another kiss.

"And appreciate you."

My hand slides down to his designer leather belt. I undo the buckle and then slide my hand down under the waistband.

"And need you."

I know I've got him when his head falls back against the headboard and his eyes close.

"Do you need me, Hunter?"

I continue stroking the length of his dick and revel in the way it elongates and hardens under my touch. He groans in pleasure but doesn't answer the question.

"Oh, you don't feel like talking right now?" I tease.

"You want me to talk? I'll talk," he promises with a deep timber to his voice. "I want you to take off your clothes, get on your hands and knees, take every inch of my dick inside your pussy until you beg me to stop, and then we'll go out for dinner."

His words have a bite to them, and my panties become soaked with desire. I want this man in a way that I've never wanted him. I want him to consume me. To fuck the last twenty-four hours out of my heart and soul.

I want to forget who I was.

And I only want to remember this.

As I strip my clothing off, I watch as he inspects the

bruises I've managed to accrue over the last few days. If I didn't know better, I'd think that it physically pains him to see them.

"Hands and knees on the bed," he orders. "Head down."

"Something bad could have happened to you tonight," he suddenly says, and when he speaks, his voice sounds different than I've ever heard it sound before.

"You're wet as fuck," he says, almost as if he's surprised.

"That's because I want you," I tell him again.

"You've said enough," he claps back. "Your body will tell me what it wants tonight. Not your mouth."

The room becomes eerily quiet. All I can hear are the sounds of our breaths as they become heavy with want for each other. Hunter slides his left hand along my spine until it reaches the base of my skull. He grabs my hair and lifts my head up.

"Something bad could have happened to you tonight," he suddenly says, and when he speaks, his voice sounds different from I've ever heard it sound before.

"I know," I say.

His right-hand rubs small, soothing circles on one of my butt cheeks.

"I could have lost you, and if I had, there would've been no consoling me. I would have raged and ripped this city to shreds."

I don't know how to respond to that except with tears.

"I'm sorry," I say because I don't know how else to answer him.

His hand moves in between my legs.

"Don't ever apologize for shit that's not your fault ever again, Megan. Your only mistake is that you didn't tell me everything a long time ago."

"Okay," I whisper through a mixture of pleasure and tears."

"Spread your knees wider for me."

I adjust my legs as he gently lowers my head back down.

"Wider," he commands.

Carefully, he places kisses on each of my butt cheeks, then between my legs as my body shudders in delight.

"That's a good girl," he praises me. "Your body is telling me that it's ready for me now."

My clit pulsates, and my hips wiggle in anticipation of what's coming. I want this badly. I need him to pound into me mercilessly. I hope he's right. I wonder if he can actually tell what my body wants without me having to tell him. That would be fucking amazing.

My hands grip the comforter of the bed when Hunter pushes his fat dick inside of me. Every time I have sex with this man, it's like my vagina forgets just how much it's going to have to adjust to make room for him inside.

Hunter is huge.

He grabs my hips with his massive hands and continually strokes deep inside me without mercy.

His words are dirty.

"I've got exactly what your juicy cunt needs."

His words are possessive.

"Whose pussy is this, Megan?"

My head gets lower and lower until I'm biting the covers. His dick feels like it's damn near in my throat as he pushes himself in and out of me in a hypnotic rhythm. I can hear the bed squeak as he thrusts forward and a small sound in the back of my throat when he slides back.

It feels deliciously good.

But ten minutes in, and I'm not even close to having an orgasm.

Hunter notices it, too, and after a while, decides for us to switch positions. Now he's on his back, and I'm on top of him in a position where I can control the tempo.

"Take what you want," he tells me. "Ride me as long as you need to."

I lower myself onto his rock-hard length again.

My hands pressed against his chest.

And I begin to work my hips up and down.

Then around.

It's one of my favorite positions and so I try all my moves.

I grab my own tits and pinch my nipples as I bounce up and down on Hunter and feel like a wanton goddess as he grunts with pleasure.

"That's it, baby. Fuck me like you want it."

But another ten minutes later, no orgasm, and now I'm tired.

Hunter has staved off his own release for as long as he could and finally puts a stop to this train wreck of a sex session.

"Let me call the restaurant," he says and gives me an obligatory tap on the ass to move out of the way so he can get up to pee.

So now I'm spread eagle on the bed.

Naked as a jaybird.

And as the tears roll down the sides of my face and onto the pillow, I'm asking myself...what on earth just happened?

What's my fucking problem now?

Chapter 30

I Don't Like Distance

Hunter

For days, I've quietly watched my lover move through her usual daily activities on autopilot. While I know Megan has been through something extremely traumatic, and I shouldn't expect miracles, something is off. Way off. She's not necessarily avoiding me, but there is definitely a distance between us.

I don't like distance.

Not from her.

Not after everything we've been through.

And especially not now that she's become such a huge part of my life.

After ringing the bell to the apartment, I can hear Naomi's slow, hobbled steps finally reach the door. Megan told me she broke her foot in some sort of accident, which is why she's been spending more time in the apartment with her instead of with me.

"Sorry to hear about your foot, but I'm glad that Megan

has something else to focus her attention on," I say as she opens the door, leaning on one crutch.

"We've always focused on each other's well-being. No need to thank me for what I've always done," she says back with a smug twang to her voice that irritates me to no end.

Struggling to find anything nice to say to this woman is a feat in itself. Why do I even bother? I can appreciate that she's fiercely protective of Megan, especially after hearing about everything Megan had to deal with at the Blue Whiskey and from her own family. So I get it, but it's just that her attitude toward me leaves a lot to be desired, especially because she does nothing to hide it. If she were anyone else treating me with such disdain...hell, I hate to think how I would have already destroyed her life if she were anyone else.

"Do you talk to all of your landlords like this?" I say, immediately pissed with myself that I'm not able to let this go.

"You're not my landlord," she says with a shit-eating grin. "You're Megan's landlord, and I'm her guest."

"A guest with her own bedroom?"

"I suppose that's why they call it a guest bedroom."

"I'm not here to trade passive-aggressive barbs with you. Where's Megan?" I ask impatiently. I've been in this apartment for damn near five minutes, and she hasn't come out to greet me yet.

"Stop stressing her. Lord knows she can hear your voice from the bedroom. She'll come out in a minute." Naomi hobbles to the couch and plops herself on the couch, finally turning on the flat-screen television. "Also, Lena is going to the exhibition in my place tonight, so you'd better take excellent pictures."

"What the hell were you doing that you even broke your

foot, clumsy?" I taunt but am cut off when Naomi shouts out.

"Megan, your landlord is out here being a dick to me!"

I give her an icy look, and she gives me a mocking wiggle of her brows.

"What's going on?" Megan appears in the room's doorway, looking harried. She gives me a narrow-eyed look when I stride toward her. "You're an ice sculpture to the rest of the world but when you're around Naomi, you pick fights?"

"I don't pick fights," I say with a smirk. "I end them."

"What are you, Don Corleone?" Naomi jeers from her seat. "Am I in the middle of a scene in *The Godfather* and didn't realize it?"

"Can't you two get along?" Megan sighs, inadvertently wiping a bit of paint across her cheek.

"No, she rubs me the wrong way," I assert.

"I wouldn't rub you with a ten-foot pole!" Naomi shouts again.

"See?" I scowl at Megan. "You want me to get along with someone who acts like that?"

"She's just very protective," Megan says slowly before adding with an afterthought. "At least, I think that's it. Anyway, why are you here? You didn't text me to tell me you were coming down."

"Were you painting today of all days?"

"Yes, I've gotten behind on some of my work for school. I have some pieces I need to work on."

I feel like an idiot that I haven't considered how Megan might be behind on her artwork. Doing well in school and in the exhibition has always been her prime aim. Her family, my club, and all the mess that comes along with it have all just been distractions.

"Should you take a break from the club for a while to catch up?" I ask.

"A break?" She looks confused. "How would I pay my bills?"

Naomi mutters a few incomprehensible words that I'm sure are meant for my benefit.

"You don't need to worry about your bills, Megan," I whisper. "I can cover everything in the apartment."

"I know you can, but I still need to make my own money, Hunter. I have to buy art supplies, food, and bus fare."

I bend my head down a little closer to hers. It doesn't escape me how she takes a slight step back.

"Just because Samuel is taken care of doesn't mean you still don't need your security detail. There are still people out there trying to fuck with me, which means they could decide to fuck with you. Security stays. They can drive you to campus and they can pick up whatever you need from the store. They have a company credit card."

"Hunter—"

"I don't want to talk about it anymore." I shut her down, then hand her an envelope. "I brought some cash for Lena because she told me you invited her to the exhibition. I want her to go shopping and pick out something pretty to wear. Where is she, by the way?"

My sister has kind of warmed up to me after Samuel's attack on Megan. I think she's starting to recognize that I'm only here to care for the women in my life, not impose myself on their lives.

"She's at her part-time job." Megan takes off her painting smock. "I'm not sure she'll have time to buy a dress, but I can lend her one of mine."

"Thank you for inviting her."

"I thought it would be a good way for you two to spend some non-intense time together. Plus, Naomi wasn't using the ticket, anyway."

Still feeling the sting of Megan's standoffishness, I wander over to a pile of paintings and sketches that have been accumulating in a corner of the room and flip through them.

"Did she say anything about quitting her part-time job at the shelter? She was a little angry with me because I insisted she leave there and just work full time at the club."

"She does have an attachment to that place. They must have been–"

Megan's words fade into a pleasant buzz in the background as I select a painting of a couple in a café. The woman's back is the viewer, but the man who is watching her has this look of burning passion in his eyes and a small, content smile playing on his lips as he listens to what the woman is saying. The features are in broad strokes, but not so broad that I can't make out who the man is supposed to be.

My breath catches for some reason as I see none of the heaviness of the responsibilities of the world in my eyes. It's completely different from her previous sketch of me. I look lighter, happier, and way more human.

"When did you paint this?" I ask her.

When Megan wanders over to see what I'm looking at, she immediately snatches it from me, blushing fiercely. "That's not for you!"

"*When* did you draw it?" I repeat.

"Paris." She looks uneasy. "On the plane ride home."

"Can I have it?"

"Fine," she sighs, handing it over. "But it's my favorite one, so be careful with it."

I don't know why, but something about the way she's captured me looking at her is making something in my chest unfurl.

"What?" Megan asks when I keep staring at the picture.

"Every time I think I'm done being surprised, you do something else and throw me off, Miss Taylor."

"Sometimes you talk in riddles, and I wonder if someone dropped you on your head as a baby," she says, giving me a wry look. "Will I ever get a translation of these random thoughts of yours?"

I grin at her before squeezing her jaw and planting a kiss on her lips. "Such a smart mouth."

She bites my lower lip in retaliation before pushing me off. "Go away. I have to clean up my paints, take a shower and get dressed. Naomi is doing our hair and makeup."

"I can send you someone from the salon at–"

"Stop hovering, Megan's landlord!" Naomi shouts from the couch. "I got this."

"I'm going to shoot her," I warn Megan as she laughs and pushes me out of the apartment with both hands on my back.

"You're not shooting her today, Mr. Middleton. Today is all about me. Now go so we can get ready."

I tuck the picture in my inner jacket pocket before sneering at Naomi. "Once she starts living with me, *her landlord* is kicking you out."

"That was a stupid move telling me that," Naomi says as she hungrily munches on some random cheese-flavored snack. She then rolls her eyes at me then looks toward Megan. "Bestie, I feel like we don't spend enough time together. Let's never live apart."

"Out, out, out," Megan pushes me again as Naomi's chest rumbles with laughter. "Pick us up in a few hours."

Megan rises on her toes and presses a kiss to my lips. And while I've been scrutinizing everything about her behavior lately, the kiss feels genuine. It feels like Megan. But after the door closes behind me, I frown.

Who have I become that I've allowed a college student and her snotty best friend to run completely roughshod over me?

This has got to change.

And it will start changing tonight.

Chapter 31

Just Pointing Out The Obvious

Hunter

"You're pussy whipped," Christian snickers once I walk back into my apartment."

"Come again?" I challenge.

"I just thought you should know," he smirks, shrugging his shoulders. "The lovely Megan has you completely wrapped around her little finger."

"No one asked you for your opinion and why are you still in my home? Get a hotel room or something," I respond, knowing perfectly well that he isn't going to listen.

"Why don't you move her in with you or marry her at this point?"

"How can I move her in when you're always here?"

"My reaction shouldn't be a surprise. Vaughn is the one who's usually caught in his feelings for a woman, not you. This is new."

"I'm not caught by anything. Megan has been through a lot of shit since she's been in my orbit."

"True, she's been through two shootings, falling through

a glass table, and then her family tried to extort her. It's almost as if a black cloud is following the poor girl."

"Exactly, and I'm just trying to be a half-decent person by checking in and making sure she's okay."

He laughs"But that's the funny shit, Hunt. You're not a decent person. Not even a half-decent one." He laughs hysterically. "There's no other explanation for why you're sniffing behind her all the time but the pussy. It must be–"

"Talk about her pussy one more damn time, and we're going to have *actual problems*," I threaten icily.

"No disrespect intended." Christian raises his hands as a show of surrender. "I'm just pointing out the obvious."

"If we're talking about obvious concepts, there's also the fact that my sister lives down there, too."

"Right, you're down there all the time for your *sister*," he mocks.

"Where's Vaughn?" I ask, changing the subject before I wring his neck.

"He's somewhere champing at the bit. He thinks he found Jonathan's ex."

"What's the point in finding her now? We already know what Jonathan looks like and that by some miracle, he was able to get away in the alleyway the other night."

"I didn't really get it either." Christian shrugs. "But Vaughn seemed insistent on looking into it. I didn't stop him because the guy is like a bloodhound when he has a lead. That's why you got him into the information business in the first place, isn't it?"

He's not wrong.

But as good as Vaughn is, it's infuriating that we haven't been able to get a step ahead of Jonathan at any point thus far.

It was only by an earlier stroke of luck when I had

Vaughn dig into the people causing trouble for Megan that Diana's expenses drew a red flag. Credit card alerts under her name were popping up at the kinds of restaurants that she shouldn't have been able to afford on what I paid her. Aside from that, what stood out the most was that all the restaurants were places Jonathan used to frequent while he worked under me. We just put all the clues together a little too late.

"I guess he figures if we follow the trail of women, we'll find the fucker, eventually. Using women to his advantage seems to be his modus operandi. It's too bad we weren't able to get to that Diana chick in time."

After the other night, we attempted to find Diana to get some answers. We knew if we could get to her, we'd probably learn a lot. However, Jonathan was a step ahead of us, and when we reached her apartment, all we found was her dead body.

"That's why Jonathan made sure to take her with him that night because he didn't want to give her up. He knew if he did, and she lived, that she'd sing like a canary," I say, regretting how that whole night went down. He caught me with my guard completely down, and my reaction was sloppy. They could have killed Megan.

"It seems that Diana had some nursing experience," Christian says as he mindlessly leafs through a real estate magazine from my coffee table. "Doesn't that feel like a coincidence?"

"And did you notice anything odd about Jonathan's face?" I recollect.

Christian has a contemplative look on his face. "When he was in Megan's apartment, he had his cap pulled down really low. However, in the alley, most of his face was shrouded in darkness."

It had been a wild guess, calling out his name. I hadn't expected that it would be him or that he'd be reckless enough to attack me at the Blue Whiskey.

"I didn't notice any deformity as well," I muse. "But he seems to need a nurse for some reason. It's also bothering me that he's far too obsessed with getting to me through Megan."

"Well, he's going to focus on your sister soon," Christian says, his voice grim. "Have you thought about how to declare her appearance?"

I've had Christian spend the most time with Lena and wonder if she's confided anything to him that she'd rather keep from me.

"Why did she say something to you about her feelings about being related to me?

"No, nothing like that."

I open the fridge and take out the bowl of assorted melons that Megan made for me. Whenever she's over at my place, she does these small things for me without asking. They're oddly touching.

"Well, I haven't made any definite plans about how I want to share her existence with the world. She's still getting used to the whole idea of being my sister, and I don't want to put too much pressure on her." I chew a piece of ripe watermelon. "I considered sending her abroad until this whole issue with Jonathan is sorted out, but I want her somewhere where I can keep an eye on her."

"I mean, if she wants to work at the club, we have our security crawling through there every night. Outside of what happened the other night, it's the safest place for her to be."

"I would have thought the same thing a month ago, but the other night *did* happen. There's no ignoring that. Which is why I'm just not so sure the club is the safest place for her to be."

"We can add more security to the building and assign her own security detail, just like Megan has."

"I'm considering all of that," I say. "By the way, Vaughn hasn't mentioned Shelly in a while."

"You're dealing with enough." Christian's face grows heavy. "I didn't think to give you an update on their drama."

"Well, I'd like one now."

"As you suspected, she was cheating on him. The investigator that Vaughn hired got some pretty damning photos of her with another man."

"Figured as much."

"There's more."

"What else?"

"She took out a life insurance policy on Vaughn as well. Two million dollars."

"You're fucking kidding me?"

"Nope, and he hasn't said a word about it to me, although he obviously knows I know."

"An affair is one thing. A fucking plot is another."

"I already started looking into the divorce proceedings. I'll handle it for him. Gonna bleed that bitch for everything she has."

The venom in Christian's voice is not surprising. Out of the three of us, Vaughn has the mildest personality and was head over heels in love with his wife. He's the last one that should have been done dirty by a woman. He's got to be hurting.

"I expected you'd kick up some dust on her, but this is going to be a shitfest."

"That's why he's staying here with his best friend," Christian adds slyly. "And it's also why his other best friend is going to need to stay by his side as well and keep an eye on him."

"While I sympathize, this is not a YMCA or a college dorm room." I point hard at my friend as I walk into my bedroom. "Call the Four Seasons tonight, book yourself two rooms, and be gone by the time I get home from my event tonight."

"Sure thing," Christian ignores me, flipping lazily through his magazine. "I'll get right on that."

Chapter 32

She's Coming In Hot!

Hunter

A few hours later, when I arrive at Megan's apartment to pick her and Lena up, I'm taken aback by what I see when I arrive. Lena has washed out the dye in her hair, and the true ashy blonde color of her hair is as striking as her dark eyes. I can't help but stare at her when she opens the door and she blinks back at me.

"What? I wanted a change, and Naomi did my hair for me."

Naomi's head pops up from lying flat on the couch.

"I did a damn good job, didn't I?

I ignore Naomi's rhetorical question and offer Lena a tight smile. "I forgot how much you looked like Mom."

It's clear that my statement makes her uncomfortable as she shifts awkwardly between both of her feet. Naomi lays her head back down as if she's attempting to step away from our private conversation.

"I do?"

"I have a picture of her if you want to see it. She was beautiful."

As we wait for Megan to finish getting ready, I take out my wallet and remove a faded photograph that is creased by the folds. The woman in the picture is holding a toddler. Both of them share the same ashy blonde hair, but my mother has gray eyes like mine.

"That's my mother?' Lena touches the photograph reverently.

"Yes, and that's you who she's holding."

"She's so pretty."

"She was. As are you," I tell her, looking at her. "When you were about two years old, I used to have long hair, and you liked pulling on it. I would pretend that it hurt so badly, and you would laugh and laugh."

I recall a small room with a faded carpet and shabby pieces of furniture. For a moment, I can recall the scent of my mom's famous beef stew cooking on the stove and the small weight of Lena on my shoulders as I ran around the room, the laughter of the little girl echoing in my ears.

My chest feels tight to the point of suffocation.

I haven't heard Lena laugh once since she's been back in my life.

Does she even remember how to?

"I'm not sure how you made it out of the house, Lena, but I'm grateful that you're here," I tell her. "And I'm sorry for not finding you before."

Lena's eyes sparkle with tears and she just shakes her head, keeping her composure. "It's okay. You found me now."

The sound of a door opening interrupts the touching moment between my sister and me, and when I see the vision walking toward me, I almost forget how to breathe.

Megan looks stunning.

She's clad head to toe in the clothes and jewelry I purchased for her, and her hair is delicately curled in soft ringlets that frame her gorgeous face. Her makeup has been applied tastefully and makes her skin appear as if it is glowing from the inside out. The black halter dress shimmers with each movement of her hips and it's a perfect fit if I do say so myself. Her shoulders are exposed, as is a part of her back, giving her a high-end look without showing too much skin.

"Well, how do I look?" she asks the room.

"Whoa, you look rich as hell," Naomi says as she sits up. "You look like you wipe your ass with hundred-dollar bills, bitch!"

Megan checks herself out again in the full-length mirror near the front door as if she's second-guessing herself.

"What do you think, Lena?" she asks my sister.

"You kind of do," Lena agrees. "You've got the whole socialite thing going on. Those earrings look like something someone from the royal family would wear."

"Shut up, you two," I order before taking Megan in my arms. "You look like the gorgeous artist you are. The dress fits you like a glove, and the jewelry is appropriate."

"For a college student?" Naomi adds. "Or a Kardashian?"

"She's absolutely stunning," I affirm, looking straight into Megan's eyes.

"Thank you, Hunter." She beams at me with a faint blush on her cheeks. "You look amazing yourself."

She confidently picks up her clutch purse and tells Naomi, "I ordered you two large pizzas. They're coming in thirty minutes."

"Two large?" Naomi gives Megan a puzzled look. "What am I going to do with two large pizzas?"

"Christian and Vaughn might drop by to watch Netflix."

"Wait." Now Naomi stands up. "You're telling me that those two adult men with full-time jobs are coming over to use our Netflix account?"

"Why are they visiting your apartment?" I scowl at Megan. "I didn't tell them to drop by here. Are they bothering you often?"

"They're not bothering me," Megan paints a coat of iridescent pink gloss on her lips. "They come over every now and then, and I didn't want Naomi to be alone. Plus, Christian is kind of cute. They might–"

"Hey," I narrow my eyes at her. "Those two are not for admiring."

"I'm not," Megan chuckles. "I'm trying to help Naomi find a man."

As if anything would happen between those two.

"Christian is cute," Lena agrees.

"Stop looking at my grown-ass friends," I growl at her. "You're too young to be dating!"

Lena just rolls her eyes at me. "No, I'm not."

"Let's go, Hunter." Megan pulls at my arm, and I frown.

"We need to talk about this," I counter.

"Not tonight."

"I'm not messing up my Netflix algorithm for any man," Naomi complains. "I have a whole movie night planned, and I'm not even wearing makeup! If they come by, I'm not answering the door."

Good, at least Naomi and I are on the same page for once.

When we arrive at the gallery, it's apparent that the

event planners have really rolled out the red carpet for the exhibition, making sure the students selected from every university art program in the city feel special. There are photographers waiting by the door, taking shots of all the guests arriving in their semi-formal attire.

As a patron of the arts in Los Angeles, I recognize quite a few faces as we go inside. Many of the art pieces on display are beautiful, but I'm drawn to the corner dedicated to Megan. Her work is a bit more simplistic than some of the other paintings but I feel a hint of pride at how thought-provoking her work is. Each piece is different and has a deep meaning.

I watch from a distance as Lena takes a lap around the gallery, looking at all the various displays, and as Megan talks to an older woman who is admiring her work and asking questions.

"So, that's your girlfriend," comes a voice from behind me, and my expression grows stiff.

"DiAngelo."

Dante DiAngelo is a popular philanthropist. He's also the head of the DiAngelo family. At the age of thirty-two, he seized the position from his brother. Nicknamed 'The Hellfire' in underground circles, he's got a reputation for being both power-hungry and having a taste for blood.

The fact that we're allies is beneficial for the two of us, but there's something about him seeing me around Megan that makes me feel uneasy. I can't let him see that, though.

"How did you enjoy my gift?" I murmur, sipping the champagne and watching him closely.

He smiles at me, the cruelty in his eyes shining through. "I always enjoy gifts from you, Middleton. However, you must've really been upset with them if sending them to me was your choice of punishment."

"Well, I do keep you in my thoughts every now and then." I shrug.

"Who are they?" he asks with an unsettling curiosity.

"They're nobody," I tell him.

A woman silently presents a tray of hors d'oeuvres in front of us. I pass but Dante takes some sort of lobster quiche puff and pops it in his mouth.

"They arranged all this in my honor," he explains vainly. "It would be rude not to try everything there is to offer." He admires the painting in front of us as he chews. "I heard you got stood up by two of our friends. It's a pity."

I don't miss the warning in his words. The fact that the two gang leaders whom I summoned refused to show up is circulating in the underground world quite rapidly. A refusal is not good for my reputation. It shows weakness.

"Well, you can't train every old dog new tricks." I smile lazily. "Sometimes you just have to get a new one."

He raises an eyebrow. "I'm hearing rumors about some-body trying to usurp you. Trouble at the Blue Whiskey. Trouble at your home. It's an entertaining thought that someone's trying this hard."

He glances at me, a smile on his lips. "I can't wait to see how you deal with this."

"Many have tried." I swirl the golden liquid in my stemmed glass. "If I remember correctly, your brother had a similar idea."

"Good thing he did." Dante grins. "Or I wouldn't be standing here as the head of the family."

I nod in agreement.

"So?" Dante looks over his shoulder, and they follow his gaze. "Which one is your girlfriend? Is it the fair-haired beauty?"

"That's my sister," I tell him, cold. "And she's not even legal, so don't even think of sniffing around her."

"So the rumors are true," Dante studies Lena with a little too much interest. "So then the woman next to her must be the one you're involved with. She looks young, too. I never really took you to be the dating type."

Megan and my sister walk over to us and I curl my arm possessively around Megan's waist as I reluctantly introduce them to Dante.

"Megan, Lena, this is Mr. Dante DiAngelo. He owns the DiAngelo Group and is a well-known art investor."

"It's such a pleasure to meet you, Mr. DiAngelo," Megan offers a little too eagerly. "I've heard a lot about you."

Dante beams at them both. "Miss Taylor, I saw your name under one of the sketches that caught my eye. I really enjoy your work. You're very skilled, and you have a lot of potential."

Megan smiles brightly at him and it makes the vein in my neck throb.

"Thank you."

"I was actually thinking of buying a few pieces, but I only managed to get one. Yours were the first to be sold out."

Megan's mouth is agape. "Wait, what? Somebody bought my work?"

I give Dante a dark look. "So you were the one who bought that sketch of me?"

"I was going to hang it in my office for motivation." He grins devilishly.

Lena chuckles but immediately straightens her face when I give her a stern look.

"I'll buy it off you," I tell him.

"It's priceless to me, Hunter," Dante says, false sincerity dripping from his tone.

"I'll sketch you a new one," Megan puts her hand on my chest, and I like the proprietary feel of the gesture. And then, she adds, "But I wonder who bought the rest of them?"

"That's an interesting question, isn't it?" He offers me a knowing grin and I want to smack it completely off of his face. He's playing games.

"I'm sure –"

Megan doesn't even allow me to finish my sentence, her eyes widening, "Please say it wasn't you, Hunter."

I have no reason to feel guilty, but I still avoid Megan's eyes because I know what she's thinking. The student who sells the most art tonight qualifies for the New York showing, and I've just fast-tracked her to the finalist spot.

"I liked them, and if I like something, there's no reason I shouldn't have it."

A defiant fire lights up in Megan's eyes. "If you liked them so much, you could've just picked something out from me personally. There's a reason why I didn't want you to pay for my work."

I hate that Dante is still here, watching this conversation unfold between us. Every interaction I have with Megan is a chance for him to learn more about me and my weaknesses. I'm fucking up.

I'm about to put an end to the conversation when a familiar someone interrupts and beats me to the punch. I just wish it had been someone else.

"Mr. Middleton!" I always wonder how Dean Darwin looks so terrified and yet reverent when he sees me. "How are you? I didn't expect to see you here tonight. Can I get you anything?"

"I'm fine, thank you."

"Just let me know. This is a fine showing, Miss Taylor. You should be proud."

"Thank you, Dean."

Megan's lips flatten into a straight line as Darwin walks away to kiss some more ass. She had no idea that I have a familiar relationship with the Dean of her school and I'm sure a lot of wild thoughts are racing through her head.

She leans into me, smelling of a tempting floral scent, and I bend my head down to hear what she clearly wants to say.

"I'm not happy, Hunter. We'll chat about this later," she whispers in my ear. It's meant to be a warning, but all it does is make my dick hard as a rock.

"It's nice to meet you, Mr. DiAngelo." Megan then takes Lena's arm. "Let's go around the room and look at some of the other pieces, Lena. Please excuse us."

Megan is pissed at me, and the gallery is quite safe, so I let the two of them roam around and enjoy the rest of the night.

Darwin finds me again and talks my ear off about some new construction project the school is interested in getting funding for. DiAngelo has no patience for small talk with unimportant people, so he escapes early on. By the time I manage to shake the Dean off, I look around and can't find Megan or Lena anywhere.

My phone rings, and I step outside to answer it.

It's Vaughn.

"I'm out with the girls," I tell him without even a hello.

"I know, but this is important."

He sounds tense.

"What is it?"

"I found the nurse, Rose. Jonathan ended up with a

severe infection after the plastic surgery. Even after additional surgeries, his condition has become worse. That's why he kept Rose around and, later, Diana. I found out something else. Jonathan is not the executioner. He was, in fact, in contact with the man called the Executioner. Jonathan gave him money. He isn't working alone."

"So this is bigger than just Jonathan."

"Everything is all connected. I think he's either working with or for the same person who's involved in the power struggle we're dealing with in the city right now. This executioner person is the key to everything."

"Shit—is there anything else?" I ask as I digest everything Vaughn has just shared with me.

"Oh, and the picture that Steve talked about was an old one of Lena's. It was sent to Jonathan eight years ago. He's been looking for Lena almost as long as you have."

My blood runs cold.

Chapter 33

I Can Only Blame Myself

Hunter

So this was all planned by some phantom executioner? I scan the room, wondering if the fucker is in here...watching me.

"Are we any closer to a name?" I ask Vaughn. "No," Vaughn says. "But stay put. Christian and I are on our way. The exhibition is too public. If they're paying attention to your movements, they'll know that Lena is there. We're bringing back up."

Shit...the girls.

"Text me when you're outside."

Cutting the call short, I stride back inside the exhibition while dialing Megan's number, but no one answers it. I try Lena's cell but get no response either.

Walking quickly, I circle the gallery, and my worst fears are confirmed when I realize that I can't find either woman.

"Mr. Middleton–"

I ignore someone trying to gain my attention as I make my way to the ladies' restroom and barge inside. It's empty, aside from one annoyed woman applying more lipstick, and that also means that both my girls are not here.

Fuck.

My heart is pounding with sickening fear as I cross over into the restricted area and take a look around. The gallery is quite large, aside from the exhibition area, because it serves as a full-fledged art gallery.

As I walk across the marble floor, I see a glint of something. Making my way over to it, I recognize the diamond earring Megan was wearing. Looking around, I see the pair dangling from an artificial potted tree. The large plant is next to a door that leads into what looks like a basement area.

I pull my gun from the back of my waistband, send a message to Vaughn before putting my phone on silent, and then proceed to find out what the fuck has happened to my girls.

Gun steady in my hands, I open the door, grateful that it doesn't creak, and start descending the steps.

Basements of art galleries are usually quite massive and they serve as a storage unit for pieces that are often rotated or have newly arrived. I see the large containers and shelves and slowly walk past them.

I notice a faraway portion of the basement is illuminated, and I make my way there.

It's difficult to keep my emotions in check right now, with fear for both Megan and my sister at the forefront.

I can only blame myself for this sickening feeling I have in my chest. A few months ago, I would have never made a mistake like this. This is what it means to have a weakness. Being connected to me has put them both in danger. And what's worse is that it's happening right under my nose.

I make sure that I'm walking in the shadows of the

pallet next to me, which is why I'm not seen immediately. Containers have been pushed back against the wall to make a large space in the center, and the lamps have all been turned on.

My heart crawls up and inside my throat when I see Megan and Lena standing still, their arms at their sides. It looks like it's just the two of them, but of course, I know better.

My eyes dart toward the shadows, and I can make out the forms of armed men standing there. It looks like a prepared stage just waiting for its last actors.

Then, out of nowhere, I hear the sounds of arrogant clapping, and Jonathan's voice reaches my ears.

"I know you're here, Hunter. It took you long enough. You might as well come out. I just want to talk for now."

If I walk in there, it's possibly a death sentence for me, but Jonathan is unpredictable enough to harm Megan or Lena if I don't comply.

I feel my phone vibrate in my pocket, and I take it out. The message I receive makes me smile grimly.

Gun in hand. I tuck my phone back and walk into the spotlight.

Megan sees me and doesn't react, her face erased of emotions. It's almost as if she's now desensitized to the violence around me. Lena, however, is new to my chaos and is struggling to compose herself. I can see the tear tracks on her face. Thankfully, they both seem to be unharmed.

"Hunter!"

"It's going to be fine," I tell them, my eyes flickering towards Megan, who watches me steadily. I can see that something is going on in her brain. She either wants to tell me something, or there's some sort of plan percolating in that head of hers. Either way, I need her to fall back.

I've got this.

"Well, aren't you going to come out and greet me?" I raise a brow, speaking out loud. "It's been a long time."

The sound of footsteps from behind Megan makes me look up. In the dim light, I can see Jonathan's face. There doesn't seem to be much wrong with it, but then I notice the red patch on his forehead. It's an odd color of red and it has traces of a greenish and yellowish hue to it.

"How've you been?" I ask casually. "And where the fuck is my money?"

"Where it belongs," he sneers at me. "You seem awfully calm for someone who couldn't keep tabs on the two most important women in his life. Shouldn't you be groveling?"

"You know better than anyone, Jonathan," I smirk. "I don't grovel. It's unsightly."

Jonathan's eyes flicker and I can see his wariness at my calm reaction, so he attempts to goad me. "You know, I was so disappointed when I discovered that Lena doesn't recognize me. I mean, overlooking the current situation, I used to babysit her. Remember how she used to follow me around all the time like a little baby duck?"

Lena turns her head towards me, but I'm careful not to show a reaction. "Well, times change, don't they? Children grow up."

Jonathan scratches his chin with the muzzle of his gun, a mocking expression on his face.

"I always wondered whether I should have apologized for framing you all those years ago, and then I thought that maybe it made more sense to apologize for leading those gang members to your home. I mean, I was quite attached to your mother and sister, but I did enjoy hearing what those men did to them."

My smile stiffens at his sudden confession, and the last

missing pieces of the puzzle come together. I've always wondered how they found my family so easily when I'd made sure to be so careful. I was young, but I wasn't stupid. Two of the men in my circle swore that they hadn't done anything to my sister. I still killed them viciously, but both of their versions of events had lined up, leading me to believe that Lena's remains were unable to be found in the fire wreckage or, later on, that someone had rescued her and was too afraid to contact me.

I never, not even once, suspected Jonathan.

My loyalty to people I trust has always been my Achilles heel.

My weakness.

Now, I'm seeing the overarching results of that mistake.

"So, you were never truly loyal to me, were you?" I say with reserve, as my blood boils with anger.

"Did you really think I would sit idly by while you stepped higher up in the organization? Did you think I'd be satisfied being your second in command? A Scottie Pippen to your Michael Jordan? Hell no."

"Where you fell in the organization was up to you. We were both young, both building up our reps."

"It was satisfying to see you break when you realized that your only family died painful deaths," he says, his gun moving with each syllable that he utters. "But then you weren't broken for long, were you? You always were resilient. You just tore through anything standing in your way, and it was later that it occurred to me that it was because you were careful to eliminate any weaknesses before they could be found. But you fucked up, Hunter. You fell in love with a girl? Really?"

"Who told you she's my weakness?" I let out a low laugh. "Do you really think I am who I am in this city by accident? You don't think all these years didn't teach me how to protect my actual weaknesses?"

"Your sister, little Lena, is right there." Jonathan points out. "Unprotected."

"That was a variable I couldn't have predicted," I say coldly.

"Men, why don't we start our game?" Jonathan says.

That's when I see two more familiar faces reveal themselves. They are the gang leaders who didn't show up at the meeting the other day.

I can't say that I'm very surprised.

I just study them, unfazed, wondering if they realize that this is going to be their last day on the earth because I'm going to kill both of them...slowly.

"I'm going to make this easy for you," Jonathan says with glee. As soon as he says that, both men take a position behind Megan and Lena, their Berettas pointed at their heads. My hands immediately tighten around my gun, but I don't show any sign of stress on my face.

Lena looks terrified, and then I see Megan looking at her and frowning as if trying to communicate something to her. Lena's hands clench the fabric of her dress, and she presses her lips together to hold her cries back even as her eyes fill up with tears.

"I will allow you to keep one girl alive," Jonathan continues. "You just have to choose. After all, I did take your family away from you once. I can't be that cruel and take away both your lover and your sister. Just doesn't seem fair."

My reinforcements haven't arrived yet, and my jaw tightens. I need to stall. I need to think of something to buy myself some more time.

Fuck!

Megan meets my eyes, and I see her move her hand slightly. It's enough for me to notice what she's holding in it. My eyes move towards Lena, who is standing stiffly, trying to hold in her fear. But when my eyes settle on her, I see a shadow move behind her, behind the pallets, and the flash of a gun. The person hiding moves just enough for me to be able to identify them.

"And what happens to the one who survives?" I ask, choosing my words carefully. "Does she get to walk out with me?"

"Always the negotiator." Jonathan smiles. "We'll figure that part out later. For now, you choose. Is it the sister you barely know any longer or the college kid you're fucking?"

My phone vibrates again, and I give Jonathan a relaxed smile.

"Then, the choice is obvious, of course," I say.

Megan meets my gaze, giving me a terse nod. Her face is pale, and my hands tighten on my gun.

"Well?" Jonathan prods.

"I have to save my sister."

Chapter 34

The Showdown

Hunter

Everything happens at once, almost as if in slow motion. The creep standing behind Lena crumples to the ground from a shot to the head just as Megan whirls silently around, slashing the steak knife in her hand at the man who was behind her.

I knew I had fallen for a bad ass, but I didn't know she had this kind of presence of mind. Her attack was a thing of beauty and I'm so proud of her for thinking on her feet. Of course, I take advantage of the chaos and shoot the man in the chest, stomach, and hand so she won't have to wield that knife ever again. It's not Megan's job to protect herself. It's mine.

Various footsteps come rushing forward, and Jonathan has his Glock pointed towards me. He stands tall and firm as if he's so proud of himself, and I wonder to myself how could I have missed that he hated me as much as he does. Do I not have a good sense of how people think? Have I been fooling myself this entire time? Maybe I'm not half as bright as I think I am.

"You're a dead man," he smirks.

"You did all of this to kill me in a basement?" I ask snidely. "How original."

"It doesn't matter where or how you die, just that you're gone."

Lena and Megan are huddled together over on the side. Megan has her arm wrapped around Lena, giving her comfort, but I know I've got to get them out of here. I don't know how many more people Jonathan has brought with him or the extent of his plan.

Suddenly, Dante walks out of the shadows with his gun now aimed at Jonathan's temple. But it's not until Vaughn enters the room that I begin to exhale. My team is finally here. If Dante and Vaughn are here, that means there are at least seven more men close by, including Christian.

"Put the gun down," I tell Jonathan. "This is over."

"Fuck that!" He protests, but I can tell that his resolve is slowly crumbling. A gun pointed at your head can do that to a man.

"With just one word, I can have your brains blown out all over this room but out of respect for our history," *and the fact that I want to kill his ass slowly in the basement of the Blue Whiskey,* "I'm going to give you a death worthy of someone who came up in the organization just like I did. Put your gun down."

While his arm is a little shaky while still aimed at my heart, I know he won't relent. This is the end of the road for him, and as I suspected, he won't go down without a fight. This is what he ultimately wanted: a showdown between us two.

"Keep those two alive," I redirect Dante, referring to the

two overly ambitious gang leaders. They've got a fresh dose of hell waiting for them when this is all over.

"And Vaughn–" I motion toward the girls. "Get them out of here."

I'm ordering the guns off of Jonathan because a part of me knows that he isn't going to pull the trigger. He's expended all this energy trying to bring me to my knees, so I figure that he's not going to let it end anticlimactic. I just want Megan and Lena left out of this. I need them safe.

"You made a mistake keeping them close to you, Hunter."

I hate how Jonathan's words echo the same ones running through my mind right this very second. I allowed my cock to do all the thinking for me when it came to Megan, and I let some sort of misguided nostalgia lead me to find my sister. I'm not new to this. I know that having people in your life you care about, especially women, is a weakness– not a strength.

"They have nothing to do–"

Before I can finish my sentence, Jonathan swings a stiff arm around, points his gun toward Megan, and shoots. It's the loudest shot I've ever heard in my life as his icy words follow it. "You said you wanted to save your sister, so now you've got your wish."

A foreign noise escapes me as I watch Megan's eyes widen in shock as the bullet pierces her abdomen. A cold feeling surrounds my heart and it feels like everything has gone still. I run to her, my body lowered to the ground beside her, and watch in horror as blood stains the cemented floor.

"Hunter," she whispers in a haunting tone as tears flood her eyes.

"I've got you, baby," I reassure her, desperately making a bargain with God in my head.

Please save her. I'll do anything.

I hear another shot, and because I don't know whose gun it's coming from, I cover her with my entire body. Suddenly, Christian barges into the room, emptying his gun into someone or a few someones. I don't know because all I care about is keeping Megan safe from further harm.

I cover Megan's ears with my hands and continue to mouth the words, "*I've got you.*"

I'm not sure when or where he came from, but Lars is suddenly beside me, pressing down on the wound.

"We need to get her to a hospital!"

His tone is urgent, and I know I'm reacting and moving, but everything inside me has gone numb. I think Vaughn has a sobbing Lena and Dante is also behind us as we rush up the steps. I don't know why I can't go faster than this. It feels like my thighs are made of concrete.

"The Downtown Medical Center!" Lars shouts at Parker as I ball up Megan's shawl and press it against her wound. She keeps looking at me, eyes blinking rapidly, not a sound escaping her.

I know what she's thinking. She's coming to terms with her injury. As if she always expected to go out violently. I don't know why that full acceptance in her eyes makes me so enraged.

My voice is low as I hiss at her, "If you even think of dying, I'll set this whole fucking world on fire! Keep your eyes open. Keep fighting. I've got you, and I'm never letting you go!"

But her eyes are growing cloudier, and it feels like somebody has grabbed me by the neck, making it difficult to even draw out a single breath.

My hands are covered in her blood, and it feels as if someone is driving nails into my heart. Her lips are moving, and she's trying to say something, maybe to curse me out for yelling at her, so I lean forward, desperate to hear anything she has to say.

"Thank you," she whispers.

My heart nearly stops.

"I – I - love you," she stutters.

Just as she finishes saying those three beautiful words, she spurts out some blood, and I order her fiercely and say, "Tell me that again after you've been patched up, baby."

She gives me a drained smile in response, then her eyes roll to the back of her head, and sheer panic settles into my soul.

"Megan!" I shout her name. "Please, don't go."

Chapter 35

You're Not Allowed To Leave

Hunter

Parker has barely pressed on the brakes in front of the Los Angeles Downtown Medical Center when I rush out of the car, holding Megan's limp form in my arms. I feel like a desperate character straight out of a medical drama, barging through the emergency room doors, bypassing the metal detector, and straight to the nurses' station.

"I need help!" I plead.

"Okay, sir, but–"

I have a visceral reaction to the word, but I immediately look around for another nurse who will help us. I notice a female doctor in an open patient area, and recognition hits me.

"Dr. Yasmin!"

She was in the middle of taking off her coat when she sees me and the limp woman in my arms. Her eyes turn grim as she gestures to the nurses, who quickly transfer Megan onto a gurney.

"What happened?" She asks firmly.

"She got shot in the abdomen. There's no exit wound. I've tried to stop the bleeding, but there's so much." My voice trails away.

The doctor touches my arm. "We'll take it from here. Let's prep an OR now," she commands the staff. "Mr. Middleton, I need you to stay here in the waiting room. I'll have someone come get you when I have more information."

Normally, I'd ignore orders like this. They're for the average person. I'm not average. I'm Hunter fucking Middleton, and I probably gave thousands of dollars to this hospital.

It physically hurts my soul as they take Megan out of my arms and place her on the gurney through the dreaded double hospital doors to a surgical room. I want to follow her, but there's another small body that throws herself at me, and I look down to see Lena sobbing against my chest.

"Is she dying, Hunter?"

My arms wrap around her lithe frame, dazed, as I watch the light turn red in the surgery room. I feel hollow as I wait, unable to process anything, barely able to breathe.

"They're going to fix her," I tell my sister because it's the only reality I will permit myself to believe.

All I can see over and over in my head is Megan's shocked look and then the way she collapsed.

Thank you.

I love you.

You can't just say statements like that to me as if you're dying, as if you're okay with dying, I think to myself as I leave Lena sitting in a chair to grab a cup of disgusting vending machine coffee.

You're going to stay alive! You're going to say it to my

face! You have to wake up, or I'll destroy everything you love! You're not allowed to leave me!

What will I do if you leave me?

"Boss?"

I look up to see Lars standing there, a weary expression on his face. "Christian and Vaughn took Lena back to the apartment. Parker's gone with them and he's arranging a full security detail around the apartment. I'm staying here with you."

I nod, feeling drained. "How long has it been?"

He knows what I'm referring to. I have no idea how long we've been here. I don't even know how long I've been standing at this damn vending machine.

"An hour."

I sigh and then slump into a waiting chair. "She'll be fine."

"Of course, she will," Lars says, his voice tight. "You fell in love with a fighter."

"Love, huh?" I look down at the murky-looking liquid in the cup. "Am I in love with Megan? Is *this* love?"

Lars looks at me with an expression I don't think I've ever seen from him before...compassion.

"You don't react the way you did if you're not in love with a woman, but I don't know what that means for you."

"What do you mean by that?" I glance over at him and repeat his words. "What it means for me."

He studies me. "You've always tried to get rid of anything you consider a weakness. Megan is your weakness. Your sister is definitely one as well, but dare I say that Megan is even a bigger one."

"I'm not going to get rid of her," I snarl at him, my face twisting. "She's in the fucking operating room. You want me to—"

"That's not what I'm saying," Lars frowns, his Danish accent growing thicker as it occasionally does. "I'm not telling you to get rid of her. Just the opposite. She's good for you. She's made you more human."

"I was always human, Lars."

"You know what I mean. You look happier and have more of a balance in your life. I think that's a good thing. It's healthy. All this power and money, what does it matter if you have no one to share it with?"

"I may love her, and she may be good for me, but what the fuck have I done for *her*, Lars. The kind of life I lead puts anyone I care about in danger," I reply, Megan's shocked face after being shot flashing in front of my eyes. "When she wakes up from this, she should run as far from me as she can," I say, knowing that the very thought might just put me into the grave.

"When you have someone to protect, it's not a weakness; it's a strength. It makes you fight harder. I've always disagreed with you on your policy about women and kids," Lars says slowly. "Imagine your life if you'd never met her. Imagine what it could be like if she stays in it."

I look towards the doors with the red light still blinking above them, and all I can think about is what her life would look like if we'd never met. She would still be a server at the Blue Whiskey, making great tips and going out on the weekends with that pain-in-the-ass roommate of hers.

"On one of the most important nights of her life, Megan nearly died tonight because of the choices I've made."

"She also could've died in her childhood home with those wretched people she lived with," Lars interrupts me. "She also could have died walking to work one night or choking on one of those damn wings at the club. Death is inevitable for all of us. However, it shouldn't stop us from living our lives."

I jut my legs out in front of me, lean back, and close my eyes. I don't want to hear any of this sage wisdom any longer. I want fucking silence.

"The only reason I'm saying all of this to you right now is because I don't want you to push her away when she recovers."

Lars is usually never this talkative, and I look away guiltily at his words as he continues his rant, "That girl has not had anyone really give a shit about her in her life. If you push her away to protect her, it'll break her heart. When she wanted to leave, you wouldn't let her, so when she wants to stay, don't you dare force her out. You've given her a life, people she cares about. If you force her out, you're leaving her with nothing again. You'd be no better than her parents."

"Careful, Lars," I say icily. "Remember your place. Even I have my limits."

"Fine, just think real carefully about I said while she's in there fighting for her life. I saw the look on your face when she was shot and when we drove her here. You love her even if you don't want to admit it."

"I have admitted it! She knows how I feel."

"Saying the words casually or in a moment of passion is quite different than backing the words up with action." After those final words, Lars gets up and walks away to probably cool off. I realize that while he cares about me, he also has grown to care for Megan and doesn't want to see either of us hurt or hurt each other. He made his point though tonight and his words linger in my ears.

I take another sip of the lukewarm brown liquid in my cup as a new realization hits me as fiercely as a thunderbolt.

Regardless of what those doctors tell me when they walk through those double doors tonight, I already know what I have to do.

Chapter 36

What Have You Done To Me?!

Megan

When I pry my eyes open, it's to the view of a plain white ceiling. My entire body feels uncharacteristically heavy as I stare up, dazed. There's a dull throb in my lower abdomen, and my head feels like it's stuffed with cotton. My mouth is parched, and when I try to move, a pain-filled moan escapes my lips.

"Megan?" Hunter's ragged-looking face pops into my line of sight, "How're you feeling, baby?"

"Feeling?" I echo. "I'm thirsty, but my stomach hurts."

"Wait." He picks up a white styrofoam cup of ice water from the side table. He inserts a fresh straw through the plastic lid and raises it to my lips. "Take small sips. Careful."

The cold liquid goes a long way in clearing my head as I look at Hunter tiredly. I feel about as bad as he looks.

"So, I guess I survived?"

"From a gunshot to the gut? Yes," he says with an odd

look as he presses a button to page a nurse. "You're going to be more than fine. In fact, there's something you should know."

Before he can say anything else, a woman walks in dressed in a white lab coat. I recognize her.

"Dr. Yasmin?"

"Well, you sure are one lucky girl," she says, beaming at me. How're you feeling?"

It doesn't escape me how Hunter's body shifts uncomfortably whenever anyone refers to me as a "girl". I haven't thought about it lately, but I think our age difference makes him much more uneasy than he'll ever admit out loud.

"It hurts to move, but it's not as bad as it could be," I confess, feeling more like myself as my body awakens.

"Well, you and the baby are fine. It's-"

"I'm sorry," I sputter, choking on my own salvia. "Me and *the what* is fine?"

"The baby." Dr. Yasmin looks at Hunter who now looks annoyed. "You didn't tell her?"

"I was just about to when you walked in."

"Wait, I don't understand." I look between the two of them, my mind barely processing the words. "I'm pregnant?"

"Yes." Dr. Yasmin smiles at me. "Congratulations. You and the baby are fine."

"There must be some mistake. I can't get pregnant. There was an accident, and I...well, my stepmother told me I couldn't have kids. She said–"

"Well, you're perfectly healthy." Dr. Yasmin frowns. "I don't know why your stepmother told you that, but she was wrong. You're actually six weeks along."

"Six weeks?"

Immediately I try recalling what I've been eating, drinking, and doing over the last six weeks. Not once did I feel sick or anything, but now that I think about it, my period was late.

"There's been so much going on," I mutter, feeling blank. "*Are you sure?*"

"Completely sure. Fortunately, your injury didn't cause you to lose the baby. And while I recommend you set up an appointment for prenatal care as soon as you're released, I highly suggest you take it real easy this first trimester. Your body experienced severe trauma two days ago. It needs time to repair and heal itself."

"Wait, I've been asleep for two days?"

"You lost quite a bit of blood, Miss Taylor. You and the baby needed your rest."

Dr. Yasmin conducts a routine checkup on me while I lay there, still processing the news. It's only when she leaves the room that it all hits me like a ton of bricks.

"You got me pregnant?" It hurts to move, but I'm at least able to tilt to the side, grab the water cup, and throw it at him. "You idiot!"

I can't think of any better insults right now, plus my hands are shaking in anger and fear.

"It's good to see that you're feeling better," he says casually as he picks up the cup and places it back on the side table. "We're going to need someone to come to mop up this water."

"Why are you so calm?" I ask frantically. "I'm having a baby!"

"I know." He smiles at me.

I stare at him, comprehension dawning on me, as I say slowly, "You're happy about this?"

He steps closer to the bed. "Until I met you, I never wanted anyone in my life. And until learning about our baby, I didn't realize I wanted a child. But I realize that with the right person, a lot of things you think you want or don't want can change in an instant."

"Oh," I mumble, my heart feeling unsteady.

"How do you feel about it?"

"Scared," I say softly. "I'm young, and I don't have any experience with what good parenting looks like. What the hell do I know about being a mom?"

"You will be great. Look at it this way: at least you know what not to do."

"What does this mean for us?" I ask tentatively.

I see a sly look form in Hunter's eyes. "Well, I guess it means that you're stuck with me."

"You want to raise it together?" I ask, still surprised by his reaction.

"Isn't that what couples do?"

"I guess but–"

Hunter takes my hand. "You said something to me when I was bringing you to the hospital. I told you to keep fighting and say it to my face once you recover. So, I want you to tell me again."

I stare at him, and when I remember the moment when I wasn't sure if I was going to survive and I just wanted him to know my true feelings, my face gets hot.

"Technically, I'm not actually *recovered* yet."

"I want to know, Megan." His voice is serious. "I waited two excruciatingly long days for you to wake up and tell me."

I don't know why I'm so scared. He just told me that he wants to raise this baby with me. All he's ever done since we met is show me how much he cares about me. Why is it so hard for me to say the words?

"I wanted to say thank you," I begin hesitantly,

watching him. "For everything you'd done for me until now. And that I love you. I am in love with you."

I retreat into myself, irrationally fearing the response. The two of us have shared tender moments before, but this feels significantly different. I was shot. And now there's a baby. This is serious now.

"When they took you inside for surgery, at first, I was overwhelmed with guilt."

"This wasn't your fault."

Hunter strokes my hair, bending down even closer to me.

"But then all I could think about was how was I supposed to go on without you? I was driving myself crazy with worry. They had you on the operating table for more than three hours because the surgery got complicated once they discovered you were pregnant."

"Oh, my God."

"I was trying to convince myself that once you recovered, I would let you go so that you could live a life that is safer than what you'll find by my side. But then, they told me you were pregnant, and I was ecstatic. I had a reason to keep you next to me."

"A reason?" I stare at him. "No offense, Hunter, but that sounds a little messed up."

He sighs and then takes my hand in his. "It was easier than confessing to you how I really feel."

My heart begins to beat wildly. "Which is?"

"That I've been falling in love with you since the day you spilled my drink on me and then dared me to shoot you. You are the most unruly, unpredictable woman that I have ever met, and you just went and made me fall in love with you. And then, when I was finally determined to push you away for your own safety, you decided to go and get pregnant."

"First of all," I sniffle, my heart overflowing with emotion. "That was beautiful, right up to the point where you half suggested that I planned this pregnancy to trap you. You just wait until I'm on my feet. I will kick your ass. If you think I actually planned to get pregnant with your devil spawn, you're crazier than I thought you were."

Hunter laughs, swallowing the rest of my protest in a kiss before saying, "I feel like I'm the one who's trapped you."

"And you're happy about this?" I ask when I calm down.

"I am." He kisses my hand. "You're giving me all the things I never thought I needed. I love you, Megan, and I'll love this child of ours just as fiercely."

My lips curve at his words and then immediately fade when he adds, "Which is why I'm adding a five-person security detail to you wherever you go."

He grins at me when I scowl.

"Not going to happen."

Chapter 37

That Was A Seduction, Not A Date

Megan

"You just can't help yourself, can you?"

I press the button on the bed controller so I can sit up and take another sip of water.

"You knew who I was when you agreed to date me." Hunter grabs the cup before I can and holds the straw to my lips. "I'll hire the entire damn police force of Los Angeles to keep an eye on you if that means nothing like this will ever happen again."

"Why do I believe you would do just that," I reply dryly. "And I can hold my own cup."

"You just cringed in pain. I'll hold the cup. Drink."

I take a longer sip and slightly choke.

"Little sips."

"I'm thirsty," I complain in a whiny voice.

"Megan, you might not believe this, but my life isn't usually this...eventful."

"Is that right?" I curve my lips slightly, wondering if he actually believes what he's saying.

"I don't feel bad about many things, but I will forever feel guilty for all that I've put you through since we've met."

"Hunter–"

"I just need you to know that we've finally neutralized the threat."

Why is he talking like he's in the Secret Service?

The threat?

"You mean the man who kidnapped me, shot me, and almost killed our baby?"

"Megan."

"If this is going to work, you're going to have to stop talking to me in abstracts and give me the real. I may be young, but let's not forget that you're fucking me, and if that's going to continue, I'm going to need you to be more transparent."

"Looks like your pain medication is finally wearing off," he says with a tight look in his eyes. "Should I call the nurse?"

"You don't scare me, Hunter Middleton. Look at me. The worst has already happened. What could you possibly do?"

"Fine," he sighs, shaking his head. "Johnathan's gone. Gone like in *dead* since you want me to be perfectly transparent."

"Were you the one who did it?" I ask softly, worried that the answer is probably a yes.

"Transparency is a new concept for me, Megan. Let's take baby steps," he warns. "Suffice it to say that the drama is over, and now we both can finally exhale and focus on the future."

"Water, please," I request coyly, and then I take another sip.

He stops the flow of the water by pinching the straw with two of his fingers. "Sip, or you don't get any more."

I roll my eyes in exasperation.

"Fine."

I don't know that I've ever been this thirsty in my entire life.

"What about college?" I ask, thinking about the human being growing inside of me and all that will mean for my future.

"You'll finish it," he says seriously. "Obviously, you might miss a semester or two because you're going to need to be careful after the injury you have. But I'm not going to allow our child, you getting shot, or anything else become an obstacle for your studies or whatever else you want to do."

A sly smile suddenly forms across his face. "Now, I have a reason to kick those two freeloaders out of my house."

"Are you talking about your two best friends?"

"You realize that they both have houses of their own, right? Nice ones."

"I'm sure they have their reasons for sticking close to you."

"We can easily convert one of my extra bedrooms into a nursery and the other into an art studio for you. That only leaves one extra bedroom besides the main one, and that will be my new home office because–"

"Wait," I interrupt. "I'm moving in with you?"

He pauses and studies me, a strange look on his face, "Megan, we're having a baby together, and we love each other. Do you really think I'm letting you walk away from me? I'm going to tie you to me in every conceivable way. Not only are you moving in, but we're going to get married."

I stare at him like he's lost his mind. "The hell we are. You haven't even taken me out on a proper date yet."

"What the hell was Paris?"

"That was a damn seduction, not a date."

"The best seduction of your life," he scoffs.

"That's highly debatable," I snicker, but I groan because it hurts to laugh.

"You need more pain meds."

"And a date."

He gives me a sullen look, and I blink.

"I don't want to jump into marriage because you think it's the best way to tie me to you, and I don't want to get married simply because of the baby. There are plenty of happy single moms on this planet. I wouldn't be the first."

"Are you threatening me, gorgeous?" he bends to kiss my forehead. "There's no way I would ever allow you to be a single mom."

"You're funny." I take his hand, squeezing it. "But you, of all people, know about my past. I've never really dated somebody properly, and I want that for myself. I want it all...with you, but let's put marriage further down the road, okay?"

My chest tightens because Hunter looks almost crest-fallen. I don't want to hurt him, but I also feel like I just cheated death. I'm giving myself permission to ask for what I want.

"Fine," he says in a grumpy voice. "But moving in together is non-negotiable."

"We already live in the same building, so yes, we can do that," I say, but then I freeze. "Wait, this is what you intended all along, isn't it? You just wanted me to agree with you on the whole moving-in thing, so you made me believe-"

Hunter smirks at me as he rubs his thumb across my knuckles. "You're overthinking, sweetheart." Then he presses a kiss on my forehead. "I'm going to go talk to the doctor for a minute."

"You liar!" I yell, but then I start coughing from the pain in my gut.

"Calm down," he sing-songs as he leaves the hospital room. "The baby won't like that you're threatening his father."

I growl as the door closes behind him.

"HIS!?"

Chapter 38

Bring A Deck Of Cards

Megan

Hearing the lightness in Hunter's voice shouldn't make me this happy, but it does. It feels as if we've been surrounded by negative drama since the moment we met, and it's honestly a relief to take a moment and sit in peace.

When the door closes behind him, I let out a huge breath and closed my eyes. My hand gently comes to rest on my stomach, and I whisper to the small child growing inside of me, "I have no idea what I'm doing, little one, but things are going to be so different for you. You're going to be so loved, and you won't suffer a day in your life. I promise."

My eyes suddenly fill with tears that I can't control. I remember the look on Hunter's face when he realized I'd been shot. His face showed a myriad of emotions: shock, anger, fear, and grief.

I understood in that moment as my eyelids started to feel uncontrollably heavy that regardless of the words he's said or hasn't said to me, that he has strong feelings for me.

250

At that moment, I understood that he cared whether I lived or died. I was important to him.

Even though we've shared some very intimate moments, I never truly expected Hunter to ever reveal how he truly feels about me. In my experience, that's not what men do. But I'm learning slowly but surely that I have to start thinking outside of my limited experience.

Not all families are toxic. Look at how much Hunter has gone through to find his sister. Not all men are liars and useless. Everything this man has done for me so far has been an expression of his love, even if he didn't know it was. Even if I didn't realize it either.

And now we're having a child together.

A whole ass human being.

And I can't believe he's beyond thrilled about it. I think I'm starting to get there too.

My lips curve in happiness.

The door opens, and when Hunter walks back inside the room, he looks carefully at me. "What is it?"

"I will forgive you for tricking me into moving in with you," I tell him. "I shouldn't be angry around the baby."

Hunter's lips twitch. "I don't think you should be making promises you can't keep."

"And I don't think you should be trying to get a reaction out of me all the time." I narrow my eyes at him. "It's juvenile."

"I can't help it." Hunter sits down in the chair next to my bed, filling out a form attached to a clipboard. "You look beautiful when you're mad at me, when you're frightened for me, and especially when you come for me."

My cheeks quickly grow hot, and I close my eyes, trying to stop thinking about the last time I was brought to climax by him.

A sudden pain from the bullet wound in my belly quickly returns my thoughts back to the last twenty-four hours of hell I've just been through.

"How did you find us?" I ask him, closing my eyes so he hopefully won't see the pain I'm in. It will only make him feel guiltier than he already does.

"I saw the earrings you dropped," Hunter replies after a long pause.

When I open my eyes, he's watching me closely. "I heard Lena's version of events, but I want to know what happened from you as well."

"After a conversation with a guest about one of my pieces, I was feeling hungry, so Lena and I headed to the buffet. Somebody pointed a gun at my back and told me to walk. I tried to give Lena a reason to go and look for you but she saw the gun, then she looked the guy right in his face, so he decided he wanted her as well."

"Was it Jonathan?"

"I don't think so, no. I really don't understand how nobody noticed us, but as we walked away from the buffet, I took the steak knife I was holding and just stuck it inside my dress, between my cleavage."

"That was dangerous, Megan."

He gently strokes my arm with the back of his knuckles.

"I'm not a stranger to knives," I say, reminding him of what happened with Samuel and my boyfriend.

"That was a different circumstance. Continue the story."

"I was scanning the room for you or anyone who may have been on the security detail but I didn't see anyone, so as we continued to walk, I took the opportunity to slip off both my earrings. I knew you'd figure out that something was wrong. I just wanted to leave you clues. And the rest, well, you know what happened."

"Lena said you were an absolute rock for her. That you helped her keep her shit together."

"I've been in worse situations in my own house. I was just trying to give her coping strategies that I used myself. Keep calm. Don't show any emotion. And if necessary, figure out a way to buy time."

That's how I survived all those years.

"And finally, I figured it out," Hunter murmurs.

"Better late than never, right?"

"Do you remember exactly what Jonathan said down in that basement to you or anyone else? Did he say anything odd, something that stuck out to you?"

"Odd?" I echo, trying to wrack my brain. "Well, he mentioned that someone was late. He kept checking his watch and calling somebody. And then he looked at one of the men and told him that they still had to follow instructions."

"What was odd about that to you?"

"I don't know, I thought he was the mastermind behind everything that's happened to you lately, but it seemed like he was answering to someone else. But to be honest, you can't take anything that I'm saying as the gospel because I was so close to peeing on myself I couldn't think straight."

"I can't believe he shot a pregnant woman."

"He didn't know I was pregnant."

"That's not the point, Megan."

"I know we agreed to baby steps, but what exactly happened to him?"

"I told you."

"I need more details."

"My team tried to question him," Hunter says grimly.

"But he had another gun and shot himself right in the head."

"So, after all the effort he went through to make your life a living hell, he decides to kill himself?" I feel disappointed. "That's hell of anticlimactic."

"You don't have to worry about any of this anymore." Hunter smiles. "All I want you to think about is our baby."

I smile at him tiredly and then sigh, looking up at the ceiling, "I want to be a good mother, Hunter."

"You will be." The confidence in his voice makes me look at him.

"When I was young, if things got too out of hand at home and I had to get stitches, Veronica would bring me to the hospital where she worked and give me the stitches herself. They were so painful, and I had to get them so frequently that I became terrified of hospitals. She didn't use anything to numb the skin, and if I cried or called any attention to myself, she would poke me with the needle. That's my example of a mother."

Hunter's hand covers mine as he looks at me with gentle eyes. "They're gone. All of them. Your family, those people who abused you, will never have the opportunity to hurt you again."

I purse my lips, nodding, "Yeah."

"I watch you work and interact with people at the Blue Whiskey every day, Megan, and they all adore you. You will be a good mother because you are a good person."

"That might have been one of the sweetest things you've ever said to me, Hunter," I say, my eyes tearing up.

Hunter uses a single finger to push aside a few locks of my hair and then peppers soft kisses on the side of my face, swallowing my tears.

"I can be sweet," he jests.

"Hey, you never told me what you discussed earlier with the doctor."

"Oh, I just asked him the basics."

"Like what?"

"How much longer you have in here, and when it's safe to make love again."

"Seriously?"

"What?" He feigns ignorance.

"You asked my doctor about sex?"

"The moment I realized at the art show that I'd somehow lost you, and worse, that you'd been taken, I probably lost about three years of my life."

"And so–"

"And so every moment together is precious."

"We're spending a moment together right now."

"Let me rephrase that then. Every moment I spend inside of you is *especially* precious. I want to make sure we capitalize on those."

He grazes his fingertips along one of my thighs, and my core instantly clenches like muscle memory.

"You're unbelievable," I say, crossing my legs at the ankles.

"Honesty is the cornerstone of our relationship," he grins, noticing the change in my posture.

Then he bends down and gives me a brief kiss on my lips.

"I have to go home and check on Lena. I've dumped her way too much on Christian. I'll be back in an hour or two. In the meantime, Lars will stay with you."

"The threat is gone. Why are you forcing that poor man to babysit me?"

"You don't get it, do you? I practically had to force Lars from camping out here 24-7. That old man has a soft spot for you, and you'd be hurting his feelings if you don't allow him to sit by your bedside for a while."

I realize there's still a lot of ground to cover in this relationship. Living together. His friends. The club. And our new baby. But for once, I'm not afraid to explore it all with this man by my side.

"Tell him to bring a deck of cards."

"Cards?"

"I heard him tell Parker that he was a card shark. I want to learn how to play poker."

Hunter chuckles as he gives me a final peck on my forehead.

"He'll love that."

Chapter 39

The Godmother Conundrum

Megan

I'm finally discharged from the hospital three days later, and for now, I return to my apartment, which I still share with Naomi and Lena, both of whom are thrilled about the news of my pregnancy.

"So, when's the due date?" Naomi asks excitedly as I look around the room at the 'welcome home' decorations.

I already had a feeling that Vaughn and Christian would be here, according to Lena, the two of them were often at the apartment. I think she may have a little crush on Christian, but of course, something between them could never happen in a million years. She's barely legal. I'm not sure how they roped Parker and Lars into being here, too, but they are.

"Sometime in November," I tell her.

"Ooh, I hope she's a Scorpio. She's going to be a wild one." Naomi immediately looks at me and asks in her typical demanding voice, "I'm the Godmother, right?"

"Wait, what?" Lena looks dismayed. "But I'm the aunt, and I want to be Godmother."

"Get in line, kid," Naomi gestures with a wave of her hand. "I was here first. Plus, you're already blood-related to the kid. Don't be greedy."

"You're not the Godmother," Hunter tells Naomi, frowning. "We've got better–"

"Congratulations," I hug Naomi, completely cutting Hunter off before he says something beyond rude. "Of course, you're the Godmother!"

"What about me?" Lena pouts miserably, and I take her hand.

"Well, you're going to be her aunt, so it's an equal privilege."

Vaughn frowns, "Wait, so who's the Godfather? Have you decided? Me or Christian?"

"You can't seriously care about any of that," Hunter gripes.

"Hell yeah, we do."

"Christian?" Hunter looks for a more appropriate response from him.

"I'd take the commitment seriously if I was selected," Christian offers, completely blindsiding Hunter. He wasn't expecting either of his friends to be so interested in the role in our baby's life.

I think it's sweet.

I smile. "I figured that Hunter wouldn't want to choose between the two of you, so I decided that you both get to split the privilege. There's no rule that a baby can only have one Godfather."

Vaughn and Christian start to spar with each other about who would be a better role model for the tiny little person inside me. Then, they drag Lars and Parker into it, asking them to pick a side and back it up with a reasonable argument.

It's hysterical and kind of messy, but it's my life now.

These people in this room are my new family. I've gone from a house filled with people who despised me to a tiny apartment where I was often struggling to make rent, to all of this.

"How are you feeling?" Hunter asks as he helps me adjust my position on the couch. "Are you in any pain?" His hand rests on my abdomen.

"I'm a little sore but nothing too uncomfortable."

I won't admit this to Hunter because he would insist that I take pain medication or, worse, go back to the hospital, but I'm still in a lot of pain. I just don't want to ingest any unnecessary medicine that could affect the baby. I don't know much about being a good mother, but what I do know is that I need to give this baby the best pregnancy I can, especially since he or she has had such a stressful start.

"Your face seems tight," he says, always the observant partner.

"I didn't say I was pain-free. I said it wasn't unbearable."

"I think you just need a good meal instead of that bland hospital crap and maybe a little trash tv?" Naomi interjects. "We can watch the new bachelorette hand out roses."

"Have you told her yet?" Hunter asks me, no doubt, purposely in front of Naomi.

"Told me what?" She frowns.

"Can I speak with you for a minute, Hunter?" I ask with a clipped tone. "Right now."

"Tell me what?" Naomi demands to know.

"I'll be right back," I tell her. "Can you order us some of that good Mexican we had like last time?"

"Uh, okay."

"Get enough for everyone."

"Everyone?"

"Here." Hunter hands Naomi his American Express card. "Use this."

"I can freakin' pay for Mexican food," she practically spits back at him, refusing the card as she walks away.

Once the two of us are inside my bedroom, I push him to sit down on the edge of my bed, and I place my palms firmly on his shoulders.

"We've been through hell and back, and I trust you with my life, but what the fuck is going on with you and Naomi?"

"I'm sorry?" He gives a subtle grin as if he's actually amused by my question.

"Don't feign ignorance now. You've been a jerk toward her since the moment you met. I need to know why."

"This sounds like a conversation you should be having with her. She's the one who can't stand me."

"Since when do you care about people liking you?"

"Sit down, baby." He gently seats me on his lap.

"Don't flirt with me."

"I'm not flirting." But he obviously is, using that sexy voice of his that can almost persuade me to do anything.

"Your friends are right outside that door. We can't flirt right now."

"Flirt or fuck?"

"Hush." I place a finger on his lips to quiet him.

He kisses it.

"Do you realize this is the first time we've been alone together in almost a week?" he asks.

Then he gingerly kisses the bit of skin revealed by my v-neck shirt.

"I'm well aware of that, Hunter, but you're changing the subject," I say as I find myself wrapping my arms around his neck, snuggling further into his embrace where I feel safe and loved.

"You're looking for some complicated reason why your roommate and I mix like oil and water. There isn't one."

Hunter's lips form a small, closed-mouth smile, and my stomach churns with unease. That smile is his tell.

"Oh my god. You're lying," I try pulling away from him, but he won't release me that easily.

"Megan, don't get yourself worked up. You just got out of the hospital."

"You're lying!"

He sighs heavily.

"Everyone who cares about you is outside in your living room, and this is the conversation you want to have right now?"

"You started it! You wanted me to tell her right then and there that I was moving out. Why?"

"What do you know about Naomi?"

"I know that she's the only real friend I've ever had."

"Who disappears for weeks at a time."

"Stop trying to make it sound so ominous. She doesn't disappear. She goes home to visit her family a lot."

"Her family in New Orleans?"

"New Orleans?" That's not where Naomi told me where she's from, but people can have family anywhere. "I never asked for her travel itinerary. I just know she visits them *somewhere*."

"Naomi's actual last name is Fabre. Did you know that? Her family has an old Creole heritage dating back to well before the civil war."

"Okay, so?"

"The Fabre's are a notorious crime family in the bayou."

"Crime family? Be serious."

"She's not using her real name, and she never told you any of this, which tells me that she's either running or working some sort of hustle for them. If I discovered who she is, then you can best believe her family already knows that she's here, so I don't trust her, and neither should you."

"Wait, you're telling me that Naomi is like some sort of a mob princess?"

"That's what I'm saying, and if you think I'm bad, wait until you meet her family. They're ruthless."

I'm speechless.

And if it's actually true, I'm hurt.

"If she's working some sort of hustle, what would it be? Why would I have anything to do with it? I'm penniless. I'm nobody."

"Don't say that. You are somebody."

"You know what I mean."

"I'm not saying that you're a target of it or that she doesn't actually care about you. She probably does. But it's no accident that a Fabre is in Los Angeles. That family is up to something. Maybe they're trying to make a move in LA? I don't know. I just know that you need to create some distance from her and moving in with me is a start. Making Lena the godmother of our baby would be another."

My heart aches.

On one hand, I'm hurt that Naomi could keep her past hidden from me like this but on the other hand, I have to at least try and understand it. It's her life. Her business. And if her family is dangerous, I can understand why she'd want to stay tight-lipped about it.

"Have you already said something to her about this?"

"No, she was the least of my concerns when I had Jonathan to contend with. But I will say...for a while, I believed that she might have had some hand in what was going on with me. Jonathan wasn't acting alone. He wasn't smart enough. Her family has the money and the cache to pull those kinds of strings."

"Wait, I need to stop you right there. You're reaching and stretching right now. Naomi had no idea I was going to work at the Blue Whiskey or meet you."

"True, but–"

"And Steve was up to no good well before I started working there."

"Maybe, but things escalated once I moved you both into my apartment. What if–"

"She would never betray me like that, Hunter! You're being paranoid about everyone and everything because of the people from *your* world...not mine."

I grimace in pain.

"Calm down, Megan. You're hurting yourself."

He uses a calm tone that feels very patronizing. A tone I've heard him use with people who work for him at the club. I stand up and back away, pointing at him.

"This isn't right."

"What isn't right?"

"This?"

"You mean us?"

His face hardens.

"The fact that you want me to cut my friend out of my life doesn't sit right with me."

"Which is why I waited to say something."

"Really, because if I didn't force you to come clean, it doesn't seem like you were ever going to say anything about your suspicions."

"I was protecting you."

"Hunter, what I need is your support, not your protection. Stop trying to control everything and everybody."

"So now I'm trying to control you?"

I can feel the anger rolling off of him.

"I just think we need a minute."

"A minute for what?"

"Let me rephrase that. I think I need a minute."

"A minute for what, Megan?" He repeats with a sterner tone. "You're pregnant with my child."

Suddenly, there's a soft knock at the door.

"Is everything okay in there?" Lena asks. "The food's here."

I'm looking defiantly into Hunter's eyes as he continues to examine mine. After a tense pause, Hunter answers his sister.

"Me and the guys will be taking our food to go, Lena."

Fine, I think to myself.

Get out then!

But I don't say any of that out loud because my heart won't allow it. Instead, I just watch him stand, adjust the cuffs of his white collared shirt, and walk out of my apartment without another word to me.

After Hunter and all of his friends exit behind him, Naomi leans against the kitchen counter, takes a bite of her burrito, and asks with a smirk, "Aww, did mommy and daddy have their first fight?"

The nerve.

I'm going to give this mystery mafia princess a piece of my mind next.

Chapter 40

Men Like What?

Megan
Two Days Later

"Are you going to lay up in this bed your entire pregnancy in your pajamas watching...wait, are they speaking Chinese?"

Naomi barges into my bedroom with a tray of snacks, plops down on the edge of the bed, and gives me a goofy grin.

I've been holed up in my room for the last two days thinking about my argument with Hunter and deciding how I was going to talk about the reason why with Naomi.

"It's a Korean drama and stop exaggerating. It's only been two days."

"Why the hell would you watch television you have to read? And I've never seen you take off work for even one day, so two seems wild and crazy for someone like you."

"People change," I say with a heavy exhalation, hoping that Naomi will magically volunteer up information about herself. Clearly, I'm having trouble initiating the conversation.

"What did you bring me?" I ask her, looking at the plate full of small bites.

"Only healthy stuff for the baby. I think this is the phase when her brain is growing. It's important for you to have brain-boosting food. So here's some nuts, a berry mix, olives, and a little French bread and olive oil dip. I know you like that good bread now that you've been to Paris and all."

"It looks good."

"You better eat up because you're probably going to become nauseous in the next month or so and won't want to eat anything."

I accept the plate and place it at my side on the bed.

"Thanks."

"Cheer up, girl. You and Hunter had a little disagreement. You can't curl up and die over it. You're bound to have many more with someone like him."

My eyes raise up to meet hers.

"What do you mean by that?"

"I'm just saying–"

"What are you saying? What do you mean by someone like *him*?"

She starts to stumble over her words.

"It's just that I've known a lot of men like him."

"Men like what?"

"Powerful. Domineering. Overwhelming. You know. the type"

"You know powerful and domineering men?"

"Megan–"

"Actually, Naomi, I've known you since I moved to LA, and you rarely talk about your family or your past."

"Neither did you, that's part of what we had in common."

"I didn't talk about mine because they were freaking sociopaths. What's your excuse?"

Naomi looks silently down at her feet, no doubt thinking of another way to avoid talking to me about the truth about her family. She's right, though. Neither of us chose to share details about our pasts, which seemed perfectly normal at the time, but now I see that both of us were hiding from each other and possibly from ourselves.

"My family is complicated, Megan."

"How so?"

She looks me dead in my eyes and inspects them as if she's searching for something.

"Did your boyfriend tell you something about my family?"

I pop an olive in my mouth and savor the salty explosion in my mouth as I chew.

"Yes."

Her entire body deflates.

I've never seen Naomi like this...ever.

"What did he tell you?" She asks in a small voice.

"That you're from New Orleans and that your family is dangerous."

"Fuck."

"Do you actually go home to visit them, Naomi, or are you in danger because–"

"There's no danger. My family is many things but they love me. No one would ever hurt me."

Like mine.

"I see, so why did you move across the country?"

"I'm avoiding something which is probably inevitable anyway."

"What?"

"Marriage."

"Are you engaged?"

I pat my hand on the bed as an instruction for her to sit down.

"I'm not engaged, I'm promised."

"Promised? What does that mean?"

"The girls in my family are always promised in marriage to a boy from another prominent family. I was promised to my fiancee when I turned one year old. There was even a ceremony that sealed our fates, and the time is quickly approaching when I have to honor that promise."

"An arranged marriage? In this day and age? I didn't realize those still happened. I mean, you can't actually want to marry someone your parents picked for you."

"I don't."

"Is he some sort of old man or something?"

"No, he's only three years older than me."

"Do you know him? Is he an asshole?"

"Does that matter, Megan? I don't love him. I don't love anyone. I just want to be a normal twenty-something. I don't want to get married. I want to become a celebrity makeup artist and stylist. Can you imagine me on tour with Beyonce or Taylor Swift? I would create fierce looks for them."

"Why don't you have an accent?"

"Not everyone speaks with a twang back home."

"I'm sorry, I just thought–"

"I get it," she chuckles. "But I attended private schools my whole life. They teach you how to speak like you're a news anchor there. That way you can blend in anywhere you go, at least in the States."

"So what will you do? How long can you avoid this marriage thing?"

"My father has given me until my 25th birthday to *sow my disrespectful oats,* as he put it, but then I have to come home and get married or there will be consequences."

I think about the many times Naomi and I have eaten Ramen noodles for dinner or how she moved with me to Hunter's building because she wouldn't be able to afford a place on her own. Does that even make sense if she comes from a powerful family like this?

"Why don't you have any money if your family is well off?"

"This isn't *Coming To America.* My parents weren't going to bankroll my escape to Los Angeles like Eddie Murphy's parents did in that movie. If I was going to disobey them, I'd have to fund it myself. They expected me to fail. They expected me to be back home three years ago."

"So what are you going to do? Your birthday is in three months."

She grabs a piece of the French baguette and dips it into the olive oil and basil.

"I don't know, girl. I'll be in deep shit if I don't go home. The women in my family have had arranged marriages for a hundred years. I'd be the first to break tradition."

"A hundred years?" I repeat in disbelief.

"My family's wealth began during prohibition. My great-grandfather built an empire on selling illegal liquor."

"Oh, that doesn't sound so dangerous."

"Yes, but prohibition ended. So the money he earned during that time was used to fund another business that exists today, and it's very dangerous. Much like Hunter's business is."

"Is that why you don't like him?"

"I never said that I didn't like him."

"It's pretty obvious you don't. Hiding your emotions has never been a part of your skillset."

"That's real nice, *prego*. I suppose your baby's daddy just reminds me of so many guys I grew up with and not in a good way."

"He's been nothing but wonderful to me and for me, Naomi. He encourages and supports my art in a way I didn't know was possible. He actually believes in my talent."

"I believe in it, too!"

"You know what I mean."

"Let me ask you this." Naomi's voice grows more serious. "Have you ever told him no?"

"Told him no?" It's my natural inclination to immediately respond with *well, of course, I have,* but if I actually think about it, I'm not sure that I've denied Hunter anything.

"He's never asked me to do anything I'd have to say no to."

"Nothing?" she asks incredulously.

"Nothing."

"I bet he didn't even ask you anything. I imagine someone like Hunter Middleton just kind of tells you what's going to happen, and that's what you do. I'm pretty sure you didn't jump at the idea of having a full-time security detail following you around."

"I didn't like it, but I understood that it was necessary. His enemies could view me as a weakness and try to hurt him through me. He only assigned the security guys to protect me."

"Are you listening to yourself, girl? His enemies? People hurting him through you? That's not normal behavior. I ran away from everything I knew back home because of nonsense like that. And now you're bringing another human into the world who will be totally connected to all of that drama."

I place both of my palms on my stomach the moment she talks about my baby, as if I'm protecting him or her from her harsh words.

"Hunter won't let anything happen to our baby."

"He can't promise you that."

"Then what do you propose I do, Naomi? He's the father of my unborn child. You want me to run away from my life like you have?"

Naomi stands.

"That's why I didn't tell you anything. I knew you'd judge me. You've changed so much since falling for him."

"This isn't judgment. This is me being taken aback that you've been my closest friend– no, my only friend for years, and I don't know anything about you."

"You know about everything that matters. You are probably the only person on this earth who knows me for the woman I truly am and not the obedient little girl I was brought up to be."

"Then let me ask you one more thing about your past, and then we can leave it behind us."

"What do you want to know?"

"Will your family come for you if you don't go willingly back to New Orleans to get married?"

Naomi shifts from side to side uncomfortably, and dread fills inside my chest once she answers.

"Yes."

Chapter 41

Snitch

Hunter

I was never the kind of kid who attended school dances or football games. To me, that was for the students who had normal families and simple lives. Unfortunately, that was never my life.

After the death of my mother and the disappearance of my little sister, I spent my teenage years trying to prove to men who didn't give a shit about me that I could be a valuable member of an illegal organization designed to use us up and spit us out. My complicated and ultimately fatal relationship with Jonathan is proof of that.

The organization taught me many things, but it wasn't until I got here out on my own that I was truly able to elevate myself and expand my reach in Los Angeles. There was no time or room for emotions and definitely no safe space for a real relationship. Relationships were the kiss of death to a man like me, so I avoided them like the plague.

But look at me now.

"Everything's been prepared to your specifications, Mr.

Middleton. Everything's set up. Is there anything else I can do for you?"

It's funny how some women have the balls to be flirtatious when they've just finished helping plan a romantic night for another woman.

"Nothing else, thank you."

The woman shamelessly pouts and sticks out her breasts, thinking that will be some sort of enticement to me. Obvious displays of sexuality were never a turn-on for me like they are for most men. It always feels like the women are trying too hard which must be why I'm so attracted to Megan.

God knows I'm doing all the work.

"Are you sure?"

"Positive. Just keep your phone handy in case I run into any issues. I'll have an envelope for you tomorrow if everything goes smoothly."

"Of course, Mr. Middleton."

Megan's been avoiding me for the last few days and I've allowed her to have her space so she could spend some time having the tough conversations I know she needs to have with her friend. But now that time has come to an end.

I miss her.

Not to mention that she's pregnant with my child.

I knock at her door, already aware that she's home, but of course, Naomi answers. The very last thing I need.

"Well, look who it is," Naomi answers the door in some sort of satin kimono with a smug look on her face.

"I'm here for Megan."

"Megan is resting. She's been through so much lately."

"I bet. She just found out her roommate is not who she thought she was."

"Thanks for confirming that you were the snitch."

"You're welcome. It was never a secret."

"Then why did you wait so long to tell her?"

"You have no idea when I discovered your lies."

"Oh, it's clear you've known since I moved into this building. You've been an asshole from the start."

"Naomi–" Megan interrupts our exchange. "Excuse us."

"Remember what I told you," she says to Megan as some sort of warning as she saunters back into her bedroom.

"And remember who's paying the bills around here," I say in response to that clear dig.

"Hunter."

"What?" I throw my hands up.

"You promised me you wouldn't throw the fact that this is your apartment up in our faces."

"I'm not throwing it up in *your* face. Frankly, I'm surprised you still have her in here after what I told you."

"You act like she's some sort of mafia hitman. She just happened to be born into a complicated family. So was I."

"Those are completely different circumstances, and you know it, but I didn't come by here to talk about your friend or her family. First of all, I want to know how you're feeling."

Megan's face starts to relax. I don't think she even realized how stressed our conversation was making her.

"I'm doing better. My stomach feels less sore."

"And the pregnancy?"

"If the doctor hadn't told me I was pregnant, I wouldn't have known. No real symptoms yet. I feel normal."

"Okay," I say not really knowing if that's good or bad.

I'm still standing awkwardly in the middle of her kitchen.

"Where's Lena?" she asks.

"At the club, working on a recipe with Billy. After all

that's happened, she says she feels most normal if she keeps busy with work."

"Is she okay there by herself?"

I've chosen not to get into the fact that I believe there was someone else out there pulling Jonathan's strings because what good would that do? The reality is that Lena and Megan's connection to me will always pose as a threat, but it's my number one priority to keep them safe or die trying.

"She's safe. I made sure of it."

"Okay."

I step closer to her, unable to avoid the strong pull I feel whenever I'm near her. I love that I tower over her minute body. And I love that a little human we made together is growing inside of her.

"So I know you're a little irritated with me, but I was hoping you'd go somewhere with me today."

"Today?" She sounds a little breathy.

"Yeah."

"Later or like right now?"

She starts fidgeting with her hair.

"I was hoping right now."

I try to sound as humble as I can.

"How long do I have to get ready?"

"Thirty."

"What do I need to wear?"

"Whatever you want. You'd look good in a trash bag."

"Flattery will get you nowhere with me."

I step closer.

"Then what will get me somewhere?"

It's almost as if I can hear her heart pattering just a foot away from me or maybe that's my own heart I hear.

"And what if I say no?" She asks softly.

"Then you say no."

But please don't say it.

"You're not moving me in right now, are you?"

"Megan–" I lift her chin so I can stare straight into her eyes. "I'm not going to make you do anything you don't want to."

She takes a moment to consider what I've said, then answers, "I'll get ready."

"Great."

She studies me for a moment.

"You're acting weird."

"That's because I'm trying to be humble, which is probably odd to see."

Megan emits a real laugh for the first time in days. It warms my insides and makes me smile inwardly.

"That's exactly what it is...odd."

"Go get dressed." I shoo her away.

"Anything in particular I should wear for wherever you're taking me?"

"You look perfect in anything you wear, baby. Surprise me."

With that, she walks over in her bare feet, rises to her toes, and pecks my lips with the sweetest kiss I didn't know I needed.

"See you in thirty, Mr. Middleton."

Chapter 42

This Is My Los Angeles

Megan

The vibrant pulse of Los Angeles surrounds me, a hum of energy and excitement. I stand beside Hunter outside the Blue Whiskey, wondering why he's brought me here, of all places.

His tall, dominant figure seems to cast a shadow even in the night and makes me all too aware of the contrast between his powerful demeanor and my own sense of wonderment. The more time I spend with him, the more in awe of him I become.

"You look beautiful," he says to me, and I blush.

"You'd probably tell me I was pretty if I was only wearing a trash bag."

"Have you ever spent the night out enjoying the city we live in?"

I cock my head to the side, not totally understanding the question. "I mean, I've gone out with friends."

"What friends?"

"That's not nice."

"I'm serious."

"Naomi and—"

"And who? Did that the boyfriend of yours from school ever take you anywhere?" he asks with a jealous bite to his tone.

"Obviously not."

"That's what I thought." Hunter captures my hand, his touch reassuring. "Tonight, Megan," he whispers, a twinkle in his eye, "I'm going to show you my Los Angeles."

While it's weird to see Blue Whiskey patrons gawk at us, I feel a flutter of excitement as we settle into the plush limousine that suddenly pulls up in front of the club.

Hunter opens the door for me like a gentleman. "Your chariot awaits."

"Wait, is that Parker underneath that hat?"

"Hey, Megan." The driver's side window lowers, and Parker peeps his head out.

"No one drives me but Parker or Lars. It's part of how I keep security around me and now you as tight as possible."

"Of course."

I've never been inside of a limousine before. The buttery, soft leather interior makes me feel like I'm back in the deluxe private plane we took to Paris, gliding us across the streets of the city.

"I stocked the limo with your favorites if you want to snack. Lift that lid right there."

The limousine has so many compartments that it feels almost like a treasure hunt.

"Ooh, there's red licorice in here."

"Yep," he chuckles.

"What else is there?" I ask eagerly as I open some of the other compartments.

"Check this one," he tells me, pointing to one at the far side of the limo.

I lift the lid and recognize instantly what's inside. There's a square-shaped, light blue box with the word Tiffany embossed and a white ribbon tied around it. I've never touched an actual gift from a high-end jeweler, but I've seen advertisements for the brand many times.

"What's this?" I ask softly.

"It's yours. Open it."

"I asked for one simple date, not for any of these over-the-top gestures," I say, suddenly uncomfortable for reasons I don't even understand myself.

"Everything I do is over the top, Megan. Just open it."

I untie the ribbon and stuff it in my purse to save. I haven't received many gifts in my life and don't want to throw any part of it away, especially because it's from Hunter.

When I lift the lid, there's another box inside which I open and find a beautiful, unique bracelet inside that almost takes my breath away. It's oval-shaped, and one side is gold, and the other side is covered in diamonds.

"This is stunning."

"Come sit here next to me," he commands, patting the seat beside him. "It's called the lock bracelet." He opens the bracelet and then clicks it in place around my right wrist. "And you should never take it off."

"Hunter, it's gorgeous, but this thing is blinding me. Of course, I should take it off. I'm scared to walk around with it on."

"You'll be perfectly safe. Promise me you'll never take it off."

"But when I paint?"

"That's why I put it on your right arm. I want you to see

it and be reminded of me every time you pick up a paintbrush."

"Why don't you pee on me while you're at it?"

He laughs at my sarcasm as I continue to admire the bracelet. I've got to admit, it's truly a work of art. I'm just not sure that such a pretty piece will go with my closet full of jeans and sweats.

"I think this is a much nicer way to mark my territory, don't you?"

I admire how the diamonds sparkle under the lights inside the limo. I'm no pro, but I can tell this bracelet must be worth a lot of money.

"How expensive was this, Hunter? I hope you don't give all of your dates gifts like this. You'll go bankrupt."

"Are you going to question the cost of everything we do tonight, Miss Taylor?" He uses an exasperated tone. "Because you know I can afford it, right?"

"Fine."

"And just so we're clear, you're the first woman I've ever given a piece of jewelry to."

"Well, what other presents have you given women?" I ask suspiciously.

"Let me rephrase that. You are the first woman I've ever given a gift to, period."

"How many women were there? The ones that didn't get gifts."

"Only you would find a way to be jealous after I've given you a diamond bracelet...and a baby." He pulls me in closer to his body, pulling me by the hips. "Sit closer to me. I missed you."

I chuckle. "What's the point of this big car if we're just going to sit on top of each other?"

"God, I wish you'd sit on me. Maybe it would help you relax."

"You're such a pervert."

"Thank you." He grins.

"And you're also a good gift giver for a first-timer," I quip, staring back at the bracelet. "This is so gorgeous I can't take my eyes off of it."

"I'm glad you like it." He wraps his palm around the back of my neck, pulls me close, and kisses me gently on the lips. "You're welcome."

Every corner we turn and every street we pass holds its own magic, and I find myself soaking in the city's allure with wide-eyed fascination.

Just when I thought the night couldn't be more surprising, our journey takes an unexpected turn. Hunter guides me to a waiting helicopter, his confident grin telling me he has something special in store.

"Before we get on, I just want to make sure that you're not nauseous," he checks with worry etched on his forehead.

"I'm fine."

"And the gunshot wound?"

"All better."

"Have you ever been on a helicopter before?"

"Aren't these questions you should have asked before tonight?"

"It wouldn't have been a surprise then."

I place a hand on his chest and tilt my head up to meet his eyes.

"I've never been on a helicopter before, but I don't have any motion sickness, and if I hadn't gotten shot, I wouldn't even know that I was pregnant right now. So let's go. I'm excited."

As the chopper soars above the sprawling city, Hunter points out various landmarks—the glittering coast, the iconic Hollywood sign, and more. Each sight seems more beautiful than the last, the world stretching out beneath us in a breathtaking panorama.

"Los Angeles seems almost magical from this view," I gush. "Not the same city where you might trip over a body in the alleyway."

"Yeah, everyone should see it this way. Maybe they'd respect it a little more," he says.

The helicopter touches down on a secluded rooftop. I gasp when I see a candlelit table set against the backdrop of the city. "I've always dreamed of dining beneath the stars," I murmur, awe-struck.

Hunter pulls out a chair for me, his usually stern face softening. "This is the closest I could get."

The night creates a whirlwind of emotions for me. What started as a simple date has turned into so much more...almost a statement of some sort. Hunter is making a point and making it well.

I feel myself drawing in closer to Hunter, the city lights below us painting a picture of dreams and possibilities. At one point, he leads me to the edge of the rooftop. The vastness of L.A. spread beneath us, its lights twinkling like distant stars.

"It's beautiful," I whisper, feeling a sense of insignificance amidst the grandeur of the night skyline.

Hunter's voice, soft and sincere, breaks through my reverie. "No more than you."

And in that moment, amidst the glow of the city, I feel closer to the stars and the man I love more than ever before.

As we sit back at the table, a cool breeze sweeps across

the rooftop. Hunter's hand reaches out, grasping mine. The intensity of his gaze makes my heart race.

"Megan, there's something I need to tell you," he says, his voice low and urgent.

I feel a lump form in my throat, unsure of what he's about to reveal. My immediate thought is that he's done all of this to let me down easy, to break up with me.

But that doesn't make sense, Megan. Get a hold of yourself.

"I don't want any bargains or compromises between us," he continues, his grip on my hand tightening. "I'm in love with you, and pregnant or not, I want to spend the rest of my life with you. I don't want you to just move into the penthouse. I want to marry you."

My breath catches in my chest as his words sink in. The world around us seems to fade away, leaving only the two of us in that moment.

"I love you too, Hunter," I reply, my voice barely above a whisper. "But I told you I wanted us to take our time."

"You've seen me at my best and my worst. There's not much more I can show you. You know who I am and what I'm about. If you want to date and be romanced, I will do that for the rest of our lives as a married couple. This is only the beginning."

His words move me, and I'm unable to keep my tears at bay, but he keeps talking.

"Marriage is a statement to the world that you are mine, and I am yours. It's a pledge you make to me to love me, and it's one I make to protect and cherish you. I realize that I'm not speaking from a place of experience, but I know enough of what not to do to make this work. With you, it wouldn't be work. It would just—"

"Yes," I say, cutting him off mid-sentence.

"What?"

"Yes, I'll marry you."

With a look of pure joy, Hunter leans in and presses his lips to mine. The sensation is electric, sending shivers down my spine. As we pull away, I see the same sense of wonderment in his eyes that drew me to him in the first place. When Hunter looks at me, he sees something about me I don't even see in myself.

Something worthy of love.

He pulls a smaller Tiffany blue box out of the inside pocket of his leather jacket and hands it to me. It's the most perfect solitaire diamond ring I've ever seen. Simple but brilliant.

He slides it on the ring finger of my left hand, then pulls my hand toward his mouth, kissing the inside of my palm.

"I can't wait to make you Mrs. Middleton."

Together, we gaze out over the city as the night stretches on. The stars twinkle above us, a reminder of the infinite possibilities that lay ahead.

Will I continue to paint? Will I become the full-time manager of the club so that I can work near him every day? Or will I become a stay-at-home mother and take care of our son or daughter instead?

But as I look at Hunter, I realize I don't need all the answers right now. Anything is possible and all things that will be will be as long as we are together.

Chapter 43

The Partition Please

Megan

I'm still on a Hunter Middleton high after being proposed marriage in the most romantic way a girl like me could have ever dreamed of.

It wasn't that long ago that I was on a trajectory of possibly ending up like so many of the nameless faces who end up dead in alleyways like the one next to the Blue Whiskey.

But I beat those odds.

And I beat them in the most satisfying way.

I belong to Hunter, and he damn sure belongs to me, and I'll never be afraid again.

I'll be loved.

"What are you thinking about, beautiful?" he asks after a few moments of me silently staring out the window of the limousine.

"I'm wondering if this is all a dream." I smile, unable to admit out loud to him that a part of me is worried that the other shoe is going to drop. That suddenly all the happiness that I feel is going to be cruelly taken away from me.

He slides across the seat and encloses me in an embrace that smells like leather and musk.

"Of course, it's a dream, but it's our dream together. It's you and me. Forever."

I lay back in his comforting warmth and close my eyes as he presses soft kisses at the nape of my neck. His head bends, and he gives me another slow kiss on the side of my neck. I lift both of my arms up, bend them back, and wrap them around his neck, pulling him closer.

"The partition, please," Hunter suddenly says to Parker, who nods and presses a button, which closes a darkly tinted window between us and him.

Hunter's arm wraps around to the front of my waist and slides the front of my pants, gently exploring between my folds.

"How long have you been soaked like this?" He growls into my ear.

"Forever," I mutter thickly, finding myself wanting Hunter in a very carnal way. There must be some truth in what women say about a pregnant woman's hormones raging because I've been wet for half the night.

"I can't have my woman aching for me like this and not telling me."

I can feel a hardness poking me at the base of my spine when suddenly he whirls me around in my seat.

He claims my mouth with his hungrily as if he's been starving for me for days, or perhaps I'm projecting my own desire onto my new fiancé.

I wrap my arms around his neck and climb into his lap, grinding myself into his hardened length.

"So greedy," he teases. "You just want to take what you want when you want it, huh?"

"When it belongs to me, yeah," I retort, and that makes the flecks of steel in his silver-gray eyes sparkle like they often do when Hunter is determined or happy.

"I belong to you?" He asks with just a hint of vulnerability in his voice.

"Of course, you do, Hunter."

Hunter instantly grabs my hips and pulls them forcibly further into him. The sudden movement takes me momentarily by surprise but only makes me want him more.

I lift my strapless silk top up, immediately exposing my breasts because I'm braless tonight, and barely get a chance to toss it aside when Hunter takes one of my nipples into his mouth.

My head falls back from the blissful feeling of my tit between his lips as he simultaneously kneads the other breast with his right hand.

"Hunter."

Fuck, I just want him inside me like right now. Why the hell didn't I wear a dress tonight?

I grab his face between both of my hands and try pulling him away.

"What's wrong?" he asks breathlessly.

"I need to take my pants off," I tell him, wiggling myself out of wide-leg slacks. "My pussy aches."

"Fuck, Megan. That mouth of yours."

It's only now that I realize that Parker has taken us completely in another direction and is driving us purposely into the Hollywood hills to kill time.

Normally, I'd be embarrassed because that can only mean that he knows exactly what we're doing back here, but honestly, I don't care. I need Hunter in the worst way, and I don't really care who's around to hear it.

My skin is hot.

So, I pull everything off.

And now I'm riding around inside a limo with nothing on but my new diamond bracelet and an engagement ring.

I feel like one of those Real Housewives; I laugh to myself.

Decadent.

Powerful.

Radiant.

Hunter is staring at me like I'm the last woman on planet Earth and as if he's the luckiest man alive. It's the headiest feeling to have a man want me like this. I could get drunk off the way this man makes me feel.

I train my eyes on him as I undo his leather belt, pulling it clean out of the belt loops and tossing it and its heavy metal buckle to the floor of the limo with a thump.

When I unzip him, his dick almost has a life of its own, springing from behind the zipper of his pants.

Hard and angry.

Weeping at the tip with want.

I lick the corner of my mouth as I stare at his beautiful penis, remembering how delicious it tasted the last time.

"Your greedy cunt can wait a little longer," Hunter says in a thick voice. "Take me in your mouth first."

But first, I grab the base of his dick with my hand and start jerking him off.

"Megan...shit," he moans.

I smile when his eyes bore into mine with an expression that can only be described as one full of desire. He's barely holding on. He's so used to being in control of every situation that he doesn't understand how to surrender.

"Megan," he mutters my name prayerfully. "Your mouth...please."

That's better.

I get on my knees in the limo in between his muscular legs and take him in my mouth. After a few moments, the telltale sign that he's close to release is when he slides his hands into my scalp to grip my hair at the roots and fuck my mouth.

When I feel him growing closer to coming, I pop his dick out of my mouth and pump it with my hand for a few final strokes.

He comes hard.

"*Yessss!*" He hisses.

And I watch with delightful satisfaction as his release drips down onto my fingers.

I did this.

Hunter's breathing is still labored as he tugs at the base of his dick a few times to get hard again. He pats his thigh and orders me to, "Come ride me, Megan."

I climb up on top of my beautiful man and then lower myself slowly down his hard length, staring him in the eyes the entire way down.

"That's it, baby. Now cup your tits in your hands."

I do as I'm told while he grips my hips, keeping me balanced as I wind my hips in delicate circles, relishing the pleasure.

"Why do you always feel so fucking amazing, Megan?"

"Shhh, you talk too much," I tell him, my eyes shut, nearing my orgasm. "Let me fuck you."

The rumble of his laughter vibrates throughout my entire body, only adding to the pleasure of feeling him inside me.

"Parker can't drive us around forever, baby. Are you close to coming?"

"Are you?" I challenge flippantly.

"Fuck, yes."

"Then come."

I press a harsh hand against Hunter's chest, and my head falls back as I allow the exquisite pleasure of my orgasm to wash completely over me.

His next orgasm chases right behind mine.

"God, I love you."

I slump in his embrace. Totally nude. Sweaty. And extremely satiated.

"I love you too, old man."

He tickles me under my rib cage.

"That's not funny." He suddenly puts on his "serious" voice.

"Oh, so now you want to pretend that there isn't a noticeable age difference between us when that's all you used to throw up in my face?"

He kisses the tip of my nose and then nuzzles the side of my neck. "Is that any way to talk to your husband?"

"Not my husband yet," I tease, blinking as my ring catches the light of an oncoming car.

Suddenly, a speaker I didn't know was in the car comes to life with Parker's voice.

"We're ten minutes away, boss," he announces.

"Oh my god, could he hear us the whole time?" My mouth drops.

"The way you don't know the man you're about to marry is shocking."

"Right," I shiver. "You'd never allow that."

"Exactly. He leans over, grabs his leather blazer off of the seat, and wraps it around my shoulders. I will always protect your privacy, your dreams, and your life, Megan. That is my promise to you. That's what this all means."

He lifts my wrist with the bracelet and kisses the inside of it exactly where my pulse is.

"I will die for you," he tells me. "And our baby."

His words soothe me like a warm cup of tea. Making me feel safe and loved.

So I tell him with a 100% surety, "Let's set a date."

Chapter 44

Back To School

Megan

When I walk into the fine arts building of my university, I enter the halls a different student. A different woman.

It's been a few weeks since the incident at the art show, and I haven't spoken to anyone in the art department since my abduction. I didn't really have to because Hunter spoke to everyone who mattered, letting them know I was safe and apologizing for any drama he may have indirectly caused at the event.

Now, things can get back to normal. Well, besides the fact that I'm pregnant and that I still have a security detail sitting in a black town car outside, looking conspicuous as hell.

There are just some things that are non-negotiable in Hunter Middleton's world, and I'm just going to have to learn how to live with it.

So will Lena.

"Hi, Megan," a girl from my sketch class approaches me

as I take my normal seat, pulling out my supplies. "Glad to see you back."

Marta Nunez is not someone who spoke much to me before I became the most famous student in the program for all the wrong reasons, but I don't fault her for it. It's just human nature for some.

"Hey, Marta. Thanks so much," I reply, offering her a warm smile. I'm determined not to let this incident and people's reactions because of it define me.

Marta hesitates for a moment, her dark eyes searching mine. "I know it might be... weird to talk about it. But I wanted you to know that we, the class, were really worried about you. Not just because of the drama at the show, but genuinely concerned for your well-being."

A hint of tears gathers in the corners of my eyes, touched by what I believe is actual sincerity in her words. I hadn't expected this level of compassion from someone I barely knew. Someone who has probably said only about five complete sentences to me since I joined this class.

"Thank you, Marta. That means a lot."

She gives a nod, her fingers fidgeting with the hem of her shirt. "You're strong, Megan. Don't let anyone tell you otherwise."

Just then, our sketch instructor, Professor Whitman, enters the room, bringing with her a rush of cold air and a powerful aura of authority. She glances around, her sharp eyes eventually landing on me. "Megan," she calls out in her firm tone. "A moment, please?"

I gulp, packing away the slight relief I'd felt just moments ago from Marta's kind words. Rising from my seat, I approach the front of the class, and Marta sends me an encouraging nod as I pass her.

"I'm glad to see you back," Professor Whitman starts,

her tone softer than usual. "We've missed your talent in this room."

"I appreciate that, Professor," I say, taken aback.

"I've pulled you aside like this because the Dean asked me to. He's on his way and wanted to speak with you privately before class starts."

"Oh."

Dean Darwin walks with purpose down the marbled hall in his off-the-rack tan suit and brown sensible shoes. Usually, when I've seen him in the past, he was busy talking to another professor or staff member, never having much time for us students–except for his favorites, of course. This time his gaze seems focused straight ahead and on me. I grow tense, wondering what he's going to say.

"I'll leave you to it," Professor Whitman says. "Come back in when you're ready."

"Hello, Miss Taylor." the Dean greets me cordially, although his posture looks slightly uncomfortable.

"Hello, Dean Darwin."

"While I had a brief discussion with Mr. Middleton about your immediate welfare right after the incident at the showing, it's good to actually see you in the flesh. You don't look any worse for wear."

What an odd thing to say to a woman who's just been traumatized at a school-sponsored event.

"Yes, well, thanks to Mr. Middleton, I was found safe and sound."

"Right." He shuffles weight between both of his feet. "I just wanted to apologize for that. For not ensuring more security at the event. We never imagined something like that could happen, but nevertheless, we should have been more prepared."

Something about his apology feels forced and disingenuous. A part of me wonders if Hunter put him up to it.

"It's not your fault," I assure him. "No one could have foreseen something like that happening. I just hope it didn't ruin the showing for the rest of the students."

I have to admit that I'm being a little disingenuous myself. I already knew that only a few people who were paying attention realized anything was going on that evening. For the most part, the drama unfolding was kept under wraps from the rest of the guests while Hunter's security searched for me. No one was the wiser until someone reported the faint sound of gunshots, and soon after, they found me. By that time, most of the student pieces had been sold, including mine.

He nods, exhaling deeply. "I assure you it ruined nothing, and I want you to know that the college is here to support you in any way you need. Take things at your own pace."

While the Dean's sudden support of me is eyebrow-raising, it almost doesn't matter why he's doing it; I just accept that he is.

He sees me.

For the first time since the twisted triangle I've been stuck in with Ashley and Ricky, I feel a glimmer of hope that maybe, just maybe, things can truly be normal for me.

"Thank you, Dean. I appreciate the kind words. It's been a challenging time, but I'm very excited to get back to work and finish my courses."

"Speaking of your work, Megan, the Turlington Gallery was very interested in a few of your pieces. Unfortunately for them, they were already sold."

I gasp with excitement.

The Turlington Gallery is a prestigious art gallery

located in the Beverly Hills section of the city. They tend to feature local artists but established ones. The fact that they were at our showcase is already exciting, but they liked one of my pieces. That's extraordinary.

"I'm sorry I missed meeting the curator," I say, for the first time feeling the sting of what I actually missed out on when I was tied up in a basement.

"That's okay because they want to commission a piece."

"I'm sorry?" I ask, swallowing thickly.

"The gallery wants to commission a work from you. I don't know all the details, but that's what you'll meet with them to find out. Of course, you can bring any professor of your choosing to the meeting just so you're not in over your head. But I guarantee you this, Megan. This commission will be life-changing for you. You will end up being one of the most successful graduates of the university if this happens. Kudos to you."

I try not to cry, at least not in front of the Dean.

"Thank you, Dean."

Once he turns away, I pull my cell phone out of the side pocket of my cargo jeans and call the one person I think about when I'm this excited about anything.

"What's wrong?" Hunter answers grimly.

"Nothing."

"Then why are you calling me in the middle of class?"

"Hunter–"

"Speak, Megan, or I'm going to break the legs of your security detail." His voice tightens. "Is something wrong?"

"Stop threatening to do things I know you'd never do."

"You clearly don't know me," he growls.

"I'm calling to tell you something exciting."

"What is it?" His voice suddenly smooths out.

The Turlington Gallery wants to commission a piece from me.

"Congratulations."

"It's a big deal, Hunter," I say, wondering why he's not more excited for me, although excitement is not a common emotion I've ever seen from him.

"I know."

I pause for a moment.

"You had nothing to do with it, did you?"

"I'm good at a lot of things, Megan, but believe it or not, I'm not all-powerful. You secured the commission all on your own."

"I better have."

"Believe in your talent."

"I do! I just also believe in your need to control everything." I think about my exchange with the Dean.

"I've got a meeting in fifteen minutes. I'll see you later at the club."

"Okay." I smile. Happy that Hunter has changed his tune about me still working at the Blue Whiskey until I physically can't.

"And Megan?"

"Yes?"

"I'm proud of you, baby."

Chapter 45

An Unexpected Crossroads

Hunter

"What can I do to help?" I ask Megan, and I can tell by the expression on her face I'm only annoying her as she buzzes around the place, assigning tasks to people.

"I've got it." She smiles, patting the center of my chest with her hand.

I've given most of the people who work at the club the night off except for a few essential employees I'm paying to manage the party I'm giving for Lena at the club tonight. It's her birthday and while I would rather throw her something elaborate with all the bells and whistles in a hotel ballroom, Megan reminded me that Lena would probably hate an over-the-top celebration.

"Did she pick out something nice to wear?" I ask her. "I didn't see any credit card alerts from the credit card company saying that she shopped anywhere this week."

Megan tells one of the servers where she wants the

high-top tables placed in the main bar area, then turns back to me.

"That's because she doesn't want to use your money, Hunter."

"She's not independently wealthy, and I'm just trying to buy her a birthday gift."

"No, you're trying to make up for lost time, which is sweet, but if you want her to spend a little more money, then maybe you should pay her better," she chuckles, trying to make light of what is a serious dilemma, in my opinion.

Megan wraps her arms around my waist and embraces me tightly in a comforting way. She knows I've been struggling with how to make a connection with Lena but continues to assure me that "it will come naturally."

"Wait, forget I said that." She smiles. "You'll just pay her some ridiculous amount of money for being the club's cook."

I kiss Megan gently in the center of her forehead.

"That's the great thing about being the boss; I can pay whatever I want. This would be much easier if she'd go to college like you do."

"I'm a firm believer in not going to school until you really know what you want to study; otherwise, it's a waste of time and money."

"Is it too much to want my little sister to have a normal experience for once?" I bluster. "She's been struggling alone in foster care and homeless shelters for a long damn time. I was working my ass off back when she was a baby so that we'd have a better life. It hurts my heart that all of it was for nothing."

Her hand palms the side of my face. While her touch is always welcomed, it makes me uneasy to be this vulnerable in the open. My employees are watching, so I pull my head slightly back.

"I know you think I don't understand how you feel, but in many ways, I do. I really like your sister, and I want her to have an amazing future as well, but I'm just saying that if you push her too hard, you might scare her away for good."

"I'd never let that happen," I say, not liking where this conversation is headed.

"Okay, listen, maybe you should have Christian talk to her since Lena's future seems to be weighing so heavily on your mind. I've got to go check on the DJ and make sure she has everything she needs."

My hands tighten around her upper arms.

"Why the fuck would I need to talk to Christian about my nineteen-year-old sister, Megan?"

Her eyes blink rapidly.

I think she's nervous.

But why?

"I'm just saying that he's been the one who's been taking care of her the most. She trusts him."

"And she doesn't trust me?"

"That's not what I meant, Hunter."

"Megan, is there something you're not telling me?"

"No, babe." She checks her texts and scurries away. "We'll talk later. The DJ needs me, okay?"

Neon lights flash, casting colorful reflections on the sleek surfaces of the club. A special section stands out, lavishly adorned with silver and gold balloons, twinkling fairy lights, and a banner boldly proclaiming, "Happy 19th, Lena!". Megan did a great job planning this.

Lena looks happy, surrounded by many of the employees I gave the night off. It's nice that they chose to spend their evening here to celebrate with her. I'll never know if it's because they genuinely like her or if they're trying to impress me, but it doesn't matter. I'm just glad that she doesn't have to spend the entire evening surrounded by people she doesn't know besides my immediate circle.

It warms something inside of my cold chest to see her laughing and chatting animatedly with a few of the servers. I can't help but smile. She's dressed in a tasteful black mini dress with spaghetti straps that I've recently discovered, much to my horror, she thrifted from a local consignment shop. I'm not even mad, though. She looks lovely.

Yeah, my little sister's growing up.

While the evening has been a roaring success, I can't forget the exchange Megan and I shared earlier in the evening, which is why I've had my eyes on Christian all night.

The man has been staying in my house, he works for me, he's one of my only friends. Is there a connection he has with Lena that's impeding my ability to connect with her? Would she rather Christian be her big brother instead of me? Am I too aloof? Too cold?

I watch proudly as she dances to the thumping bass of the music in the center of the club with Megan, Naomi, and some of the servers who normally work here.

When the female DJ smoothly transitions into a popular tune, the crowd erupts in cheers, and the girls form a circle around Lena, egging her on to keep dancing.

From the corner of my eye, I notice Christian's gaze fixed on Lena, and I feel a twinge of unease. Immediately, I approach him. I'm not one for beating around the bush.

"You're staring, man."

"Was I? Damn, I just... got lost in the vibe."

But as the night wears on, I can't ignore the magnetic pull between Lena and Christian. It's in their stolen glances, the casual brush of hands, and the way she smiles when he speaks to her.

This is very fucking wrong.

Vaughn approaches me with two highball glasses of whiskey in either hand.

"Here."

I accept it but keep my eyes on Christian and how he is now actively avoiding any eye contact with Lena.

"You've noticed, haven't you?" Vaughn says to me.

"How long has this shit been going on?"

"Nothing is going on," he tries reassuring me. "I promise you."

"So what is it that I'm noticing, Vaughn?"

"Your sweet sister has a crush on our boy and for very good reason. Christian has been her rock since your world turned to shit. Let's not make a federal case out of it."

"She's nineteen."

"There are nineteen-year-old girls fucking their professors in college."

"You're not helping!" I growl.

Before I can get into it any further, a spectacular cake makes its entrance. "19" candles flicker brightly as we all gather around, singing "Happy Birthday." Lena looks elated, making a wish and blowing out the candles. It doesn't escape my notice how she gives Christian a brief glance afterward.

Once the applause dies down, I pull Christian to the side, and I feel the tension rolling off of him. He's not his usual laid-back self. That bothers me more than anything.

"How long have we been friends?" I ask him.

"A long time."

"I know all your secrets. I know where all the bodies are buried. That's because we're brothers."

"Of course."

"So let me be clear. That's my baby sister over there celebrating her nineteenth birthday. A girl who's literally been through so much alone out in the world without my protection. That is not how she's going to spend the next nineteen years of her life, I promise you that."

His eyes drop.

"That's great, man. You know I'm glad you two are reunited."

"I'm not saying you'd ever betray me, Christian, but if you are even the least bit tempted by her, then walk away now. Go home. I don't want to have to ever pick between the two of you because I think you know what my choice will be."

We stand there, locked in a stare-off, two old friends at an unexpected crossroads. The music blares, and the party continues, but there's a palpable shift in the air. Christian hasn't admitted or denied anything, but his silence speaks volumes.

This is going to be a fucking problem.

Paint And Sip...Well Kind Of

Megan

I step out of a long and luxurious shower to my cell phone, vibrating along the marble countertop. When the face of the caller flashes on the screen, my lips curve into a smile.

"Hey, baby daddy."

"Why are you naked at seven in the evening?" he practically growls.

"I was just grabbing a towel. One second."

"You're not answering me, Megan."

"I don't understand the question," I tease.

"It's not bedtime."

I can see him walking through the main room of the club and almost chuckle at the reactions of the servers preparing for opening. Their backs stiffen, and the looks on their faces grow very serious as if Hunter is some sort of military commander. It's hysterical. Little do they know how sweet he is...or rather, he can be.

"Your age is showing," I giggle.

He glares hard at me.

"It's girls night–remember? That's why Lena isn't coming in tonight or me."

"Right," his face softens. "I forgot."

"Totally understandable; you've got a lot going on."

He rakes a hand down his face clearly affected that he actually forgot about my plans. Hunter strives to have control over all of the moving parts in his life and part of control is remembering the important things. In his world, forgetting important pieces of information can lead to disaster, although forgetting that I'm hanging with the same women I always do to paint is not a life-or-death error.

"This is the whole paint and sip night, right?"

The girls and I have planned a relaxing night of painting, complete with wine and dinner. I will be having apple juice with my dinner, but it's still going to be a great time.

"Yep, I'm going to teach Naomi and Lena how to paint a high heel."

"A shoe?"

"Yep."

"Have you been working on your commission piece?"

"Of course I have, Paw-Paw," I tease, knowing he hates it whenever I give him a name that reminds him of his age.

"Megan–"

"Calm yourself. This is just a night for me not to have to worry about work, about you, or about my piece for the gallery. I just want to hang out with my girls and kick back."

"Right, of course, and I want you to do that as often as you want to. If it were up to me–"

"I wouldn't work at the Blue Whiskey anymore. I know, Hunter, you're like a broken record. But I think you and I both know that there's no completely safe place. I'll be just as safe at work as I am here tonight. The security dudes Vaughn hired are scared shitless of you."

That elicits a small smile from him, the one I find so sexy.

"Yeah?"

"Yep."

"Okay, well, have a good time tonight. I'll be home at the usual time."

"Kiss me when you get home."

"Right between your legs."

I chuckle as my nipples pebble at the mere thought of Hunter's mouth in between my legs. These pregnancy hormones are wild.

"I can't wait."

<hr>

I set up the large television to mirror what's displayed on my laptop. That way, Naomi and Lena can see exactly what they should be painting.

"Is that a Louboutin?" Lena asks about the image we're painting tonight.

"Yes, Naomi's favorite shoe brand." I grin.

"Aren't they expensive?"

"Yes, ma'am, they're high as hell but worth every penny," Naomi replies, taking a sip of her pinot noir in a long-stemmed, Olivia Pope kind of wine glass.

"How can you afford them?" Lena asks.

It's a reasonable question.

A few months ago, neither one of us could barely afford dinner, and now we live in one of the most expensive high-rise apartment buildings in downtown Los Angeles. But now that I have new information about Naomi's family, some of her expensive tastes make more sense.

"I, um– I can't."

"Then how do you know they're worth every penny?"

"I own one pair."

"Oh, really? Can I try them on? I think we may be the same size," Lena says animatedly.

"They're not here in LA. I had to leave them at my old house. I had to pack light when I moved out here."

"Oh, okay," Lena sounds disappointed, and I think of the conversation Hunter and I had last week.

"If you really want to try them or even buy a pair, you can, Lena. That's why Hunter gave you the credit card," I tell her.

"Oh, I wouldn't waste his money on frivolous things like expensive shoes. It's enough that I live in this building. My foster brother would shit his pants."

Lena now lives with Naomi in my old apartment downstairs now that I've moved in with Hunter.

"You don't feel guilty about your new life, do you, Lena?" Naomi probes. "It's not like you stole it from someone else. This is supposed to be your life. You were always Hunter's little sister."

"Maybe if I grew up as his sister, I'd be a different person and enjoy all of this wealth, but I didn't. It's very new for me."

"You'll make the adjustment," I tell her matter of factly because she's going to have to. Hunter won't rest until Lena accepts her place in his life. He just won't. "It'll just take some time."

"And who's this foster brother you're talking about? You never mentioned him before."

Lena offers up a small grin as she pops a small piece of bread spread with brie cheese in her mouth.

"He was in my last group home."

"What's the story with him?"

"No story—he was just the only kid in the house who ever looked out for me. I think I reminded him of someone from his old life."

Naomi and I give each other a knowing glance. With everything that's been going on around here, neither one of us has taken the time to talk to Lena about her past. We have no idea what she's been through or any clue as to what scars she may be carrying around.

"Do you still keep in contact with him?" I ask, knowing that she's been completely on her own for at least a year. "Does he know that you've found your biological brother?"

Her eyes flash open.

"Don't tell Hunter," she rushes to say.

"I won't," I quickly reassure her. "But why not?"

"Leo has his own life."

"I'm not sure I understand," I say.

"I get it," Naomi interjects. "You don't want Mr. Dark and Stormy all in your brother's business."

"Hunter is her brother," I say firmly, reminding everybody.

"I haven't talked to Leo in a while," she continues. "And I probably won't. There's no need for them to ever know about each other. They probably will never meet."

"So you're never going to talk to your foster brother again?" I ask incredulously. "Why? What did he do, Lena?"

"He didn't do anything. We just had a misunderstanding and I'm embarrassed about it."

"Enough to cut off someone who cares about you?"

A strange look crosses her face. One that tells me that

there are layers to Lena that none of us have yet to peel back.

"Yes," she says resolutely. "Cutting off people comes easy to me."

"Yep." Naomi nods her head as if she completely understands Lena's line of thinking. "Survival mode."

I take a gulp of my apple juice, pretending it's a nice glass of Pinot Grigio. "Let's paint."

An hour later, I've painted a damn good black Louboutin stiletto, Lena is tipsy and has made a good attempt at her pump, and Naomi is definitely drunk and gave up on painting fifteen minutes ago. Right now, she's singing along with the 90s radio station I selected on Hunter's fancy music sound system. She started with the Back Street Boys' *I Want It That Way*, then to *Loser* by Beck, and now she's (badly) serenading us with *No Scrubs* by TLC.

"How do you know all these songs?" Lena laughs as she eggs Naomi on.

"My mom can never stop talking about the 90s. It was her favorite decade."

"You never talk about your mom," Lena says, and it's obvious she's feeling a lot more comfortable talking now that she has a few glasses of wine in her. "Do you look like her?"

"People say I'm a perfect blend of my parents, but that's because I think they don't want to hurt my dad's feelings. Honestly, I think I'm the spitting image of my mama."

A moment of clarity strikes me like a thunderbolt.

The three of us are almost like three wounded baby birds. I didn't know it about Naomi until recently but it makes perfect sense why the three of us get along so well. We all have a great deal of pain in our pasts that none of us wants to deal with.

While Hunter provided me with some sort of closure by dealing with my horrible family, I still haven't done the real work of dealing with the trauma of it. I have nightmares about them, about what they made me do, and mostly about what kind of mother I'm going to be because of it.

Naomi suddenly hits a note that almost makes me spit out my mouth full of juice. The girl can't sing to save her life, but I can't lie— she definitely tries to, like no one is listening.

"You better sing the song, Naomi!" I applaud and Lena joins me as we stand to join in the chorus. There were three members in the group, after all.

When we finish, all three of us collapse on the cloud-like sofa in the living room and laugh with whole-hearted joy...until Naomi's phone rings.

The moment she sees the name on her screen, her face drops, and any euphoria she may have been feeling while singing is quickly extinguished.

"What's wrong?" I ask her on pins and needles, already fearing the answer.

And in the smallest voice I've ever heard my extroverted roommate and friend ever use, she tells us, "My fiancé."

Chapter 47

Daddy Problems

Megan

Lena and I do the work of pretending to clean up our paint and sip as Naomi takes her phone call. Naomi's body language is strikingly different than her normal presentation. She is sitting stoically on the floor with her back up against the sofa, knees up, staring down at her red-painted toes. I've never wanted to eavesdrop on someone's conversation as badly as I want to right now.

After ten excruciating minutes, she ends the call, and Lena and I immediately stop what we are doing.

"Well?" I say as Naomi continues to stare into space. "Are you going to finally talk about what's going on with you and what the hell that conversation was all about?"

"Am I missing something?" Lena asks, staring between the two of us.

"My father is in trouble."

"Your father?" Lena echoes.

"But who is your father, Naomi?" I ask, my mouth in a serious line.

Her head pops up, and she looks directly at me.

"You know?"

"Not much, apparently," I say.

"Know what?" Lena demands.

"Naomi has not been totally truthful about who she is," I say.

"Does Hunter know?" Naomi whispers.

"Is that all you care about right now, if Hunters knows? It sounds like you have bigger fish to fry than Hunter Middleton."

"Did he tell you, Megan?"

"He told me your real last name—Fabre. He told me that your family is from Louisiana and not wherever the hell you said you were from when we first met. He told me that your family is powerful down there and definitely dangerous."

"Holy crap!" Lena says, covering her mouth with a hand in shock.

"He told you a lot," Naomi says regretfully. "Maybe too much."

"No, Naomi, you didn't tell me enough or rather anything at all. I've been friends with a virtual stranger. I don't know anything about you. It's fucking weird."

"How long have you known?"

"Not long enough."

"And let me guess, your baby's daddy doesn't trust me now?"

"Do you blame him? He thinks you're up to something."

"Megan, you know me better than anyone else in my life. I am not up to anything. Your boyfriend thinks too highly of himself if he thinks that any of this is about him."

"Fiancé," Lena corrects Naomi but I give her the big sister stare.

"Not now, Lena," Naomi scolds.

"Then tell us what is going on. If we're friends like you say we are, like I've always believed we were, then tell me about this fiancé of yours."

"His name is Gabriel, and I've known him my entire life. Our families hate each other."

"Then why is he your fiancé?" Lena asks, rightly confused. "Or are you two like star-crossed lovers or something?" she asks a little too excitedly.

"Trust me, we're not star-crossed. We don't like each other."

"Then why does he have your phone number? I saw the call come in. You have his number saved," I say, sounding like a Nancy Drew novel.

"We have one thing in common. Neither of us wants to marry the other. So, he was the one who helped me get out of New Orleans undetected. I went to Texas first, then Mexico, and finally, I settled in Los Angeles. He's the only person who I kept in contact with from my old life and that's only because it was the only way he would help me. It was part of the deal."

"Why would you have to marry someone you don't want to in this day and age?" Lena asks.

"My life in New Orleans is different than the normal one a person lives. We may live in a modern-day age, but familial expectations of me were established long before women had a voice in our family."

"Yes, but you have a voice now."

"No," Naomi shakes her head. "I don't. There are sacrifices people made from every generation in my family so that my family could thrive in America. I am expected to honor those sacrifices."

"By marrying a man, you don't love?"

"By marrying a man who understands the sacrifice," she

says in a voice that is not hers. It's clearly something that's been said to her by someone in her family, probably many times.

"Do you have brothers or sisters, Naomi?" Lena asks.

"A brother."

"And you two aren't close?"

Naomi's posture changes, becoming increasingly uncomfortable.

"He was murdered ten years ago."

"I'm so sorry," I tell her, but she continues.

"By the same family, my parents want me to marry into."

"Wait, what? Gabriel's family?"

"That's right."

"Oh my God. No wonder you don't want to go through with it. I mean, there are lots of reasons why you wouldn't want to, but that's got to be top of the list. Does this Gabriel guy know this?"

"He has never claimed or denied his family's part in my brother's death, which makes me hate him all the more. He tries to act like he's Switzerland in all things when you can't be Switzerland. You have to pick a side. You just have to."

I place a hand on Naomi's shoulder as I watch her become increasingly upset.

"You're a hundred percent right, babe, but what was the call tonight about? Does he call you often?"

"He called to warn me."

"About what?"

"My father knows where I am."

Just as Hunter predicted.

"And what does that mean?"

She emits a heavy sigh.

"It probably means that he's coming to get me."

"To do what?"

"To take me back home. To force me to do my duty. Be a good wife. A good...mafia wife."

"What about your mother? What does she think?" Lena asks, her tone filled with worry.

"My mother is a prime example of who my father wants me to be. She married a man chosen for her. She bore him a son and a daughter. And she keeps her mouth shut. Trust me, she does not have my back. If anything, she'll probably pack my father a bagged lunch for the flight he's going to take to come here."

"Why are the three of us such damaged goods?" Lena whispers, plopping down on the couch beside Naomi.

"We're not damaged goods," I defend vigorously. "I'm pregnant and getting married to the greatest man in the world, your brother. You are making food that everyone raves about at the Blue Whiskey, and Naomi is going to be the perfect celebrity hairstylist. She just needs that one client."

Naomi looks at me and offers a half smile.

"I am never going to be a hair stylist, Megan. It was a fool's dream thinking that I could ever outrun my father. I bet he's known where I've been since I got here. Hell, I bet Gabriel was the one who told him. I know my dad. In his mind, he's let me sow my wild oats like Eddie Murphy did in the movie *Coming To America*, but now it's time to come home and do my duty."

"Your father wouldn't hurt you, would he?" I ask, considering the gravity of the situation.

"No, but he'd definitely hurt anyone who stands in his way."

"Do you want me to ask Hunter for help? He seems to know a lot–"

"No!" Naomi exclaims. "I don't want Hunter anywhere near this. My father will perceive it as a threat. And a threat to Hunter is a threat to you. And if anything happened to you, to either of you, because of all that I've kept from you guys– I'd never forgive myself."

"But no one should have to get married against their will. This is insane!" I protest.

"Actually, Megan," a deep voice interrupts as he walks through the front door of our apartment. "It's none of our business."

I stand to face Hunter.

Hands seated on both of my hips.

"My best friend is our business."

"Only for the next twenty-four hours."

"And what happens in twenty-four hours?"

"Mr. Marc Fabre will land at the Los Angeles airport, and when he does, I don't want you or Lena to be any part of that business. I won't fucking stand for it."

Chapter 48

A Delicious Distraction

Megan

My back bows off the pillow-soft surface of our bed, and my body is so arched that the top of my head is almost flush against the mattress. My legs are bent at the knees and spread wide. My lips slightly parted.

While I realize that this moment is a strategic tactic on my fiancé's part to distract me from worrying about Naomi's arranged marriage predicament, God knows I don't mind it.

Hunter's mouth, that exquisite lush mouth of his, is right in between my legs— caressing my core, sending me straight to orgasmic bliss.

"This is a fucking fantastic way to start the day," I say after my last sweet release, totally spent.

"*Fucking* fantastic, huh?" His rhetorical question is dripping in judgment. I don't usually curse unless I'm angry or trying to seriously punctuate my point.

"I thought this was a no-judgment zone?" I ask, affectionately sliding one of my hands into the roots of his scalp.

"It is." He smiles against my skin, placing small kisses along my inner thighs and hips. "Not judging. How are you feeling?"

"Me? I feel spectacular."

"No nausea or anything?"

"Should I be concerned that you sound a little disappointed? Do you want me to be sick?"

"Don't be ridiculous, Megan. I just read that nausea is a sign of a healthy pregnancy."

"Ahh, I see. Well, you worry too much. In fact, I was just telling the girls the other day that there's nothing about my body that actually *feels* pregnant. Nothing but this. I have this insatiable need for you and everything we just did all the time, especially in the mornings."

"I guess hormones are a wonderful thing."

"Thank you, Dr. Spock." I twist my mouth into a sarcastic smile. "I know that it's hormones driving my need for you."

He stops kissing my thigh and looks up at me with a serious look on his face."Let's not give hormones all of the credit. It's obvious you want me because I'm fantastic in bed."

"Oh, is that what you've heard?"

"That's what I know." He smirks. "And every time you come for me, I'm assured that the rumors are true."

"Oh, for Pete's sake. Could you be any more full of yourself?"

Hunter stands, and immediately, I miss his warmth between my legs.

"Where are you going?" I ask, wishing we could lounge around in bed all day.

"To feed the growing baby inside you."

"But I'm not hungry."

"The baby is hungry."

"Let me rephrase, we're not hungry."

"Who are you kidding? You say you don't feel pregnant, but it seems like you're always hungry these days," he smiles.

And he's right. I could absolutely eat a freakin' bacon and egg on a bagel right now, but it's just that I don't want him to leave.

I want more of us.

I stare in awe at the chiseled man standing in front of me and rake my eyes along the powerful dips and valleys of his muscular chest and abdomen, which leads me to one of my favorite parts of him.

"I don't think we should eat until I take care of that," I say, referring to his rather large and probably very frustrated dick.

"I'm fine, Megan."

"Aww, but it looks like it hurts."

Hunter won't say it, but I think he's a little skittish about having sex with me, and I'm not sure if it's because I've recently been shot or if it's because I'm pregnant with his baby. Lately, he tries to satisfy me with oral sex but then suddenly has all these things to do when I'm ready to go to *pound town*...like get breakfast.

"My dick is always hard for you. It'll eventually settle down." He talks about his penis like it lives in its own separate area code.

"But why would we need it to settle down?" I ask, my voice practically purring as I slowly crawl across the bed toward him. "When I can give it what it needs. What you both need."

"Megan–"

"What?"

"Stop crawling like that?"

I chuckle to myself.

"Like what?"

"Like we're in the middle of a goddamn porn movie."

"Aren't we? What you just did to me was deliciously pornographic."

"And I'll do it again for you another time, but right now, we eat."

By this point, I've crawled to the end of the bed where he's standing. His stance is defiant, but his eyes tell me something completely different. His eyes are practically smoldering, and my skin feels hot. I'm so close I can practically taste him.

So, I decided that I would.

Still, on my hands and knees, it's easy to guide the engorged length of Hunter with just my hungry mouth. I open wide and lean forward, easily guiding his hard penis along the wet warmth of my tongue.

"Fuck, Megan," he says in a guttural tone that I wasn't expecting but am excited to hear.

Keeping one hand on his head and one in my hair, he grips the roots hard as he rhythmically strokes himself inside my mouth.

My pussy pulses and aches.

There's something about giving head that turns me on just as much as the receiver.

"You're not playing fair at all," Hunter accuses in a voice thick with want.

"Don't be afraid to fuck me," I tell him, matching the depth of his tone. "You won't break me."

Suddenly Hunter pulls out of my mouth, and I worry for a moment that my frankness has pissed him off.

"Stick out your tongue," he orders with a fierce growl.

Oh wait, he's not pissed at all. This is about to get freaky.

I do as instructed, and his face contorts, eyes fiery, as he ejaculates into my mouth.

"You see what you made me do," he spits angrily.

"I made you come," I laugh in a throaty way as I swallow his release down.

"And now you're going to make me come again." He advances himself onto the bed. "Stay right where you are. Strong hands and knees. Ass up."

Hunter sounds angry.

But in the best way possible.

"Finally," I mutter under my breath, but I think he hears me and gives one of my ass cheeks a smack.

"Quiet. All I want to hear from you is yes and more, and thank you."

I lower my head and smile.

"Yes, sir."

He bends over me, wrapping one hand around to palm my pussy and the other to guide his dick inside of it from behind. I almost lose my breath when he quickly fills me to the hilt.

"Is this what you want?" he asks in an almost bitter tone as he pounds my wet pussy, my thighs jiggling.

"*Yesssss!*" I hiss. "Thank you."

"Why is your pussy so wet?" Hunter growls out the rhetorical question as if my vagina is one of the seventh wonders of the world. "And tight. And perfect."

"We're perfect," I say, white-knuckling the sheets as he adjusts his position, stroking me at an angle that he knows is one of my favorites.

With his fingers still working my clit, I tumble into my second delicious release of the morning.

"*Ooh*," I cry out.

"Megan." My name rolls off Hunter's tongue in the most reverent way as he releases inside of me with a powerful grunt.

The two of us collapse softly into the sheets and in each other's arms, both of us still breathing hard. As we cuddle, Hunter plays with a few strands of my hair and kisses me once on my forehead.

"Are you okay?" he asks, gingerly skimming his fingers across the scar on my abdomen.

"I'm better than okay." I turn my body further into his embrace. "How about you?"

"I think you're going to kill me before the baby is born if we keep this up."

"It only gets better, doesn't it?" I say with awe.

"You're not fully healed, Megan. We have to be more careful."

The area of my wound is admittedly sore, but there's no way I want him treating me with kid gloves.

"I love you," I tell him, knowing that emotional confessions of this kind often stop him dead in his tracks.

"That's not what we're talking about," he bristles.

"I disagree," I say, leisurely running my fingers down the center of his chest. "I think love is at the center of everything we talk about."

He doesn't respond but simply bends his forehead to meet mine, and with this simple gesture, I know exactly how he feels.

"I underestimated my opponent and overestimated my power in this city, Megan. I failed you. But I'm not going to allow that to happen again. Not while I still draw breath."

"You can't promise me that," I tell him.

"Do you doubt me?" His head draws back as if I've smacked him. "Do you not trust me anymore?"

"That's not it, Hunter. I'm saying that you can't promise that I'll never get hurt again. The Blue Whiskey has a reputation and a notoriously powerful owner. There's no getting around that. And because of that, people will always come after you and sometimes that may mean indirectly through me. I've accepted that truth, and I still choose to stay. To love you."

"You've been talking to Lars," he grumbles. "I can tell."

"Does that even sound like something Lars would say?"

"His beliefs. Your words."

"Does it matter?"

"Yes."

I'm not snitching on Lars or Parker...ever. Outside of Lena, they're probably my only true allies in Hunter's inner circle. Vaughn and Christian are nice guys, but they have Hunter's best interest at heart, not mine.

"My beliefs." I place my palm against the side of his face. "My words."

He kisses me gently on the lips and I close my eyes as our tongues do a delicate dance around each other.

"You are everything to me, Megan. I know I don't tell you enough but I love you, and I love the little human you're growing inside of you. You are the only things that matter."

"Well, there's Lena."

"That's different. Of course, I love her, but we don't really know each other yet. Hell, I don't even think she likes me."

"But you're working on that," I assure him.

"Yeah, I am."

I finally manage to free myself from the warmth of our

shared bed and use the bathroom. When I check the time, I realize I need to make a call.

"Ooh, I need to call Naomi," I say as I enter back into the bedroom, tip-toeing on the cold hardwood floors. I notice when his gorgeous face drops.

"Why?" he asks incredulously.

"You know why. She's going to meet her scary ass father in like three hours, and I want to make sure she's okay."

"You already know she's not going to be okay, but there's nothing you or I can do about it. It's none of our business."

I exhale a long sigh.

"When have you ever cared about something not being your business?"

"She lied to you."

"She withheld some things."

"You thought she was your friend."

"The fact that she is from a complicated family doesn't change anything between us. She's still my friend."

"Don't call her." His voice hardens.

I stare at him cautiously, standing against the bathroom doorway with my cell phone in my hand.

"You've spoken to her father, haven't you?"

His eyes dart to the floor.

"Hunter?"

"I don't expect you to understand the intricacies of my business, but I cannot allow a man with Fabre's reputation to land in Los Angeles and not recognize his presence."

"He's that powerful?"

"He's very...connected."

"Will he hurt her?"

"I don't think so. He seems to care about her a great deal. I'm not sure why Naomi has cut him off like she has, but he seems genuinely worried. I assured him that she was safe."

I take a moment to digest what he's said and what he's not saying.

"And if something happened to her while she lived in this apartment building, would her father blame you?"

"Probably."

"Which is why you would rather she go back home with him."

"Naomi is not a complication I was expecting, nor do I want. If it wasn't for your friendship with her, I would have handed her over to her father on a silver platter a long time ago."

"Hunter–"

"You want honesty from me, right?"

"Always."

"Well, there you have it."

I stare at my phone again and reluctantly place it back on the charger. This is her father she's meeting, not some evil overlord. Hunter's right. Naomi is my friend, but she has a right to privacy and a right to make decisions without my input. If she needs me, she'll call me.

She's nobody's wallflower.

Chapter 49

Tying Up Loose Ends

Hunter

The Blue Whiskey always feels different to me during daylight hours versus in the evening. Maybe because the city feels differently at night, too, it's dark and dangerous and unforgiving. Something I learned quickly growing up on the streets of Los Angeles.

My sister approaches my table in simple black pants and a t-shirt with an apron tied around her waist. She's holding a large plastic platter of assorted hors d'oeuvres that look damn good.

"I thought you all could try some of these. I'm thinking about adding some of them to the menu."

Lena's smile is wider than normal and the reason why doesn't escape me. The fucker to my left is the reason why.

"It all looks really great, Lena. Thank you," Christian says.

I give him a side eye which silently communicates to him to shut the fuck up.

"Thanks, Lena," I say. "Add whatever you think is good to the menu."

"Ooh, stuffed mushrooms are my fav'," Vaughn says as he grabs a cocktail napkin and helps himself.

"I thought you'd decide," she says carefully to me. "Maybe pick your favorites?"

Of course.

I'm an idiot.

She wants my approval.

"Right," I agree. "Then why don't you just leave the platter on the table so I can sample it while we finish our meeting."

"Okay, then." She offers me a slight smile, avoiding Christian's eyes. "Just don't let your friends eat everything."

"I won't."

"I'll leave you to it then," she says to the three of us, walking confidently away, and I swear if he weren't my best friend, I'd jab a knife into one of Christian's eye sockets — he's clearly watching her ass.

"She's getting comfortable with you," Vaughn notices. "That's good."

I nod quietly, waiting to hear what Christian is going to add, but he doesn't say a thing, only making me feel more uneasy about his obvious growing feelings for my sister. I've been trying to lean into Megan's advice for me to not obsess about something that hasn't even happened between them yet but it's hard as hell.

"Damn, this mushroom is good," Vaughn comments looking between the two of us with newfound curiosity. "What the fuck is wrong with you two now?"

"Nothing," Christian says.

"This isn't what we do," Vaughn says. "The three of us

have never lied to each other, and that sounded like a big one."

"I didn't ask you here to talk about whatever issues Christian and I may or may not have," I say in a steely voice. "I brought you here to help me tie up loose ends so we can all move forward. I've got a business to run, and you two have lives you need to get back to. You can't babysit me forever."

"And so I'm just supposed to ignore that there is tension among us?" Vaughn asks, chewing his food obnoxiously.

"Not between us," I correct him. "It's between me and Christian, and for once in your life, it's none of your concern."

"Chris?" Vaughn looks over at Christian, who gives me a once-over before answering.

"Hunter's right. It's between me and him. Let's drop it."

"Well, you two better work it out fast. This uncertainty doesn't sit right with me. We work better when we're a tight unit."

"We are a tight unit," Christian says resolutely. "There's nothing to worry about, Vaughn," he says, grabbing a chicken wing covered in some sort of sticky honey-colored sauce. "Besides, why are you pretending like you don't already know what's going on?"

"Like Hunt said, it's none of my business, right?" he scoffs. "Well, all right then, gentlemen. Let's talk about tightening up loose ends."

By the time we've finished our platter of appetizers and a round of drinks, the three of us have figured out a plan to assure my business associates that the Blue Whiskey is safe and that I'm in complete control of all of my business affairs. While we still haven't figured everything out regarding who may have had a hand in Jonathan's ill-fated plan to destroy me, it doesn't matter. Whoever it is knows now that I'll crush anyone who comes for me, and more than likely, they have made the smart decision to rethink their position.

We agree that while the club will always remain my central hub, I should consider moving myself and Megan to another location. The one thing I always hoped was to keep private where I lived, but now that they have violated my home, we're fair game for any random Tom, Dick, and Harry who doesn't know any better. And since I know Megan will protest raising a baby under the protection of armed guards, my only alternative is to relocate us.

"What will you do about the friend?" Vaughn asks about Naomi.

"She can stay at the apartment if she chooses, but I'm sure her family will have a few things to say about that."

"Not sure Megan is going to like that," Christian says.

"You're right. She won't. But I can stand a little heat at home as long as I'm protecting it."

Christian's eyes harden, knowing that my comment was partly for his benefit.

"How's everything over here?" Lena approaches again.

"Great," Vaughn answers. "The food was delicious, Lena. Where'd you learn to cook like that?"

Her lips straighten into a line as if the question has made her suddenly uncomfortable.

"In the shelter."

Shit.

I hadn't asked Lena much about her life before she came back into mine, partly because there hasn't been time for heart-to-heart conversations, and I guess the other reason is that I didn't want to really know.

"Well, they taught you well, girl. I'm sure Hunt is going

to have a tough time picking what items to put on the menu."

"Yep," Christian agrees. "It was all really good."

"I think there's room for them all to go on the menu," I say.

"We're not a restaurant, Hunter," Lena says as if she's reminding me about what I already know. "We only have the capability of serving a few items a night."

"Why?" I ask her, pulling another chair to the table for her to sit down.

"Well, it's a kitchen designed for just a few people to work in. You don't have the room for a full kitchen staff. Plus, it's expensive. Keeping your menu streamlined to a few bestselling items is the best approach for a place like this."

I raise an eyebrow, delighted that Lena has an opinion about how the kitchen should be run. It means that she's starting to feel a part of it. Sometimes, the Blue Whiskey has that effect on people.

"Just my opinion, of course," she adds.

"You're allowed to have an opinion at this table," Christian says, and I give both him and Vaughn a look that tells them that I want them to leave. I need to talk to Lena alone. I can't put this off any longer.

Without another word, the two of them rise from their seats.

"I have to call my divorce lawyer," Vaughn says.

"And I'm going to make sure he asks all the right questions," Christian says. "Or she'll take his ass to the cleaners."

Now, it's just the two of us at Table 21, staring at each other with a bit of reserve. Lena blinks a few times with a quiet unease that I'm learning is part of her personality. In time, I hope that will change, at least when she's around me.

"Lena–"

"Yes?"

"Can you tell me what you remember about your childhood?"

"You mean how I came to be in the foster care system?"

"Yes, do you remember any of that, or do you know from some other way?"

"I was told by a social worker that my parents were deceased. I wasn't told how they died. Based on the records that were shared with me, I was placed into the system at two years old. I lived in several decent foster homes over my elementary school years until I ended up in a group home at twelve."

I stop her there.

"Why were you placed in a group home?"

"Most families don't want to bother with a teenager, and my foster mother at that time was older and having health issues."

"So she just gave you up?"

"It was never a permanent situation. I knew that."

She makes the statements as if they're just simple facts about her past, but I can hear the pain in them even if she can't.

"And the group home?"

"Was...hard."

My stomach hardens as her eyes sink to the floor.

"Why?"

"It wasn't a living situation that I was used to."

"Did someone hurt you there?" My jaw tenses.

"There was a hierarchy, and I wasn't at the top of it."

Her body shifts in her seat. This is making her wildly uncomfortable, but I've been avoiding asking the questions for so long that I have to move forward.

"How long were you there?"

"I managed to stay for three years, and then I left."

"And went where?"

"I was on the streets for four months when I met Kurt."

My stomach twists in a tight knot.

My kid sister was homeless?

"Who is he?"

"Kurt was a friend and an advocate for the homeless. He spotted me in a coffee shop and approached me with a hot tea, a breakfast sandwich, and information about a local shelter."

"You've never mentioned him before."

"He passed away when he had a fatal asthma attack."

"Oh, I'm sorry."

"Anyway, I was lucky. You hear about shelters being very dangerous places, especially for women, and they can be, but Kurt and a few other people at the shelter looked out for me. I ended up staying there and getting a job in the kitchen as my way of giving back to the kindness of so many people who I met there. That's where I met Billy."

"And he told you about the possibility of working here."

"Yep."

"You know, we could go on a talk show with this story." I smile. "What are the chances that the little sister I've been looking for half of my life walks through my front door on her own?"

"Yeah, it is a wild coincidence."

"Hey, maybe it's Mom pulling strings up there."

"Maybe."

"I know you don't remember her, and she definitely had her issues, but she loved the hell out of you. She just could never catch a break, you know?"

"Yeah."

I want to touch Lena's hand, maybe to comfort her in some way, but that may be a little strange for both of us. I don't really do comfort, and I don't think she does either.

"I know I've said this, and maybe Megan has to, but I need you to know that I looked hard for you once I realized that you didn't die in the fire."

"I know you did."

"I hate that you had such a hard life."

"You're not responsible for any of it, Hunter. You have to realize that."

"But it was–"

I'm startled when Lena places a hand on mine, but I make sure to keep mine still and benefit from her touch.

"I know it was bad people who set our house on fire, Hunter, but you were just a kid yourself. You had no idea what they'd do. And don't worry about me holding any of it against you because up until a few months ago, I didn't even know you existed. I'm just grateful to have you in my life. That's the truth."

My head hangs for a moment, shielding my sweet sister from the emotion welling up inside of me. Then, I quickly realize that she deserves to see my emotions. I at least owe her that.

And so I lift my head.

"Thank you, baby sis'. I think I really needed to hear that."

She stands, leans over, and gives me a chaste kiss on the cheek.

"Not any more than I really needed to say it."

In this moment I feel the connection between us shift. This was a long overdue conversation we needed to have without the interference of anyone else, and damn, it feels good. It feels so great that I consider leaning in for a hug when I notice Parker approaching with a look of dread that I know all too well.

"What now?"

Chapter 50

Something Is Off

Megan

I'm in a relationship with a complicated man. I've known that for quite a while now, yet he still manages to surprise me with some of his decisions. This time, he came home, took a shower, poured himself a scotch, and then proceeded to tell me that we would be moving out of our luxurious penthouse apartment to an undisclosed location in a week.

I mean...what in the actual fuck?

I'm pregnant, and I like this place. I don't want to move.

"This is not what I signed up for, Hunter," I tell him, attitude etched in the forehead lines of my face.

"I realize that this isn't ideal timing, but this is what's best."

"What's best?" I say, rubbing my growing belly. "Best for whom?"

"For all of us."

"When did you make this decision? I didn't even realize that moving was even a consideration."

"I promise you it's going to be a nice place, nicer than this one."

"Do you really think I care about that?" I scoff. "What I care about is that you've made a decision about my life without even consulting me. Is this what I have to look forward to for the rest of my life if I marry you?" I ask, staring down at my engagement ring. "Does me wearing this ring mean that I'm supposed to say yes to whatever you say?"

"If you marry me?" His face hardens.

"Yeah, if!" I am sure to punctuate the word and then I begin to feel slightly queasy.

"Calm down, Megan." He notices.

"You want to tell me how to feel as well?"

"Megan, this is not a big deal. We were never going to raise a family in this building anyway."

"Uh, we weren't?"

"Don't you want a backyard for our kid, maybe a view of the water or a house nestled in the Hollywood Hills?"

"I am perfectly happy with what we have now and this is the first I'm hearing that you aren't."

"My happiness is not the issue. Your safety is."

"Is that how you're going to try to win every argument we have? By throwing the word safety in the mix and hoping that shuts down anything further from me?"

"This is not me trying to win arguments."

"Please," I suck my teeth. "All you ever do is try to win arguments with everyone in your life including me."

Hunter takes another swallow of his drink and clanks the glass on the kitchen island.

"We're moving and that's final. I've already settled on the house and Parker and Lars are at your disposal for the week. They'll help us with whatever we need including managing the team the moving company sends over."

"I need a drink," I huff, completely exasperated with the direction this conversation is going–which is nowhere. He really doesn't get it.

"You're pregnant."

"I know that! I didn't say I was going to have a drink, I just said that I want one."

"When do you want to go by the place so you can see it?"

"Funny, you asked me if I wanted a house in the hills or by the beach but it appears as if you've already made the decision and bought it. So what the hell do you need me for?"

His eyes lower for a split second as if he's finally ashamed of what he's done.

"You're right but I wanted to move quickly on this particular property. It's in the Pacific Palisades area and a gorgeous piece of real estate. We have ocean views and a gorgeous neighborhood. It's far enough away from the club and perfect for children."

"Sounds utterly boring."

"You haven't even seen it."

"I need to be closer to downtown, closer to the art galleries, or did you forget that I'm trying to build a career?"

"We're only thirty minutes away from downtown LA. Lars can probably have you anywhere you want to go in twenty. He'll be your personal driver and security from now on."

"Oh, is that right? Another decision was made *for* me without consulting me. Wonderful," I say acerbically.

"Megan–"

Hunter moves toward me as if he's coming in for an embrace.

"I need a minute," I cut him off by throwing my hand up in front of his chest. "Your assumption that I'm going to just fall in line with anything you say is frustrating, Hunter. You've always been the one with all of the power in this relationship, but it feels like you're throwing it around like a big bag of dicks."

I grab my brown leather purse that's sitting on a nearby chair and walk into the elevator.

"Megan," he calls for me, sounding somewhat nervous.

"I'll be back," I promise. "I just need some air."

"Parker brought me home and is still downstairs in the lobby. Let him take you wherever you want to go."

"I'm just going for a walk. I don't need him to take me anywhere."

As soon as the elevator doors close, the tears roll down my face. I'm not sure if they are tears of sadness or frustration, probably a little of both.

When I finally reach the lobby of our building, I don't see Parker and figure he's probably sitting in the car waiting to be told he can end for the day from Hunter.

After the attempt on Hunter's life, he hired his security to work the lobby entrance of our building, but I noticed that the guy who's usually down here isn't at the desk either. A foreboding feeling crawls along my spine.

Something is off.

I stand at the locked glass doors of the building and look outside for a moment to see if I can spot either Parker or the security dude.

I can't find either of them, but what I do see is a large black Audi with tinted windows and the silhouette of two people in the backseat arguing.

I'd know that nose anywhere.

It's Naomi.

Immediately, I exit the building and knock on the window, fearing that she's in trouble. As I wait for a window to roll down, the driver gets out of the car.

He's a formidable-looking man with a thick black beard and cold dark eyes.

"Can I help you?" He says with a distinct southern dialect that reeks of danger.

"I want to speak to Naomi?"

I point to the backseat.

"You have the wrong car."

I squint my eyes and watch as the two people continue to talk to each other, and I am more sure than ever that I have the right person. I know her profile. I know my friend. But maybe her real name isn't Naomi? Could that be it?

"The woman in that car is a friend of mine. I recognize her. I just want to talk to her."

"Can you step away from the car, miss?" He says, asking the question in a very rhetorical fashion.

"I'm standing outside my home where you happened to be parked. You can't make me leave the area."

The surly man presses the ear pod in his ear and takes a call. He grunts an "okay" to whoever is on the other end and then suddenly gives me the oddest look.

After that, things happen at breakneck speed. The man lunges toward me while simultaneously grabbing me around the waist with one arm and placing the opposite hand over my mouth.

I kick out my legs and they flail in the air.

I scream against his calloused hand, "Help!" My cries muffled.

I try reaching backward with my fists so I can gouge his eyes out or at least fight my way out of his grasp.

But it's all to no avail.

It doesn't take him long to pull me into the passenger seat of the vehicle and lock the doors.

I'm breathing heavily, tears streaming down my face, when I notice that Noemi and another strange man are staring stoically at me.

"Noemi!" I cry. "What's going on?"

"Quiet," the piece of garbage next to me says as he lifts a hand so close to my face that I'm positive it's a warning of something much more sinister if I don't shut my mouth.

"I'm sorry," is all she says as she bends her head down in a completely defeated way. The usual light in her eyes dimmed to almost pure darkness.

Now that I look closely, I notice there's a strong resemblance between Naomi and the man next to her. This must be her father. The man she's been avoiding all this time. The man Hunter warned me about. He's watching me with an off-putting sort of curiosity.

"Are you a friend of my daughter's?" The man asks me, and Naomi's eyes widen. I think she's trying to communicate something she may want me to say or not to say but I don't know what it is— so I just go with the truth.

"Yes," I answer with an obvious quiver in my voice.

"The roommate, right?"

"Yes, that's me."

"Perfect," he says, giving a nod to the driver. "She'll need someone to stand up for her at the wedding."

Wait...what?

The car makes a turn onto a familiar ramp near the apartment that leads to an interstate highway.

"Where are you taking me?" I ask the man, two seconds away from a full-fledged panic attack.

"You say you're Naomi's friend, then you should attend her wedding. My daughter was rude not to invite you in the first place. Please accept my apology on her behalf."

Is this man on drugs?

I look at Naomi for answers but mostly for help, but she doesn't say one single word.

Not one.

"My fiancé will worry if I just leave town without him knowing," I say, cursing at myself for leaving the house without taking my cell phone.

"Perhaps then he'll understand how it feels."

"Understand how what feels?"

"He harbored my daughter in his apartment without my or her fiancé's knowledge or consent. Imagine how worried we were about our Josephine."

"Josephine?" The man laughs mockingly.

"My daughter is quite the weaver of tales. This life she has carved out for herself out west is a complete lie. She is not a hairdresser or makeup artist or whatever those folks call themselves, and Naomi is not her real name. Her roots are in the bayou. Her name is Josephine Fabre, and she is getting married in less than five days to the love of her life. A wedding that you will attend and witness since she decided to bring you and your fiancé into this."

As we grow closer to the airport, full-on panic settles into my chest, and I feel nauseous. I've got to get out of this car.

"Sir, I'm pregnant."

"Is that right? Well, congratulations."

"So, as you can see, I shouldn't really travel."

"We'll take good care of you, Miss Taylor, don't you worry."

He said my name.

Holy shit.

Naomi's father knows exactly who I am.

"And if all goes well, we'll return you to Mr. Middleton in better shape than you are right now. My man Eddie here will make sure of it."

The driver turns his head and gives me a sinister grin, and that's when I know for sure.

I've been kidnapped.

Holy hell! Our girl Megan is in big trouble, I fear. I wonder how our Hunter is going to react. 😱 Want to know what happens next?

Hunter and Megan's story will conclude in **Possession,** and girl, it's going to get crazy!

All He'll Surrender To Is Her...

POSSESSION is the heart-stopping finale of Hunter and Megan's story—raw, real, and packed with the kind of love that conquers everything.

There's nothing I wouldn't do for Megan. She's the one thing in my life I got right, even when the rest of the world tried to tear us apart. I've fought the demons of my past and eliminated some of hers, and now she's back where she belongs—in my arms, carrying my child, building our forever.

But peace doesn't come easy for men like me. The ghosts of what we've endured still linger, threatening to pull us under. Only this time, I'm not letting go. Megan and I didn't come this far to lose now.

We've earned this love.

We've bled for it.

And now, nothing will stop me from giving her the life she deserves.

She's mine.

Finish The Series And Get Possession!
https://geni.us/possessionLLB

Thank you SO much for reading Submission. If you've enjoyed the story so far, please leave a review at the retailer where you purchased it. —Lisa

Acknowledgments

This trilogy features one of my new favorite couples, Hunter and Megan, and was first drafted exclusively for my phenomenal Romance Ninja Insiders over on Patreon.

Ladies, without your support, I would not have been able to indulge my muse and write stories outside of my usual romances. Thank you so much for joining me on this ride! 🤍

NINJA ADDICTS
Lisa Lopez
Beejay Johnson
Breaking The Epigraph
Dawn Gilmore
Marguerite Goosby
Susan Williams
Tahkeiya White
Victoria Nogales
Pat Chrisp-Langston
Cheryl Cutaia
Lisa Adams
Melissa A Pratt

NINJA GROUPIES
Dorothy Morris

Ashelt

Char

Chafonta Whatley

NINJA SUPPORTERS

Dolores Shortt Mawhinney

Angie Lauridsen

C Kennedy

Michele Handal

Valeria Collins

Jazman Diggs

Johanne Levesque Murray

Dee Puffer

Edana Walker

Serena Fritz

Nikki Afetian

Erin Marshall

Martha

Louise Jeffcoat

Norma

Karen Niles

Jamie

Amy Mikelson

Fran

Special Invitation

Do you love stories like this one? Would you like to read the next new romance I write before everyone else? I write new books like this one exclusively for readers in my Romance Ninja Community over on Patreon. I can't wait to see you over there!
—Lisa

Learn More Here

Also From Lisa Lang Blakeney

****Discounted Book Bundles****
Ultimate Masterson Book Bundle
Ultimate King Brothers Book Bundle
Ultimate Nighthawks Book Bundle
Ultimate Alpha Book One Bundle

The Masterson Series
Devour this addictive series about the possessive bad boy,
Roman Masterson, who falls hard and fast for the girl he's
promised his family to protect.
Masterson
Masterson Unleashed
Masterson In Love
Masterson Made
Joseph Loves Juliette

Masterson Next Generation Series
The crazy hot fruit doesn't fall far from the tree. Dive into
this second generation of Masterson men!
Knox - Knox & Gigi

Bronx - Bronx & Karma
Seven - Seven & Sasha

The King Brothers Series
Dive into this series of interconnected standalones featuring 3 alpha hot brothers and the women they lay claim to without apology.
Claimed - Camden & Jade
Indebted - Cutter & Sloan
Broken - Stone & Tiny
Promised - All King Brothers

The Nighthawk Series
Sexy & sweet sports romances set in the professional world of football. All standalones.
Saint - Saint & Sabrina
Wolf - Cooper & Ursula
Diesel - Mason & Olivia
Jett - Jett & Adrienne
Rush - Rush & Mia
Freak - Freak & Willow
Brick - Brick & Kaya
Dak - Dak & Katrina

Valencia Ice Mafia Series
Hot hockey romances set on the college campus of Valencia City University.
Neo - Neo & Violet
Shane - Shane & Kennedy
Bass - Coming Soon!

The Middleton Series
(Club Blue Whiskey)

Dark, age-gap, romantic suspense trilogy, set in the underbelly of Los Angeles featuring dangerous billionaire Hunter Middleton and the object of his obsession, Megan.

Obsession

Submission

Possession

Where You Can Find Me

MY VIP LIST (Get the nitty gritty)

I have a VIP Reader mailing list. I only send free books, new release, sales or special giveaway information to this group. No spam. You can join here:
http://LisaLangBlakeney.com/VIP

MY READERS GROUP (Casual fun)

Join my online Readers Group on Facebook also known as my "Romance Ninja Warriors" where I share all things new going on, celebrate birthdays, post teasers, yummy pics, giveaways and just chit chat.
http://LisaLangBlakeney.com/community

ROMANCE NINJA INSIDER (Early access!)

For exclusive serials, early access to all my releases, and more goodies become a romance ninja insider over at my Patreon community.

Get started with this 7 day free trial!

About the Author

Lisa Lang Blakeney is a USA Today Bestselling author of contemporary romance sold in more than 28 countries. Worried that her fellow PTO moms might disapprove, she wrote and published her steamy debut novel Masterson under a different title and pen name in August of 2015.

Thanks to strong reader support of her alpha male character, Roman Masterson, she was encouraged to continue with the series and published the entire Masterson Trilogy the following year. She hasn't looked back since and continues to write novels featuring strong alpha men and the smart women they seek to claim.

A romance junkie for sure, you can find Lisa watching a romantic comedy, reading a romance novel, or writing one of her own most days of the week. If she's not doing that, she's outside in the garden tending to her roses.

Lisa is the wife of one alpha (whom she met in college), mother to four girls, and two labradoodles. Get news on releases, sales and giveaways when you become one of Lisa's VIP readers at : http://LisaLangBlakeney.com/VIP